SO BLOOMS *the* DAWN

SO BLOOMS *the* DAWN

NOW COMES THE MIST

BOOK 2

JULIE C. DAO

Podium

Cover design by Podium Publishing

ISBN: 978-1-0394-5749-2

Published in 2025 by Podium Publishing
www.podiumentertainment.com

For the women in my family who crossed oceans so their daughters could dream.

SO BLOOMS *the* DAWN

Cast down headlong in the sea,
She fell at last;
Pleasure past and anguish past,
Is it death or is it life?
—Christina Rossetti, "The Goblin Market"

CHAPTER ONE

The train is an elegant affair, painted gold and royal blue and polished to a high sheen. The wheels flash through clouds of silvery smoke billowing through the legs of hundreds of travelers hurrying along the platform. Newsboys wave papers, porters shout as they wheel trolleys and lift trunks, and conductors in crisp uniforms study schedules and glance at their pocket watches, looking grave and important.

In the midst of this teeming life, with new smells and sights and sounds, I forget for a moment what I am and what I have become. I forget that I have left everyone I love behind me, perhaps forever, and that I am alone in the world and may be for centuries yet to come. I am simply Lucy Westenra, twenty years of age and fluttering with excitement at the prospect of her first journey. For years have I envied men their ability to wander the world and see unknown cities, and now I shall do the same. How Mina would marvel if she could see me now! The thought of my beloved friend dissolves my joy in an instant, and my dark veil ripples as I sigh, the weight of memory pressing my shoulders down once more.

A porter doffs his cap as he approaches me. He has a charming smile for the other women on the platform, but his face is sober when he sees my elegant black mourning gown. I look like a grieving young widow of means—exactly the impression Vlad wishes me to give. "May I take your trunks, ma'am?" the porter asks, low and deferential. He has come close enough to see a hint of my face through my translucent veil, and I smell his blood accelerating at my wide, tilting dark eyes and deep red lips. His veins carry a warm and spicy fragrance like cinnamon.

His heartbeat quickens as my mouth curves into a sweet smile. Always, the venom inside me is fighting to survive, and in its quest for self-preservation, it knows exactly how to make me irresistible to my prey. I could have this man in the blink of an eye. I could summon the mist to conceal us, press him against the side of the train, and lower my mouth to drink every drop of life from the throat he would gratefully bare for me. Shame, cold as ice, dissolves my hunger. I press my tongue angrily against the sharp fangs just beginning to descend from my gums.

"Yes, please. I will carry this on my person." I indicate my small leather handbag. No human nose could smell the raw venison within, not when I have carefully wrapped it in several layers of waxed paper, but I find the acrid scent of blood and sinew comforting. Animal blood is thinner and blander than that of humans, but this paltry meal shall be my insurance against any harm I may do to another person. I can sustain myself on it. I *will* sustain myself on it.

The porter lifts my trunks onto a trolley and leads me to the first-class car. He deposits my belongings in a storage compartment and gives me a slip of paper. "Give that to any porter when you arrive in Dover, ma'am. He will be glad to help you recover your belongings."

I climb into the gilded, ostentatious car, which has a low polished ceiling and walls of rich mahogany. It is lined with seats upholstered in royal-blue velvet, small wooden tables, and large plate-glass windows, and it is still empty enough for me to cautiously lift my veil and look around in appreciation . . . until a horrifying sight catches my eye.

A small woman stands directly to my right, swathed from head to toe in black. Her veil is raised in one slender hand to reveal a pale face splattered with blood. Scarlet drops crawl across her cheeks like living organisms, and even the whites of her eyes are speckled with red as though someone sliced open an artery and an unholy wind blew the spray of gore all over her.

She gasps and drops her veil, and I realize that I am looking at my own warped reflection. This train car is lined with mirrors, one of which is showing my ghastly shadow self, the proof of what I am now and what I have chosen, which can only ever be seen in a reflective surface.

Someone clears his throat. "Excuse me, ma'am."

"I'm sorry," I say, blinking out of my trance as a queue of impatient passengers forms in the aisle behind me. I secure my veil and walk on, knowing it would not do for anyone to see that monstrous image. "You will never speak of me to anyone," Vlad had commanded. "You will never expose me." A laugh, high and hysterical, threatens to escape me as I imagine explaining to him how I had sent an entire train car into a panic. "For some reason," I would say, "they did not like my blood-splattered reflection." Perhaps, in response, he would finally tear my head from my shoulders as he often threatens to do. His newest, most troublesome bride, already endangering his time in England before she could be safely shipped off to his castle in the wilds.

But I wonder: *Would* he be angry . . . or puzzled? He does not appear in mirrors at all; the alchemy of light, glass, and silver cannot see him. This curse manifests itself differently in me, a fact which I have been careful to keep secret and not think upon for long, knowing Vlad can read my thoughts. Perhaps someday, I may be able to use it to my advantage.

Sunlight pours into the train, bathing me in its soothing warmth. It is another way in which the infection differs in me. To Vlad, the sun feels like knives shredding him apart at the seams, but I can still lift my face to the sky as though I had never transformed. As though I were still the old Lucy with her quick, light step, dancing up the cliffs at Whitby to breathe the sea air before returning home to her mother and to a young man whose hazel eyes glowed to see her.

The memory of Arthur Holmwood touching my face and pressing his lips to my hair forces me to lean against a table as grief creeps in, sinking its teeth into my cold, dead heart.

"Ma'am?" asks the impatient gentleman behind me. I smell the contents of his veins and of the other people entering the car. Everywhere is the heady fragrance of blood, salt, and sweat, and though I made certain to feed well before I came, I ought not to remain in the midst of so much temptation. Not when Vlad could be watching my every move from inside my mind.

I hurry toward the rear compartments, which have sliding glass doors and curtains for privacy. It would be best to shut myself away from curious eyes and veins engorged with blood.

I notice a man down the corridor in a hat and a long, tan sporting coat. His back is turned to me, but something about his confident stride is so familiar that my breath seizes in my throat. I can almost believe, from his form and figure and athletic gait, that the man is Quincey Morris. Any moment now, he might turn and I will see his handsome face with its broad nose, ebony skin, and dark brown eyes crinkling as he smiles at me. But he will never smile at me again.

Quincey, who had loved me—who had longed to take me to the New World.

Quincey, who now wants me dead.

The man disappears into a compartment, and though I know it cannot be my friend—who is surely on a ship bound for America by now—grief slips once more through the cracks of my shattered soul. Once, death had called to me in gentle, honeyed tones and I had opened my arms and my heart to it . . . to the dream of reuniting with the ones I have loved and lost, particularly my dear papa. But now that I have given myself over, inextricably linked to death for eternity, I know that I have been a fool. For one by one, everyone I know will vanish and I will linger on forever in this cursed existence, trapped and lonely and full of regret.

A sob rises in my throat. I cannot lose control. Not here, where so many people might see. If I want to cry, I must find a safe and quiet place to hide myself away. But every seat seems to be occupied, and my panic rises . . . before dissolving abruptly into hope and wild joy.

In the compartment to my left, I see Mina in a dove-grey suit with a hat perched rakishly upon her upswept golden hair. Her face is turned away, gazing out at the bustling platform, while a young man drones on across from her. He is perhaps twenty-five, with fair hair, a weak chin, and watery blue eyes. He notices me staring and frowns, but I ignore him.

When his companion turns, however, I see that she is not Mina. She is only a stranger who looks like her, for my friend would not have worn her hat at such a flirtatious angle or met another woman's gaze so boldly. She looks brazenly back at me with a face that is at once strange and familiar, eyebrows arching above sky-blue eyes and lips curving at my obvious admiration of her. The man says something I cannot hear through the glass, but his peevish tone is clear enough. I turn away, feeling unsteady. I could have sworn my lifeless heart gave another beat at the sight of Mina's beloved face on a stranger.

"Do you need somewhere to sit?" a voice asks, frail like parchment, and cultured, with a western European accent. It belongs to an ancient woman in the compartment across the aisle. She has dark eyes that are incongruously young in her heavily lined face, and she wears several thick gold rings and a traveling gown of rich burgundy velvet.

"I hate to disturb you—" I begin.

She gives an imperious wave of her wrinkled hand, in the manner of someone used to being obeyed. "Nonsense. I am traveling without my maid and would like company. Come in."

I had promised Vlad to travel discreetly . . . but it *would* be far riskier to sit in a crowded car for four hours than to shut myself away with an old lady whose stale-smelling blood does not tempt me one bit. And she has invited me in, the force of it like a rope pulling me toward her. Vlad and I may differ when it comes to sunlight and mirrors, but we share the compulsion to accept the invitations of our prey. I enter and slide the glass door shut with a nod of thanks.

"Am I not to see my fellow traveler's face?" she asks as I take the seat opposite hers.

"I am a widow who must respect the dead," I say, more out of duty than anything else. My veil has been irritating me all morning, so I lift the dark crape fabric up over my hat. After a moment's hesitation, I take off my long black gloves as well.

The old lady's eyes move from my face to my hands, studying my jewelry. On my right hand rest two rings: the first one silver with a green jade stone, an heirloom from Van, my great-grandmother who had been a lady in the court of the emperor of Vietnam, and a gold band with a diamond flanked by two emeralds, the engagement ring Arthur had given me. I had thought about wearing it on a chain hidden beneath my dress to save myself the heartache of missing him whenever I looked at it, but I could not bear to remove it. On my left hand is a brass ring with a bloodred garnet, placed smugly upon my wedding finger by Vlad to claim me as his own.

"You are very young to be a widow," the old woman remarks.

"I do not feel young," I say with a humorless laugh. Is it a lie to claim widowhood when I am the bride of a man no longer living . . . or is it simply the truth? The woman's unblinking stare holds an odd, wary recognition. "Have we met?" I ask pointedly. "You examine me most thoroughly, as though trying to remember where you have seen me before."

She shrugs. "I have never met *you*, but I have met someone like you." There is a long, charged moment of silence in which I wonder how she could have detected the wrongness in me so quickly, and then she adds, "That is, a woman with Asian heritage."

The tension in my muscles eases a bit. "My great-grandmother was Vietnamese," I say. "My great-grandfather took her back to England with him, and their children and grandchildren married English people. But I still have something of her in my face." Papa had often told me that my dark eyes came from Van—or Vanessa, as she had renamed herself after marriage—and that it often felt as though she were looking out at him through me.

Grief, again. Grief like a grave yawning before me, over the edge of which I am forever teetering. I take in a slow, ragged breath and see my companion's face soften.

"I am the Baroness Elisabeth von Bassewitz," she says.

"Lucy Westenra."

A smart rap sounds upon our compartment door, and a conductor enters, holding his hand out for our tickets. At once, I am on edge at the heat of the blood that courses through him, swirling in his veins with vitality. I taste my own blood as the tips of my fangs threaten to snap down. *I have fed*, I tell myself forcefully. *I do not need his blood. He is safe from me.*

He punches the baroness's ticket, chatting cheerfully away. When he turns around, I am thankful for yet another way in which the venom behaves differently in me: hunger turns Vlad's eyes into black orbs ringed with poison red, but my eyes remain my own. The conductor takes my ticket, his steady conversation faltering when he notices my beauty.

"Is the sun too hot, ma'am?" he asks, his eyes darting to the window. "It is shining full upon your lovely face. Shall I lower the shade for you?"

I shake my head. "No, thank you. I like looking outside."

"It will be only buildings and streets for some time," he insists. "Let me pull down the shade for you. You can open it later, when there are more trees and the sun is not so strong."

The conductor means well, and he has no idea what I am, but his determination to shield me from the sun tries my patience. "I prefer the window uncovered, please," I say, but something about my face seems to have taken hold of him.

He beams as he reaches for the shade. "Allow me to do you this service. I—"

I take hold of his wrist. I meant for it to be a light touch, but his face goes pale and his jowls quiver as he backs away. When I let go, I can see the impression of each of my fingers on his pale skin. "I b-beg your pardon, ma'am," he stammers, then turns to leave so quickly that he almost knocks over someone standing in the doorway behind him.

"Have a care, my good man," says an amused voice, female and American, with broad, stretched-out vowels. Once again, memories of Quincey Morris flash into my mind: his drawl, his bright laugh, his hand on my waist as we danced . . . and the glint of moonlight on his pistols pointed directly at my heart. But when the stranger speaks again, I realize her accent is slightly different from Quincey's. "You almost flattened me there."

The flustered conductor apologizes and leaves, with a final nervous glance at me.

Standing in the doorway is the stranger who looks like Mina, so much so that my throat almost closes with longing. I try to focus on the differences in her appearance: her height, which is too tall; her waist and shoulders, which are slimmer; and her jaw, which is sharp and defined where Mina's is soft. She also speaks in a rich contralto and not in a clear sweet voice, like Mina.

"Eleanor Wright-Davies, at your service," she says. "My husband is asleep at last, thank goodness, so I thought I would come and greet you. May I sit here awhile?"

The baroness inclines her head. "You may, Mrs. Wright-Davies."

"Just Nell, please. I haven't been married long enough to enjoy that prim and proper name." To my disappointment, the newcomer sits beside the baroness. But when her eyes find my face, I realize that from that vantage point, she can look at me all she likes . . . and I her. She raises her eyebrows when the old woman and I introduce ourselves. "A baroness? England is positively cluttered with lords and ladies. One never knows if one is speaking to royalty."

"Your accent is not that of Texas, I think," I say.

Nell laughs. "English people think we all talk like cowboys," she says good-naturedly. "I'm from New York. And in the style of a true American, I'd like to boldly ask you all about yourselves. How about you first, Baroness? You look like an interesting lady."

"Perhaps," the old woman says dryly. "If you consider someone who has now buried every last family member as of yesterday and now awaits death herself *interesting*."

"Oh, I'm so sorry—"

The baroness shrugs. "Everyone dies. I came to London for my sister's funeral, and now I return to Germany to await my own demise. In whatever form it chooses to come." There is a prophetic quality in the baroness's voice as her gaze moves from Nell to me, and I almost shiver.

Nell glances at me, her eyes soft, and I have a powerful urge to find that shade of blue in paint and cover my bedroom with it. "And you? You're an Englishwoman?"

"My people are from London," I say. "Are you and your husband on your honeymoon?"

She twists the gold ring on her finger. "Yes. It happened so fast, my head is still spinning. We met at a party in April, where Charles won my parents over with his plummy accent and double-barreled name. He proposed a month later, and my mother . . . *encouraged* me to accept, due to my advanced age. We married last week in a whirlwind of satin and bickering bridesmaids and have now embarked on a tour of the Continent, like any couple of means. Romantic, no?"

I smile at her playful, irreverent tone, and even the baroness looks charmed. "Your mother was worried about your age?" she asks Nell. "I thought you looked quite the child bride."

Nell chuckles. "This young face is merely a tool with which to shock and disarm. I am five-and-twenty, much too old a girl to be unmarried among my set. Mother had almost given me up when Charles appeared. He seemed as good a choice as any."

"What would he think if he heard you speak of him so?" I ask, amused.

She flashes me an irresistible grin. "He would think me an angel. He's pleased with my money, but I do believe the silly old bear loves me." My heart gives a sudden wayward tug for Arthur as I watch her twist her wedding ring. "You have been married, of course, Baroness? I assume you stole many a heart in your day."

The old woman is startled into laughter. "Certainly not. I was neither pretty nor sought-after. My husband's offer was the only one I got, but we were married fifty years until his death."

"And did you love him?"

The baroness hesitates. "Love does not come easily. But what other option have we as women? He gave me a home, a good name, and our son, and that is all I asked."

"And you?" Nell asks me. "Did you love *your* husband?"

I glance down at Vlad's garnet ring with a dark chuckle. "*Love* is not the word I would use. But at least I can say that I made the choice wholeheartedly."

"Your husband is not a pleasant man, I gather?"

"Decidedly the opposite," I say, hoping Vlad can hear me. "In fact, he often behaves as though he has lived five hundred years and knows everything there is to know."

"You speak as though he is still alive," the baroness says.

I lift an eyebrow. "I suppose I still feel connected to him, though he is not here."

"These pesky husbands leave a lasting mark, don't they?" Nell gives me another disorienting smile. "What would you do if you hadn't gotten married? I would have run a glamorous hotel somewhere, dripping in diamonds and flirting with everyone who came in."

"How adventurous and American of you." Before I can stop myself, I add, "My friend Mina would be shocked if she were here. Marriage is a most serious topic to her."

"She does not have modern and outlandish ideas of independence, then? I suppose that would make her the perfect woman of the age to most men."

A jolt shoots through me at her unknowing echo of Vlad's words. "She approves of female independence," I say. "She was my governess for a time, but married in the end."

"I should have liked to do a great many things had I not married," the baroness says in a wandering voice. She closes her eyes and we wait for her to continue, but a moment later, she begins to snore lightly. Nell and I look at each other, shaking with silent mirth.

"Shall I go?" she whispers.

"No, stay." My answer is too quick to be proper, but I find that I do not care. "You might disturb your husband if you returned to him now."

"How thoughtful you are," Nell says playfully. "I *would* much rather stay here. Poor Charles is no one I want to stare at for hours on end. Not like you. And I think you feel the same. You did make him rather uneasy with your rapt attention earlier."

I blush. "I was struck by your face. You look astonishingly like my Mina."

"I resemble this perfect woman? How long have you known her?"

"For much of my life. And I will love her for as much of it remains." *Though she no longer has need of me*, I think, as a knot of pain forms in my chest.

"Forgive me," Nell says quietly, hearing the change in my voice. "I know nothing of you and Mina, but I will hazard a guess that your love will always mean a great deal to her."

"How could you know that?" I ask, moved. "I am a stranger to you."

"Some strangers can feel more familiar to you than your own family . . . and I sense you may be such a person to me." Her eyes take me in, as intent as a painter studying thier subject. "There is something so *alive* about you, Lucy Westenra, in the way you speak and laugh and look at me. You have a spark I have not found elsewhere. I suppose that was why I stayed unmarried for so long. I didn't fancy shackling myself to someone with the sensibilities of a dead fish."

I choke out a laugh. "Charles is lucky you did not think of him as such."

Nell gives a careless shrug. "Oh, Charles! I had given up on finding the perfect person for me, and he seemed as good an alternative to spinsterhood as any. But you—" Her cheeks grow pink. "If I were this Mina, I would be glad to know someone who burned as brightly as you do. You fill this drab grey world with color . . . and we all need a bit of color." She gets up and smooths her skirt, looking embarrassed by her own outpouring.

"Are you leaving already?" I ask wistfully.

"I should return to Charles," she says, sighing. "He will pout otherwise. But I hope to converse more with you later. Are you bound for France as well?"

"Yes. I will be sailing to Calais."

"Good. As will I." Nell reaches for my hand, enveloping my ice-cold fingers in her warm ones. And then, without another word, she slips out of the compartment, leaving behind a trace of floral perfume, the memory of sky-blue eyes, and the lingering heat of her hand on mine.

CHAPTER TWO

The train reaches Dover in the late afternoon, and by the time it pulls into the station, the sky has become a deep, foreboding grey. Heavy rain pours down in sheets, propelled by a cold wind. "Are you ladies planning to take the boat to Calais?" a porter asks the baroness and me. "Please gather over there. The conductor has a message for all those traveling by ferry."

"That sounds ominous," the baroness says, peering at the sky. "Do you think the journey will be delayed? I would rather stay in town for the night than toss about on the waves."

I murmur something vaguely agreeable, distracted by overpowering nostalgia as I gaze out at Dover. A cobblestone street winds through a town of neat buildings, full of people with umbrellas and carriages clattering past well-lit shops. Beyond this, a wall of white rock spills into the raging water, and the breath of the ocean is sharp, salty, and unbearably seductive. If I closed my eyes, I could imagine myself back at Whitby in the grip of a summer storm, spending languid evenings with a stranger who seemed to see into the depths of my unhappy heart.

I picture two people gazing out to sea, brought together by dreams: a man, at once there and not there, and a woman full of inexplicable yearning. If I could speak to her now, would I stop her? Would I warn that silly, thoughtless Lucy not to indulge in that poisonous need—scold her for having both Arthur's and Mina's love, yet wanting more and wandering up just such a cliff in just such a storm to face her dark destiny by the sea?

I hate myself for missing Vlad as he used to be, when he would hold me and listen to my troubles as though he would take them and make them his own. But that man never truly existed. I had seized his paltry crumbs of affection and painted the portrait of a fantasy, not of reality. And now, even though I know the truth, that portrait is etched permanently inside of me.

Lucy, you will never be free of me.

A loud voice breaks into my thoughts. "What a damned inconvenience!" Charles Wright-Davies is berating a conductor in front of the other train passengers. "The ferry will not leave until tomorrow? My wife and I wish to go to Calais tonight. I find this highly irregular!"

Beside him, Nell flushes with embarrassment. "My dear, what do you want this poor man to do? I hardly think he can control the weather."

The conductor gives her a grateful look. "I am sorry, sir. I am only delivering a message from the docks. All boats are delayed, and the first ferry sails at nine o'clock in the morning. Might I suggest the White Cliff Hotel for all of your needs?" he adds as the crowd murmurs discontentedly. "Tomorrow you may come to the docks by half past eight."

"The White Cliff Hotel sounds charming, doesn't it?" Nell asks her husband, and I feel a pang for her, being tied for life to this man. Her eyes find mine. "And look, there are my friends, the Baroness von Bassewitz and Lucy Westenra. It will be pleasant to see some familiar faces."

"A baroness, you say?" Charles squints at us without recognition.

I lose sight of them as the crowd leaves the train station. The baroness and I find a carriage, and I slip the driver extra money to ensure that we travel alone. I cannot trust myself in close quarters with anyone else, not when I can recognize the tightening in my gut, sharpening even at the unappetizing chalk and faded lace smell of the old woman's blood.

"Are you feeling all right, Lucy?" she asks. "You are tired . . . and hungry, I suppose?"

"Yes."

Thankfully, it does not take long to reach the hotel, which glows with welcoming light. I recognize other passengers from the train but do not see Nell and Charles as we enter the lobby and the dull roar of a thousand heartbeats assaults my senses.

Breathing shallowly, I pay for a room at the front desk while the baroness accepts her room key from a chatty employee nearby. "You will not lack interesting company here, ma'am," he is saying. "There is such a mix of people! Only ten minutes ago, I helped a doctor who insisted upon seeing our guest list. I refused, of course, to protect our guests' confidentiality."

"Why did he want to see your guest list?" the baroness asks.

"We often host important people, you see. A famous soprano stayed here last week, so I thought he was hoping to meet someone like that. But he asked about foreign-looking guests. Not *foreign*, mind you, but foreign-*looking*. Odd, I thought." He sees me and gives me a small bow, noticing my olive skin and dark eyes. His voice rises with ingratiating haste. "We welcome people of all nationalities here. We do not discriminate."

I turn to the baroness, unsettled. I am not certain why the thought of a doctor asking strange questions should unnerve me so. "I wish you a restful night, Baroness."

"Will I see you in the dining room later?" the old woman inquires.

"Yes, perhaps." I follow two bellboys carrying my trunks up the stairs, glad to leave the teeming mass of bodies behind. I try to tell myself that it is normal for a doctor to ask about other hotel guests. This unease I feel is only grief; I am only missing everyone from my past life.

That must be why I am thinking so much of Mina, Arthur, and Quincey.

That must be why the brilliant Dr. Abraham Van Helsing is suddenly on my mind. Sharp, clever Dr. Van Helsing, who broke into the Westenra mausoleum to destroy me and who is now as bent upon my demise as Quincey. But surely the physician is home in Amsterdam and not in this rain-soaked seaside town hunting a woman he knows to be undead.

The bellboys are panting by the time we reach my room. I tip them and lock myself in with a sigh of relief, muting the cacophony of smells and sounds.

My room is small and comfortable. There is a bed with a blue flowered spread, an old armoire, and a simple desk and chair. I approach the window, averting my eyes from my horrid reflection, and only when my nose is pressed against the glass do I dare to look out at the ocean, barely visible in the thick fog. There is barely the slightest churning of white-capped waves to distinguish it from the sky and the mist, both of them an impenetrable deep grey.

I am seized by the sudden urge to climb the cliffs above the crashing waves. The violence of the rain would calm me and help dampen the smell of blood that seems to be everywhere . . . but there are too many people who would see me, and who would be faced with my increasing hunger. First things first: I must feed.

I pull out the raw venison steak. Pain pinches my gums as my fangs snap down and I eat, tasting my own blood along with that of the animal. This bland meal is nowhere near as satisfying as human blood . . . but I push that thought aside at once, for still lingering in my mind are the faces of the people I murdered: the vagrant I found the night I transformed; the young, miserable woman Vlad had forced me to kill; and a man I had encountered near the docks. All three are now soulless bodies wandering in the mist, empty shells stumbling through the world of fog where Vlad hides his victims and has commanded me to hide mine. I see them as clear as day, like a photograph of my darkest deeds, and my throat tightens with remorse.

Vlad kills without conscience. He can drain a ship full of sailors without a thought and drink from a lonely widow to amuse himself, perhaps even smiling at the memory. *But I will not be like him*, I vow. *I will never take pleasure in inflicting pain and death.*

I catch sight of a plate on the desk, holding a selection of cakes and biscuits as an offering of hospitality. An involuntary smile touches my lips when I see a flaky strawberry pastry, which had been my favorite treat as a human. I finish my pathetic meal, clean my face and hands, and tentatively pick up the light, airy dessert. I take a small bite and close my eyes, instantly flooded by a barrage of images and sensations.

I see strawberry seeds taking root in dark soil and shiny fruit springing to life on the vines, plump, red, and summer-warm. Butter being churned, the milk turning into sweet yellow clumps that are stirred into a bowl of flour and sugar. Sweet-smelling dough turning golden-brown in the oven. Mamma in the parlor, laughing as she and I each devour a pastry. Mina in the garden, our fingers sticky with jam and entangling as we share a cake. White lawn dresses in the breeze, bare feet on dewy grass, and honeysuckle vines, heady as a half-forgotten dream.

This time, when the grief comes, I invite it in. I crumple to the floor, my hands smearing jam on my dark skirt, and allow the sobs to rack my body. It is not regret for the existence I have forsaken—not entirely. But I begin to see that it is possible to miss a life I never asked for, along with all of the people, joys, and experiences I will never have again, for soon I will be shut away in Vlad's castle atop some wintry mountain. By the time my tears stop, I am weak with sadness, loneliness, and the bone-deep need to see Mina and Arthur again.

My eyes find the fog outside the window and I sit bolt upright, gripped by hope. Vlad had first found me wandering in my dreams—I had sleepwalked straight to him as though the mist were a road between the waking and the dreaming, the living and the dead. His body had been on a ship far away, yet he had also been with me. I knew the touch of his hands, lips, and tongue before he had ever even reached England, and I am not nearly as far away now from Mina and Arthur. Could the mist carry *me* into their dreams in such a way?

I get up and hurry to open the window. "Take me to Mina," I plead as the mist streams into the room and curls around my hands. "Take me to Arthur."

Nothing happens.

I lean against the desk, thinking. Vlad had called himself a dreamer like me. Perhaps he, too, had been asleep on that ship when we had found each other in the mist—or as close to sleep as a monster like him could be to such a humanlike action. There, he would have been enclosed in one of his many wooden boxes of earth, for only nestled in the dark soil of his homeland, safe from burning sunlight and human curiosity, is he able to find rest.

I lie down on the bed, fully clothed, and let the mist blanket me as I shut my eyes and conjure Arthur in my yearning mind: a tall and lanky frame, brown hair sweeping back from a high forehead, and eyes that fluctuate between hazel and green depending on the light. One perfect kissable dimple and a low, soft voice murmuring my name. But though my beloved comes to life in my mind's eye, the mist refuses to bring him to me in the flesh.

Tossing and turning, I shift my thoughts to Mina instead: her blue eyes shining, her nose crinkling with a laugh, her lily-scented hair falling in rippling golden waves like that of a fairy-tale princess or candlelight spun into something tangible. I hold on to her memory and breathe, allowing my longing to consume me. *Please*, I beg the mist. *Please take me to her.*

The lamps in my room go dark.

My eyes fly open.

I am standing in a home I do not recognize. The strangest revelation is that I can feel the divide, the split in my physical self—half of me lying upon a hotel bed *and* the other looking around this dark hall with walls papered in forest green, weathered wood floors, lavender in a vase before an ornate mirror, and windows that look out upon a rainy, tree-lined street.

I move toward the flowers and breathe in their soothing scent, remembering how Mina has always loved lavender. My movements are slow and dreamy, as though I am sleepwalking again. When I lift my head and catch sight of my reflection in the mirror, it stops me dead.

The image is of me as I was before. Black hair swept into a knot, arched brows over wide eyes tilting upward at the corners, and full lips parted at the revelation that my skin is flawless. There are no bright red drops speckling my skin or swirling in the whites of my eyes. Gone is my shadow self and the proof of what Vlad did to me. In this mirror, somehow I am as I ever was.

I run my trembling hands over my face. "What is this?" I whisper. "Where am I?"

Down the hall, something is knocked over with a clunk.

I hurry toward the sound, possessed by wild hope, running toward the joy of reunion like a lost sailor coming home. Somehow, my efforts have succeeded—persuaded the mist to work in my favor. And if it cannot bring me to Arthur, perhaps it has at least taken me to Mina.

I stop in the doorway of an office papered in dark red, a soft maroon rug upon the floor and a fireplace illuminating shelves of leather-bound volumes and brass figurines. A mahogany desk faces me, positively littered with paper covered in smudged and untidy handwriting. An overturned jar of ink seeps into the pages as the person at the desk makes a futile attempt to stop it with a handkerchief and the sleeve of a dark blue dressing gown.

The instant our eyes meet, I realize that the mist has not brought me to Mina, as I hoped.

It has taken me to her husband instead.

CHAPTER THREE

Jonathan Harker and I stare at each other. My emotions range from disappointment to surprise to the resentment I feel whenever I look at this man. I have never bothered to think of him more than necessary, and now we are alone, without Mina to serve as a bridge between us. He looks much older than his four-and-twenty years, as though he has aged a full decade since the engagement party Mamma and I held for them in February. My existence has shifted beyond imagination in those seven months, and judging from Jonathan's appearance, *his* has as well.

In the firelight, there are new glints of grey in his dark gold hair. His jaw, normally clean-shaven, is covered in an unkempt beard. Shadows deepen the hollows of his thin cheeks, and I am startled to see a tremor in the hand holding the handkerchief. I have never seen him afraid or unsure. His calm demeanor had always annoyed me, as had his smug certainty of who he is, where he belongs in the world, and how he could deserve a woman like Mina.

Only in his piercing grey eyes do I see the Jonathan I remember, the lawyer's clerk with a quick mind and intelligent conversation. But no . . . not a clerk anymore. Mina's last letter told of how her husband had inherited Mr. Hawkins's fortune and practice upon the lawyer's death, effectively bestowing means, position, and power upon Jonathan. Bitterness roils in me at the ease with which such blessings find him. This world, which saw fit to shackle me to one path—that of a wife and mother—is only ever kind to these men who take freedom as their due.

"I am dreaming," Jonathan says slowly, fear and disbelief on his face. The handkerchief drips black ink onto his dressing gown, but he does not notice. "This is only a dream."

The mist follows me into the office. "Where is Mina? I wished to see *her*, not you."

"Why are you in my dream?" he demands, ignoring my question. "*You*, of all people, my wife's dead friend. I have never strayed from her even in my innermost thoughts. How can I be unfaithful to her now in my sleep, hard-earned as it is?"

"Unfaithful? You've done nothing but gape at me."

He rubs his tired face, staining his cheeks with ink. "But I am dreaming about another woman. A *dead* woman. A woman I never even liked."

"I beg your pardon!" It is true *I* have never liked *him*, but it seems a different matter entirely to hear *he* has never liked *me*.

He opens and closes his eyes as though hoping I will disappear between the blinks. "I never understood how Mina could love someone so vain, spoiled, and selfish. So different from herself. Is it not enough that the woman coerced three good men into proposing marriage to her? Now *I* have to dream of her, too? Is no one safe? Be gone, specter, and never return!"

I scowl. "Are you always this rude in your dreams? I never understood how Mina could love *you*, either. Swaggering about and so arrogant, even though all you are is lucky."

Jonathan twitches in his chair. "Excuse me?"

"Fortune favors you. That is all, yet you act as though talent flows from your—" I almost trip over a pile of paper. Irritated, I snatch up a few pages. "Mina used to make me organize my dresses by color, but lets you clutter your study like this? Why is it like a rubbish heap in here?"

Something about my movements frightens him even more. "You're not truly here, are you?" he whispers, then utters a groan of frustration. "Of course not! I haven't slept well in months, and my mind is troubled! I am asleep, and Lucy Westenra is—"

"Dead. Yes. You have already said so." I roll my eyes at my friend's intolerable bore of a husband and glance down at the paper in my hand. I see a date scrawled at the top, June 3 of this year, followed by *The castle seems to be vast, from what little I can see of it, and a strange, cold draft permeates the halls, though all of the windows are shut securely* . . .

Jonathan bolts around the desk at the sight of me reading. "You are not to look at these!" he cries, trying to snatch the pages away. "Give them back to me at once!"

I tighten my grip. "Why? They are just diary entries—"

"They are private!"

Our hands brush, and it is as though a current has run through him. He falls backward onto the floor and presses himself against the desk, terrified. My cold skin must have felt too real to him, the way Vlad had always felt to me. But *my* dreams of Vlad had been languorous, pleasurable, and laced with dark desire. For Jonathan, this vision of me is a nightmare.

"All right, I won't read if it upsets you," I say, taking pity on him. I try to put the pages back where I found them, but it is a hopeless task. "Is there no order at all to your papers? How can you live like this? What sort of lawyer—" I take a deep breath and crouch down to meet his eyes. There are several feet of distance between us, but he still flinches. "I mean you no harm."

"Why should I believe you? You're supposed to be dead."

I sigh. "Listen to me. I will explain as best I can. You are indeed asleep and dreaming, but I am also here with you in the flesh. Both are true."

"B-but . . . how?"

"The mist allows me to make contact with those who sleepwalk or sleep lightly." I sit back on my heels, startled. "That must be why it didn't take me to Mina. She sleeps so heavily. One summer in Whitby, I knocked over a chair whilst sleepwalking, and she never even stirred."

Jonathan shudders. "Mina talks about you as though you're still alive. I thought it was only grief and denial, but I overheard her and Van Helsing when they thought I was asleep."

"Van Helsing is still in London?" I ask, surprised.

"He told her you might return. I don't know what the bloody hell is happening anymore. Everything has been like a mad, tortured dream since . . ." Slowly, his fingers find the left side of his neck, where two badly healed scars stand out in contrast to his pale skin.

Chilled, I stare at the proof of what he endured in Vlad's castle in the Mountains of Deep Winter. I, too, would have such scars had this vampire venom not rendered my skin flawless. My intake of breath brings Jonathan back to himself, and he manages to level a hard gaze at me.

"Why are you here, Lucy? Have you come to kill me? To finish what *he* started?"

"Finish what *who* started?" I ask quietly. I want him to say it.

"You know who!" Jonathan jumps to his feet, and though I am an immortal being who could destroy him before his next breath, I cannot help startling, for he is much bigger than I am. "I heard what Van Helsing said, and I believe him, even if Mina does not."

"What did he tell her?"

"That you are now the devil's own servant, an agent of that foul old man who lured me to Austria-Hungary. That hell-spawned monster in the guise of a kind, grandfatherly nobleman."

I frown. "Old man? *Grandfatherly*? But he is a—"

A sudden, all-encompassing pain racks my body. It feels as though I have stepped into the fire and the flames are eating away at my skin. I stagger into a side table, convulsing. Vlad's command that I never expose him to anyone has penetrated the very marrow of my bones, punishing me with agony whenever I even attempt to speak of him. This, too, I had forgotten.

"What's wrong?" Jonathan asks, alarmed.

I do not answer, and the pain vanishes at once, rewarding my silence. I collapse into a chair, shaking with the memory of torment like boiling water peeling back layers of my flesh.

"You tried to tell me something," he says, wary and on edge. "About that . . . that man."

I struggle to catch my breath. Vlad has always appeared to me as a man of about forty, with dark wavy hair and a cruelly handsome face, but I know he can change into a wolf, a bat, or even the mist itself at will. Why not a gentle, harmless elderly man?

Jonathan is eyeing me, thoughtful and wary. "You're not allowed to speak of him, are you? It *hurts* you. I thought when he sent you to me, you would fill my ears with poison."

"You read too much Shakespeare," I say witheringly and then pause. "*When* he sent me to you? You expected me to come?"

"I don't know what I expected. I only knew I had not seen the last of him, not by far, even after he left me in that castle . . . with *them*. And for some reason, they let me go." As he gazes into the fire, lost in his memories, I see strange, shimmering threads of mist emerging from his head. They dance in the air around his face, but he does not seem to notice.

Enraptured, I focus on one of them, and a vision blossoms in my mind, clear as life.

Jonathan is standing at the doors of an ancient sprawling castle. Under the cold moon, its bones whisper of ages long gone: narrow windows set high into walls, turrets reaching for a bleeding sky, and corridors ringing with the screams of people impaled upon stakes or boiled alive in cauldrons of oil. The doors creak open, and Jonathan is welcomed inside.

I blink, and I see a suite of rooms with a roaring fire, books, and a bed hung with garnet brocade. As comfortable as the space seems, an air of cold desolation hangs over it. Perhaps it is the wind whistling through the icy stone walls, the mountainous snowdrifts outside the windows, or the multiple brass locks adorning the door . . . not just inside, but *outside*.

I blink again, and Jonathan sits at a dining table eating a simple feast of roast chicken, brown bread, and wine. A stooped, white-haired man sits opposite him, flanked by two women, both of them dazzlingly beautiful. One is tall, elegant, and queenly, with deep brown skin, tight black curls cropped close to her skull, and downcast eyes full of despair. The other looks how my great-grandmother, Van, might have in her youth: warm olive skin, tilting brown eyes, and black silk hair. *Her* expression could not be more different: silent rage smolders in every line of her exquisite face. She holds a goblet as though she would like to kill someone with it, and as her eyes cut to her left, I think, *Were I that old man, I would not dare to fall asleep in her presence.*

"I do not blame you for thinking me partial to *Richard III* or *Macbeth*," the old man says in a deep, accented voice. "You would believe me to be drawn to plays of power, war, and politics. But of all Shakespeare's works, I am attracted to the romantic and whimsical. Forbidden love and secret identities, all twisted together like a . . ." He pauses. "What do fishermen use?"

Jonathan smiles. "A net?"

"Precisely! A net. Ah, my English will improve so much with you here, Mr. Harker. I am sure of it." The man beams, warm and genial, but his eyes hold the iciest depths of the ocean.

Jonathan turns politely to the women. "Do *you* read Shakespeare, Hong? Thabisa?"

Hong and Thabisa. I study them with an eagerness bordering on greed, knowing I will soon meet these other brides of Vlad's, all three of us united by sorrow and brutality. *And anger*, I think, as Hong of the black silk hair directs her scalding gaze toward Jonathan.

But the elderly man does not allow her to answer. "Do not feel obligated to converse with them, Mr. Harker," he says lightly. "They are here to please your eye and nothing more."

The vision changes. Jonathan is in a washroom, wearing only his trousers and holding a straight razor that gleams with blood. He frowns into a hand mirror at the cut upon his chin. "You must be more careful," the old man says from right behind him, and Jonathan gives a violent start, clearly having believed himself to be alone. "I do not allow mirrors in my castle." He seizes the tiny looking glass, which slips from his fingers and shatters on the floor. Jonathan jumps out of the way, but his elderly host is busy staring at a photograph propped against the washbasin. It shows a young woman with shining golden hair and a beautiful, heart-shaped face Jonathan could not bear to be parted from, not even whilst shaving.

Another vision. Jonathan lies naked on a bed, his wrists and ankles tied to the posts. The old man laughs as Hong and Thabisa crawl up Jonathan's legs, white silk slipping off their shoulders, their sinuous movements at odds with the fury and reluctance in their eyes.

Another vision. Perspiration runs down Jonathan's temples as he pounds on the door of his room, kicking the locks and shouting. "You cannot imprison me here!" he screams.

Another vision. The rising sun stains the sky blood red as Jonathan runs through a hall curving downward in a dizzying labyrinthine spiral. He holds a wicked silver blade the length of his arm from elbow to fingertip, glinting sharp in the light.

Another vision. Jonathan covers his mouth, looking sick, in the musty bowels of the castle. A candle illuminates a box of earth in which the old man is lying perfectly still, as though dead, though his blue-green eyes are open and his bloodstained lips curve upward.

Another vision. Heavy wet snow plummets from an iron-grey sky. A frigid wind grips the trees as Jonathan climbs down a tower choked with blue ice, slowly and painfully, shivering in his thin clothes. There is blood on his torn fingernails, gashes on his arms and legs, and two weeping wounds upon his throat. He falls to the wet ground at last, shaking with fatigue.

"Here! Take this and follow the eastern path away from the ravine," calls a soft voice from above. A bundle lands beside Jonathan, containing a warm cloak, food, and the blade he had carried earlier, now sheathed. He looks up at Hong and Thabisa in the high window, his confusion palpable, before seizing the bundle and stumbling away through the heavy snowdrifts.

"Lucy!" Jonathan cries, his eyes wild, and suddenly I am back in his firelit office. "Are you ill? You have been staring at me for minutes without blinking or breathing."

I press my hand to my heaving chest. "I-I saw it. All of it. Everything that happened to you. The castle, the mountain, the dining room with Hong and Thabisa." He jerks at the sound of their names. "The broken mirror, the blade, the tower you climbed down. Forgive me. I think . . . I somehow slipped into your mind and saw your memories. I did not mean to."

"You *what*?" he croaks.

"Mina's photograph against the washbasin. Hong and Thabisa watching as you limped away. I am sorry. I didn't mean to invade your thoughts, I swear." My throat tightens with guilt. I am no better than Vlad, but whenever *he* plunders my brain, I feel it like a thousand hot needles in my scalp. "You did not know? You felt no discomfort?"

"No!" Jonathan sputters, his face a mask of horror. "You saw my thoughts?"

"Please. I am sorry—"

He grabs a letter opener and points it at me. "You are evil and foul," he seethes. "What sort of monster have you become? Be gone! You are *never* to come here or see Mina again!"

"Please believe me, Jonathan," I beg, clasping my hands in desperation. "I am still learning my own capabilities. I know I am failing miserably, but *please* do not keep me from Mina." Tears sting my cheeks as I turn my back on him, falling to my knees before the fire. "I will not look at you. That way, I cannot invade your memories further."

There is a silence.

"You saw everything?" he asks gruffly. "Even the night where I lay . . . the women . . ."

I bow my head. "I will not tell a living soul what was never my right to know. That includes Mina. Your secrets are safe with me."

"Why?" he asks, very low.

"Because you were forced against your will. And because I would never hurt Mina, not when she would give her last breath for you. I care not one jot about you, it's true. But you are her one true, enduring love, and I would sooner destroy my own self than erode her trust in you."

Another moment of silence passes, and then I hear the letter opener clatter onto the desk.

"I will leave now," I say, getting up without looking at him. "And I will tell you what I told Mina not so long ago: *never* invite a stranger into your home. Listen to Dr. Van Helsing and do everything he tells you to do. That man is someone to be reckoned with, and—" I stop myself before I can add *if anyone comes close to being a match for Vlad, it is he.* "Do not go anywhere alone or at night. And promise that you will keep yourself safe above all." I risk a glance at him.

"Keep *myself* safe above all?" he repeats, his grey eyes narrow.

"I had to watch Mina's heart break when she thought she had lost you, and I don't ever want to see her go through that again." I swallow hard, my eyes burning with unshed tears. "Will you tell her . . . tell her that I love her, always and forever? And Arthur? I tried to see him, but the mist would not take me. He sleeps too deeply, I think. How is he?"

Jonathan's mouth forms a grim line. "Devastated. I have never seen a man more so," he says, and I cover my face, trying not to sob. "If I didn't know how honest he and Mina are, and how they do not love where it is undeserved, it would be so much easier to hate you."

"They are better off without me," I say softly. "I will leave them in peace, even if every day apart cuts like a knife. I was never gentle and good, like Mina, and now I am being punished for it, justly so. There is no going back, no point in regretting my mistake. All I can do is learn as much as I can . . ." I hesitate, choosing my words with caution. "So I can protect the ones I love."

Just as I am about to leave, Jonathan speaks again.

"He wished to purchase property. The old man. But the transaction was not completed, at least not by me. I was in a state of confusion toward the end. Some devilry, some trance through the taking of my blood. I only began the paperwork for him, but never finished."

I fold my lips. Vlad would have found a way around that. He would have had Jonathan sign where necessary and then arranged everything else himself to acquire Carfax, in Purfleet. Carfax, meaning crossroads, where legend has it that dead murderers come back as vampires.

"Write down everything you remember, exactly as you have been doing," I urge Jonathan, gesturing to the mess of paper around us like ink-splattered snow. "Share as much of it as you can with Mina, Arthur, and especially Dr. Van Helsing."

Jonathan cocks his head. "Especially him? Even though he and Quincey now hate you and believe you to be a monster like the man who tricked me?"

I nod through the sting of his words. "You must be as honest with one another as you can, for withholding secrets will keep none of you safe. I want Van Helsing to know you and I spoke tonight, and that I understand he is trying to protect everyone the way he tried to protect me."

The ink on Jonathan's hands has long dried, but he wipes them on his gown anyway, desperate for something to do in this awkward pause between us, this uncertainty as to what we are, be it allies or enemies. He clears his throat. "Where are you? Outside of the . . . the mist?"

"Dover."

He frowns, and then his face clears. "You are taking a boat somewhere. Are you going *there*? To the mountains?" I do not even dare nod, afraid of the pain that might come. I keep my eyes on the floor and my lips closed. "You're not going of your own free will, are you, Lucy?"

"It doesn't matter anymore." I wipe my wet cheeks. "I will not come back again. Remember everything I have told you. I cannot emphasize the danger you are all in."

We do not say goodbye or whatever barely friendly acquaintances might say under normal circumstances. But as I sweep the cool, silvery mist around myself and allow it to take me back to Dover, to the White Cliff Hotel where the other half of my physical body still lies, I feel somewhat lighter than I have since leaving my old life behind.

CHAPTER FOUR

The next morning, I surprise myself by sleeping straight through breakfast. I am forced to hurry to make myself presentable and summon the bellboys to carry my luggage, what with the ferry leaving in less than an hour. Slumber is not as restorative to me as a vampire—always, there is an alertness that I may be discovered and attacked at any moment—but reaching through the mist and the charged confrontation with Jonathan must have exhausted me.

I slip into the hotel kitchens to steal some cuts of raw meat to wrap and conceal in my bag. I leave money on the counter and enter the lobby to find the baroness preparing to depart.

"There you are, Lucy," she says, peering at me. "You missed dinner *and* breakfast, and I thought perhaps you had left without saying goodbye."

"I would never do that," I say, taking her arm as we go out to hail a carriage to the docks.

The rain stopped sometime last night, but thick clouds still hide the sun. I gaze out of the carriage window, thinking of Arthur and Mina and of how Jonathan and I had fought through our mutual dislike to become . . . what, exactly? Not friends, but not enemies, either. He distrusts me, but he does not seem to hate me as Van Helsing does. The doctor dislikes loose ends, and he must consider my existence to be a most bothersome one. He thinks me a monster now, murderous and corrupt, and I have a feeling he will not let me slip away so easily.

I pray silently that the ferry will leave on time.

A crowd is already waiting at the docks when we arrive. The driver hands down our trunks, and I cover my face with my veil, studying the boat tossing in the restless grey water. I had left London by train calmly enough, but this leg of the journey feels different, like the closing of a chapter. Today, I will sail away from the only home I have ever known, and the moment I set foot upon that vessel, the old Lucy Westenra will truly be gone.

I turn back to the cliffs and find myself saying farewell not to Dover, but to Whitby—for it was there that I first began to transform from the girl I was into what I am now. Soon, I will be swept away to far-flung lands, and beneath my melancholy and regret is awe that everything I have wanted, I have caused to happen by one fateful choice.

"We will be traveling with quite the coterie," the baroness says, breaking into my thoughts. "I count eighteen passengers, including us. And look, there are Nell and her husband."

The couple are far from being the only newlyweds sailing to France. I see several others with gleaming rings, one pair—a tall lanky man and his dainty blond wife—attracting my eye in particular as my heart gives a tug for Arthur and Mina. Perhaps this is yet more punishment for my choice, that wherever I go, I will see the ghosts of the ones I love and can never have again.

"Good morning," a uniformed man addresses the crowd. He looks to be in his sixties, with a white mustache and a brassy voice that carries over the wind and water. "I am Captain Clare, and I have the honor of bringing you across the English Channel today.

Unfortunately, the skies are threatening more rain, and the wind is growing stronger, so our arrival in Calais will still be delayed. In fair weather, our voyage would take five hours. But because I choose to proceed with caution, my crew will be taking a longer route, and we will arrive tomorrow instead."

Murmurs of concern ripple through the crowd. I glance at Charles Wright-Davies for a reaction, and he does not disappoint. "Good *lord*, another delay!" he cries, as Nell murmurs to him. "I don't care if they can hear me. It's a nuisance, and I am well within my rights to say so!"

"I apologize, but I am sure you can all appreciate that we sailors are at the mercy of the elements," Captain Clare says calmly. "Comfortable accommodations await you, as do delicious meals, fine wine, and cigars for the gentlemen." He raises his snowy eyebrows, and some of the men give appreciative chuckles. "We will ensure that you have a pleasant voyage. Thank you." He walks back onto the ferry as two crewmen begin collecting tickets.

The baroness takes my arm. "Well, what do you make of this, Lucy? I shall never refuse a night of rest and fine dining, but this is yet another day's delay!"

"I am in no hurry to reach my destination," I say, shrugging.

"What *is* your destination, my dear? You never said."

"I am going to stay with some . . . distant relatives in the Carpathians."

Before she can question me further, we reach the front of the queue, and the crewmen take our tickets. As we step on board, I hear one of them mutter, "Eighteen passengers out of twenty. I suppose the captain won't wait for the last two," to which his companion replies, "We leave at nine sharp. Tick off the other names and leave those be. Foreigners, eh? I rarely come across another Dutchman. It's nice to see a Van-something every now and then. Reminds me of home."

I stop in my tracks, gripped by overpowering unease.

"Come along," the baroness says, shivering. "The wind is so cold."

I barely hear her. In my mind is the voice of the clerk at the White Cliff Hotel: "I helped a doctor who insisted upon seeing our guest list. . . . He asked about foreign-looking guests."

"Go on without me," I say as my dark veil whips across my face. "I would like to stay out here awhile and watch the ferry depart. I . . . I want to say goodbye to England."

"Of course," the old woman says, her face softening as she leaves.

The crewmen ignore me as I brace my hands on the railing, gut twisting with disquiet. I keep my eyes on the horizon to hide the fact that I am listening intently, waiting for them to say more about the tardy passengers—one of whom is a Dutchman whose name is Van-*something*.

A third colleague joins them. "The captain says we are to depart in five minutes. Anyone left behind will just have to take the next boat out."

The knot in my stomach loosens a bit. Captain Clare is impatient to go, and I will be safe.

Suddenly, the man adds, "Wait. What's this?"

Two people are running across the docks, holding their hats tight against their heads in the wind, and I am sick, *sick* with dread because I know who they are. Even before I can see their faces, I recognize their scents. One smells of mint, tobacco, and gunpowder, and I know his coat conceals the pair of silver pistols he had pointed at me only a few nights ago. The other smells of medicine, soap, and clean linen, exactly the same as when he had sat by my bedside, frowning in concentration as he pressed his fingers to the wounds upon my throat.

Dr. Van Helsing lifts his hand to the crewmen. He runs faster than Quincey Morris, who is broader and heavier and is carrying weightier luggage. Both men pant as they run up the metal walkway to board the ferry. "Good morning!" the physician calls breathlessly.

"May I help you gentlemen?" the third crewman asks. His voice is polite, but his body is tense and suspicious at the sight of two such *different*-looking men.

Dr. Van Helsing offers a smile, clearly practiced and designed to put Englishmen at ease when exposed to his deep olive skin and narrow dark eyes. When he speaks, there is not a trace of his Chinese heritage in his perfect English, which is tinged only by shades of Dutch and German. "I am Abraham Van Helsing," he says. "My friend and I would like to purchase passage aboard your ferry. We are eager to reach France as soon as may be."

"The name's Quincey Morris. I hope we're not too late," the other newcomer adds, his voice deep and calm, and the crewmen all stare at the sound of his drawling American accent and the sight of his ebony skin and athletic stance.

Move, Lucy, I urge myself. *Find your cabin, lock the door, and stay there.*

But my feet will not obey me. All I can do is stare at these men from my former life—once my friends and now my hunters. If they get on this ferry, there will be no hiding from them unless I refuse to leave my cabin. The raw steaks in my bag will have to last me until we dock in France tomorrow, for it will be far too risky to creep into the ferry kitchens for more.

Suddenly, Quincey turns, sees me, and doffs his hat as he would to any other lady. I dip my chin in acknowledgement, praying that my veil is thick enough to obscure my features. It must be, for his expression remains neutral as he turns back to face the crewmen.

"We do have a vacancy," one of the men is telling Dr. Van Helsing, "but it is a single cabin with only one bed. A couple was meant to travel with us, you see—"

"We'll take it," the doctor says without hesitation.

"I repeat," the crewman says, looking even more tense and suspicious, "it has only one bed. It is not suitable for two gentlemen such as—"

"Does it have a chair?" Quincey interrupts.

The man pauses, long enough to be insolent. "Yes."

The cowboy shrugs. "If I can sleep on the ground by a campfire, then I can certainly spend one night in a chair. The good doctor can have the bed. It's no hardship to me."

Dr. Van Helsing pulls out his bulging pocketbook. "I have plenty of money, and I will pay whatever is necessary. Our business is our own, but I think I may tell you that we are in pursuit of a deadly killer and wish to ascertain if she is on this boat."

"She?" the man echoes. "A deadly killer who is a woman? Who has she killed?"

Quincey does not answer. His gaze is fixed upon the passenger list. "Are those the names of all of the people sailing today? May we have a look?"

The crewman holds the list out of reach. "Are you officers of the law?" he asks tersely. "No? Then you are not privy to this information."

"Fine," Dr. Van Helsing says, frowning at Quincey, who shrugs his broad shoulders. The ache in my chest intensifies at the familiarity of their voices and mannerisms. Not so very long ago, they had done everything they could to fight for me and protect me, and now . . . I close my eyes briefly and then, as calmly as possible, turn to head across the deck of the ferry.

The doctor's eyes find me, attracted by my movement, and whatever he was about to say to the crewmen dies upon his lips as his attention sharpens on me.

"Look!" one of the crewmen says, pointing. "Those must be our last two passengers."

Everyone turns to watch a couple hurrying out of a carriage—everyone, that is, except Dr. Van Helsing. Quincey glances at him, sensing his stillness, and follows his gaze to me.

Slowly, I put a hand over my face as though adjusting my veil and turn away.

"Excuse me, madam," Dr. Van Helsing calls to me. "One moment, please!"

Every nerve and muscle in my body is telling me to run and find my cabin. But I know that any other woman, innocent and unknowing, would turn and look at the doctor. And so that is what I do, tilting my head questioningly at him as I continue fixing my veil.

But then the newcomers are running up the walkway, breathing as hard as Dr. Van Helsing and Quincey had a moment ago. The man is wheeling two heavy trunks while his wife holds up a pair of tickets. "We are here," she gasps in accented English. "Please, we are here."

"Mr. and Mrs. Van Beek, you're just in time." The crewman adds a few words in Dutch, then looks at Dr. Van Helsing and Quincey. "I am sorry, but we are at full capacity. Another boat is scheduled to leave in a few hours, though with the impending storm, it may be tomorrow."

"Van Helsing?" Quincey asks, but then the crewmen are unceremoniously shooing him and the doctor down the walkway as though they are a pair of unwelcome cats. They stare numbly as the metal walkway is folded and pulled onto the boat, forbidding their passage.

I'm safe, I think, as the tightness in my gut eases. *For now.*

On the docks, Dr. Van Helsing cups his hands around his mouth and shouts a name. "Lucy!" he cries, barely audible over the rushing wind. "Lucy!"

I know that he cannot see through my veil now—not at that distance. He is only guessing and trying to see if I react. He expects me to startle and run, perhaps. And so I keep my eyes on him and give a slow, confused shake of the head. At once, I see that my calm, puzzled demeanor has given him pause—I have succeeded in making him doubt.

A crewman approaches me. "Do you need assistance in finding your cabin, ma'am?" he asks, and I hand him my ticket, just as any innocent passenger would. I take his offered arm and do not turn to look at my friends again as we climb a set of metal stairs, where I let myself into cabin twelve and shut the door securely. Only then do I collapse to the floor and press my hands over my heart, which would have been thundering had I still been human.

But had I still been human, I would not be on this boat. I would not be running away, leaving everyone I love, and sighing with relief to hear a horn signaling our departure. Shaking, I kneel on the narrow bed and call silently to the mist. Outside the porthole window, it rises, obscuring the rear of the vessel from sight—and I will take care that it does so for the remainder of our voyage, until we reach land and I can disappear. I press my face against the glass. I cannot see the docks from my cabin, but I know the doctor and Quincey are still standing there.

I think I will never see them again.

I *pray* I will never see them again.

CHAPTER FIVE

An hour later, when I step out of my cabin to join the baroness at our midday meal, the wind is even colder and fiercer than before. But as noisy as the gale is, Charles Wright-Davies's nasal voice is louder. He and Nell are leaving their quarters a few doors away from my own. "How dare they relegate us to the bloody *bowels* of this ferry?" he is complaining. "It was sheer luck that I could coerce that couple into trading cabins with us, so we could be up here."

"The crew is doing their best, I'm sure," Nell says patiently, and then her face blooms like a flower at the sight of me. "Ah, Mrs. Westenra! How do you do?"

My heart gives a squeeze at the name that belonged to my mother. Nell must assume that Lucy Westenra is my married name, and I do not correct her. "Mr. and Mrs. Wright-Davies," I say. "What a pleasant surprise to see you again."

Charles surveys me through watery blue eyes. "It seems we cannot get away from you, Mrs. Westenra. You were on the train with us from London, and now here you are again."

I look at him, amused by his jealousy. Nell has likely never smiled at *him* so brightly. "We are all bound for France," I say lightly.

"Travelers with the same destination often take the same conveyances, do you not agree? I assure you that I am not following you."

"Won't you lead us poor, helpless women to the dining room, darling? I'm dreadfully hungry," Nell says, and as her husband moves grudgingly toward the stairs, she takes my arm and sighs. I feel a twinge of pity, though I know she chose her marriage as surely as I chose my new existence. Perhaps we did not know everything we would face, but at least we can say that we decided for ourselves. "I saw the baroness dining alone at the hotel last night and wondered what had become of you. Is she going to Calais as well?"

"She is, and I am to meet her for this meal." I look sideways at her with a playful twinkle. "I was overcome with exhaustion last evening. I'm sorry that you searched for me in vain."

"Take care that I do not do so again," Nell says, laughing, and her husband glances over his shoulder at us, perhaps hearing the flirtatious lilt of her voice. When he turns back around, she leans in close, enveloping me in her honeysuckle perfume. "Walk with me tonight, Lucy. I should like to continue our conversation when Charles is asleep."

I feel a delicious thrill in my abdomen—either a reminder of my storied past of flirting or the knowledge that this is another invitation I will be compelled to accept. "When?"

Her sky-blue eyes shine at me. "When the moon is bright."

We enter a narrow dining room that runs almost the length of the ferry. The walls are of dark weathered wood, as are the tables, almost all of which are occupied. The space would be much too hot and uncomfortable for me had not a porthole been opened, allowing a breath of fresh, cool air to mute the smell of blood in all of these warm bodies. Relieved that I thought to dampen my hunger with an animal steak, I look around to find the baroness seated near the window.

Nell pouts. "Must you go? Wouldn't you and the baroness like to join us?"

"My dear, these tables are much too small for four," Charles says at once. "You and I will dine alone, as befits a honeymooning couple."

I smile and move away, and the baroness lifts her eyebrows when I approach her. "You enjoy playing with fire, I see," she observes. "Have a care when you are walking on deck later. That husband of hers would happily push you into the sea."

"I have given him no good reason to do so," I say, though I see the sense in her warning. This casual flirtation is not wise in one who is meant to travel discreetly—particularly with one's former friends in pursuit. Even now, Dr. Van Helsing and Quincey must be awaiting the next ferry to France. I shiver, wishing I were melting into the crowds of Paris. The servers bring us wine and bowls of fragrant consommé, and I try to shake off my unease. "This smells delicious, does it not?" I ask with forced cheer, admiring the bright green herbs floating atop the clear soup.

My friend, however, is not put off so easily from the subject. "That young man may be a fool, but he loves her. Steer clear, Lucy. Surely you remember how it was to be a newlywed?"

I look down, avoiding her gaze, for I certainly do *not* remember.

Arthur's ring winks up at me, the diamond between the sparkling emeralds that are as green as his eyes in some lights. By now, I should have been his. Lucy Holmwood. Lady Godalming, young mistress of the estate, perhaps planning our first ball as a newly married couple. We should have had a beautiful wedding day, surrounded by friends: Mina and Jonathan, newly married themselves; Jack Seward and Quincey Morris, eager to celebrate our joy; and Dr. Van Helsing, who would have taken the train in from Amsterdam. Instead, Arthur and I will be a sea apart.

He, a lord without a lady . . . and me, an undead being without breath.

The baroness touches my hand, seeing my sorrow. "Forgive me for paining you." Her eyes take in the whole of my face, and I fidget in my chair, for her scrutiny reminds me so much of Mamma's attempts to untangle the thoughts in my head. "I know you think me too bold and that I am a prying old woman. But if you need a friend, I am here."

"Thank you," I say softly. I sip the broth, hoping we will move on to safer topics. But the soup reminds me of Mamma, who had favored mild dishes such as this—the opposite of Papa, who had relished the spices of his grandmother Vanessa's country and passed his tastes on to me. I struggle to tamp down the grief of remembering my parents and how much they had loved me.

The old woman is still watching me. "So you do eat. I wondered."

"You suppose that because I missed dinner and breakfast I can go without eating?"

"Without eating food." She pauses. "*Human* food, that is. I know what you are, Lucy."

The spoon slips from my hand and clatters against the bowl, but the room is noisy and no one pays any mind. "I don't know what you mean," I say curtly, my hands clenching into fists.

The baroness waves my words away. "You don't need to pretend. I knew what you were the moment I met you on the train. I can smell it on you, the lingering essence of human blood."

My mind becomes a dizzying whirl of panicked thoughts: how she could possibly know the truth, what she might do with it, and how Vlad will react when he finds that I have somehow revealed myself to a human. I ponder how to confuse and persuade the old woman that I am only a dream, a figment of her imagination, should she decide to tell someone. Killing her is out of the question. I will not be like Vlad. But perhaps I could use the mist and put her into a trance . . .

"Have no fear," she says, interrupting my frantic thoughts. "Your secret is safe with me."

Through the cacophony of smells in the dining room, I pick out the scent of her blood, thick with history and a life long lived. "You tell me to have no fear," I say. "But why aren't *you* afraid? You sit across from a creature who could kill you before you took your next breath."

To my surprise, she laughs. "You think death frightens me? I am too close to the end to fear it. No, my dear. I trust in your strength and deadliness, but you will not use them against me." The servers bring the main course: flaky white fish cooked in herbs and butter on a bed of crisp, colorful vegetables. She begins to eat, and I know the tremor in her hand is only from age.

The tension ebbs from my body. "How did you sense me when no other human has?"

"On the train, you asked if I had ever known someone like you. Well, the truth is, I *did*. And here I am not speaking of just your heritage."

Realization dawns on me. "Not a human woman, but a—" I break off, not daring to say it. Not when I remember the blinding pain that comes whenever I risk exposing Vlad.

The Baroness von Bassewitz, however, has no such qualms. "Yes, I knew a vampire. Two, in fact, who happen to live in those very mountains to which you are going."

I sit back in my chair, hard. She knows Vlad's other brides, in whose exile I will soon take part and with whom I will be imprisoned in that castle in the wilds of Austria-Hungary. Out of sight and mind, so that he might continue spreading his venom without concern for us.

"Your food is growing cold. Eat, and I will tell you all." She gestures to my food, and I numbly pick up my fork, like an obedient daughter. "I am of an ancient family on both sides, my father descending from German nobility and my mother from the royalty of Austria-Hungary. My maternal grandfather owned several ancestral estates, the grandest of which lay in a forest at the foot of the Carpathians. This region has a lovely name," she adds, and proceeds to pronounce it slowly and clearly. "It has many translations, such as the Horns of Ice or the Midwinter Peaks."

Or the Mountains of Deep Winter, I think. That was the translation Mina had told me, the one Jonathan's client—none other than Vlad in a cunning disguise—had favored.

"From the windows of the estate, I could see the great castle atop the peak, half hidden by trees and mist. My brothers and sisters and I were told many times never to play outside the gates of our land, for the villagers warned of a strange, dark evil that haunted the mountain." In the mischievous smile playing on her lips, I can see a hint of the girl she was. "But I didn't listen. I never did. I was the favorite, beloved by my grandfather for being the bravest of the children."

"You climbed that mountain?" I guess.

She shakes her head. "The mountain is much too steep. But one afternoon, during a game of hide-and-seek, I slipped out of the gates and encountered the women who lived up there."

I grip my fork. "Did you meet anyone else?"

"No, and they never spoke of another." She lowers her head, remembering. "They were so different from other adults, not just in the way they spoke to me, as though I were grown and not a child of six or seven, but also their looks. I had never seen anyone so beautiful, with skin that gleamed and eyes as luminous as the stars. That was why I stared at *you* on the train. It was another way in which I recognized you. One of them was tall, with skin as rich and black as earth and a quiet way about her. She had a lovely singing voice, sweet enough to bring one to tears."

"Thabisa," I whisper.

"The other was more like you. Small, with hair and skin like yours. She looked as fragile as a bird, but there was such strength and confidence in her gaze . . . and ferocity, too."

"Hong." A memory springs into my mind. On the cliffs of Whitby, beneath the star-strewn sky, Vlad had told me that he knew a lady from my great-grandmother's country. Now, I know that he had meant Hong, who was one of his brides. Who *is* one of his brides.

"They were fearsomely educated and spoke every language in existence. They talked to me about astronomy, history, art, and literature, and I paid more attention than I ever did at any of my lessons." She chuckles. "They were amused by me and never rebuffed my questions the way other grown-ups did. Thabisa laughed when I asked if they liked living in that old castle. She said they had little to entertain themselves, which was why they came down often to walk."

"They must have needed to feed. Were you afraid?"

"Never. They showed no sign of wanting to hurt me. They were like doting aunts, and I invited them onto the estate to play with my siblings and me."

I gasp. "You *invited* them?"

"They did not accept," she reassures me. "I think they could not. Just as we children were bound by my grandfather's rule to stay inside the gates, so, too, were Hong and Thabisa forbidden to leave their mountain. They could walk along the base of it, but they were restricted from going farther than that. They never explained why or by whom."

I look down at my untouched food, breathless with realization. The baroness had befriended Hong and Thabisa by day, indicating that these other brides share my ability to still walk in the light. And though we have never met, I feel a strange sense of connection and of sisterhood to them. "They told you what they were?" I ask.

The old woman nods. "We were talking of food, and I assumed they were teasing me when they said they only fed upon animal blood. But over that summer, bit by bit, they spoke of other things—mirrors, invitations, and the mist, and how they had lived hundreds of years. I don't think they expected me to believe them. I was just a child who thought they were spinning fairy tales. Perhaps it was a relief to unburden their truth to a harmless, innocent little girl. But our friendship ended abruptly." She sighs. "My nursemaid found me talking to them and told my grandfather, who forbade me from playing outside. Afterward, he sold the estate, and I never saw my friends again, though I remember leaving them a farewell present. I stole my brother's paints and made a rather clumsy portrait of them. I haven't thought about all of this for an age!"

I cannot help smiling at her wonder. "Do you think they have forgotten you?"

"Perhaps," the baroness says, shrugging. "I imagine, with such a long life, that many memories come and go. But then again, they had such remarkable minds."

"You must have been a welcome diversion, trapped as they were. As they *are* . . . and as I will be," I say with quiet despair. "I chose this existence, thinking it would give me the freedom I craved, but now I see that I have only given up one kind of shackle for another."

"It is natural to regret our choices," the baroness says gently. "That is the human part of you that will never go away. But the fact that you sit here as you are implies that you at least made the choice with all your heart. Is it not so?"

There is something so like Mamma in her kindness that it makes the tattered remnants of my soul ache with unbearable yearning for my mother. I cannot speak, so I simply bow my head.

"Let me tell you what I have observed in my long life, for you are young yet," she says. "Men make choices every day, some of which affect people's lives and shake the foundations of empires . . . yet they do not doubt themselves as we do. They leap into risk and uncertainty, and they take the consequences, come what may. Why shouldn't *we* do the same?"

Tears burn my eyes. "Why shouldn't we?"

She lays a hand over mine, her face full of tenderness. "Women *always* have a choice, my dear, even if it isn't obvious. And when yours came, you seized it with everything you had. I can't tell you what will happen, but I *can* tell you that you were not meant for an ordinary life."

I think of that last night in the churchyard with Arthur and Mina, who had looked at me with such horror, and Quincey, who had aimed his guns at me with shaking hands. This choice I have made has created irreparable harm, but I must live with that. There is nothing to be gained by regret. "Thank you, Baroness. I am grateful to have a friend who accepts me."

"I think you are special, Lucy Westenra, and I think we were destined to meet. But now," the old woman adds, sitting back with a weary sigh, "I believe I shall have a nap. No, do not get up. Enjoy the dessert they are bringing out. I can find my own way back to my cabin."

As I watch her leave, I catch sight of Nell and Charles. Nell is watching me avidly, and when Charles turns to speak to a server, she lifts her wine in a secret toast. I nod, trying to ignore the fluttering in my chest and remind myself what happened with Mina, Arthur, and everyone who had once cared for me. I ought to keep Nell at arm's length.

A server lays coffee, dessert, and a folded note before me. I open it to find a message written in smooth, flowing script. *Greetings to a most colorful lady, who paints every room she is in with light. Do not forget to meet me on deck tonight.*

I look up, expecting Nell to punctuate her note with a secret smile, but instead she looks worried. In a moment, I understand why, for Charles is standing over me with a frown. Quickly, I tuck the note away and ask, "Is there something I can do for you, Mr. Wright-Davies?"

"Where exactly are you going, Mrs. Westenra?" he asks, low and acidic. "You have been guarded with your plans. Will you stay in Paris?" His gaze flickers to Vlad's ring on my finger.

"Why this sudden interest in my plans, sir?" I ask lightly.

"I have a right to know when my wife is forever adjusting our honeymoon to include you," Charles says, his jealousy tainting the air like rank sweat. "At the hotel, she wished to find and invite you to dinner, and today she bids you join our midday meal. 'I cannot do without my friend Lucy,' she says, even when I tell her you cannot possibly wish to come between us—"

I lift an eyebrow in cold distaste. "And what can *you* know about what I wish?"

"I must insist that you leave my wife alone on our wedding journey. You were a bride, too, were you not? Or was that merely a charming story you made up to amuse my wife?"

He is only a weak fool, but the command in his voice nettles me, implying that it is his right to speak and my duty to obey. Nell appears at his side, looking apprehensively between us.

"Well, Mrs. Westenra, what of my request?" Charles prompts me, narrowing his eyes.

I do not back down from his pale stare. "Request? It sounded very much like an order."

"What is happening, my dear?" Nell asks him. "What have you ordered her to do?"

Charles ignores her. "You and Nell may say your goodbyes, Mrs. Westenra. As Paris will be our destination for a few weeks and not yours, now is the time for farewell."

I look up at him with mingled rage and amusement, wondering at his sheer gall. I had no intention of staying in Paris, not with Van Helsing in pursuit and Vlad expecting me to go to his castle. But a stay in the City of Light may be just what I need before my long imprisonment. "I've heard Paris is remarkable, full of grandeur and beauty," I say, smiling at Charles. "France may not be my ultimate destination, but it would be a shame to pass through so quickly."

Nell brightens as her husband's face turns purple with helpless rage. "Oh, yes!" she exclaims. "It would be wonderful to have a friend in the city. We are staying at the Destin-Savoir until November. They will have a masquerade ball in a few nights."

My smile widens with vicious delight as I rise to my feet. "What a coincidence, for I also plan to stay there! Now, as Mr. Wright-Davies clearly wishes for my absence, I will wish you both a good afternoon." And then I sweep out of the dining room without looking back.

I know full well that this is not a wise decision, but Charles Wright-Davies's attempts to control me are as good as an invitation.

And the good lord knows I can no longer refuse an invitation.

CHAPTER SIX

I do not remember falling asleep. I only recall watching the mist rise and the cold rain weep against my cabin window as I ached for my home and my friends, yearning for Arthur and imagining him slumped in an armchair in his great empty house, his eyes dim with sadness.

And then, suddenly, I am here and *there*—at once lying on a boat tossing in the fog on the English Channel and standing in a room so dark and sprawling that at first, I cannot see the corners of it. The only light comes from dying embers in the hearth, which cast a sickly orange glow upon gilded ceilings, stately paintings of woods and rivers, low comfortable chairs on a rug the color of autumn, and windows upon which the rain beats an uneasy rhythm.

I do not recognize where I am until I see the case of hunting trophies and fine old rifles on display. Lord Godalming had been so proud of them when he had lived. The *former* Lord Godalming, I should say, he who ought to have been my father-in-law.

Slowly, I move deeper inside the grand drawing room of Ring, the Holmwoods' estate—and the home that should have been mine. I should have been lady of these rooms, these halls, and these lands. I should have known the art on the walls, the pillows upon the well-used settees, and the vases I would have filled with flowers I picked from my own gardens.

And there, crumpled in an armchair, I see the man with whom I would have shared it all.

To a casual acquaintance, Arthur would not look as though he had changed at all in our time apart. But someone who loves him as I do can see the new slump of his shoulders and the wrinkles in his suit, so at odds with his once proud posture and meticulous attention to dress. His hair is mussed, his cravat is untied, and the hand half covering his face does not hide the worry lines around his mouth. His breathing is slow but uneven, only drifting along the edge of sleep rather than submerged in its embrace.

Over and over have I tried to reach him through the mist, and over and over have I failed. He neither sleepwalks nor sleeps lightly, and I do not know what is different about tonight or how I have managed to come to him at last . . . only that my whole body is afire with longing.

I touch his shoulder gently, and he stirs and looks up. I expect him to cry out or leap away, but instead, he gazes at me with tears in his eyes and asks, hoarsely, "Lucy?"

At once, he pulls me down and locks me in his arms, his strong heart pumping against my still one as he sobs into my shoulder. I stroke his hair and feel my own tears escape. His blood smells of pine, the blossoming heather of the lands surrounding Ring, and the crisp tang of cigar smoke. He smells like home. He *is* home, and the hunger I feel is not for what runs through his veins, but for the intangible—his laughter, the shine in his eyes when he looks at me, and the way I feel safe and protected when he is near.

"Arthur, my love, my dear one," I murmur as he trembles with emotion.

He pulls away to look at me. His face is bleary with crying and his chin is rough, but he has never looked more beautiful. "It worked. I *knew* it would, however Seward doubted it."

"What worked?"

"The hypnosis." Arthur stares at me the way a wanderer in the desert drinks water. "Mr. Harker told us you had come to him through the mist and not to his wife, because she sleeps too deeply . . . like me. So I asked Seward to try the procedure on me."

"Procedure?" I look him over, alarmed, as though I might find stitches or scarring.

"He learned it from Van Helsing. It's a technique that helps dislodge thoughts and memories from a person's mind. They use it on patients with trauma, I think. I didn't understand everything he said. He told me it was a kind of trance, a light sleep, and it had been effective at the asylum, and that was all I cared about. I was so afraid it wouldn't work," he adds, his breath hitching on a sob. "We tried it for hours this morning, to no avail! But tonight—"

"I was thinking of you as I drifted off to sleep," I say with wonder. "Perhaps at the very moment Jack Seward put you into this trance."

"May it last forever," Arthur says fiercely, his hands pressed to the sides of my face. "I hope I never wake up again. I don't want to go on anymore without you."

"Don't say that, love." I lean my forehead against his, unable to bear the grief in his eyes. "My dearest love, who I miss every minute of every day, who I would give anything to be with again. Oh, Arthur, how I have longed to kiss you—" I lean toward him, hungry to feel his lips on mine, but to my surprise, his expression changes and he turns away.

"We shouldn't."

I sit back, hurt, wondering if he thinks I am a monster now, too. "Why not? Are you afraid I will attack you? I would *never*—"

"No, it isn't that." He glances at my hand, at the finger that should have worn his ring but bears Vlad's instead. "We shouldn't kiss . . . because you are not my intended anymore."

His words cut me to the quick. "Arthur—"

Gently, he pushes me away and kneels by the hearth, poking at embers as though his life depends upon it. "Do you know what I think of when I sit here alone? I think of what you said the night you disappeared." His voice is as emotionless as it was passionate a minute ago. "You said that you have always longed for freedom. For the ability to live and to roam as men do."

I wait, looking at his downcast face limned by firelight.

Arthur turns back to look at me in the shadows. "You said there was nothing more in life for you," he says slowly, "than to belong to me. *Belong*. That was the word you used. As though you would be nothing more to me than a possession."

"I was only trying to—"

"As though I would treat you like any item I owned, a saddle or a horse or a gun! Can you truly believe that of me? Do you even know me at all?" This time, the tremor in his shoulders is from rage. I try to take his hand, but he pulls it out of my reach, his voice choked with tears. "It would have hurt less had you told me you loved me no more."

I take a deep breath. "I accepted your proposal because I love you, but also because marriage is the only path that was ever open to me. Belonging, yes, *belonging* to any man who would have me. I knew I would be lucky to have that man be you. But oh, Arthur, the world! I want to climb mountains, sail oceans, see cathedrals . . . to go wherever and do whatever. To be *free*. Not just a smiling doll of a wife whose only purpose is to decide what meal to serve, what dress to wear, or what name I should give our next baby."

Arthur stands and leans wearily against the mantel.

I get up and clutch his arm, desperate to make him understand. "I would have had *you*. I would have had your smile, your hand in mine, and your warmth beside me each night. It would have been a kind of happiness . . . but never everything I want in the depths of my soul. Yes, I am a selfish being. I chose this existence because I thought it would still give me *you*, but also—"

"A life without me," he says bitterly.

"A life *after* you. And all the world before me at last." I lean my throbbing head against his shoulder. "I hate that I hurt you. But I did this with all the love I bear you, and will have for you until the day I leave this earth. Please, *please* believe me."

There is a long silence, punctuated only by the crackling of the fire and the pattering rain.

Arthur sighs, and when he speaks, the anger has faded from his voice, leaving only despair. "I believe you, but I cannot forgive you, Lucy. Not yet. My heart is still in pieces on the floor. I don't know how long it will take to put it back together, and even if I can, even if it is whole again someday . . . until then . . ." He trails off. "I would have us be friends."

I swallow past my gathering tears. "Friends?"

"Friends. Just two people who share a mutual regard, who respect each other, and who can sit and talk comfortably together. I need more time, and I cannot hope to heal if your hand is in mine and your lips are . . ." He glances at the armchair where we had been wrapped in each other's arms just moments ago, then back at the fire. "I need more time."

I want to crumple at his feet. I want to sob and plead and tell him not to torture me like this—to be so near, yet forbid me from kissing him. But I can feel this is important to him. It is what he needs after all the pain I have caused him, and so I quietly step away. "Yes, of course," I say, my throat tight. "You will have all the time you need, my lo— Arthur. Let us be friends."

He nods, his eyes clouded. "Thank you."

I perch on a settee, and he returns to his armchair. The drawing room furniture is arranged companionably, set close together to invite low conversation and quiet laughter on winter nights, and I can feel Arthur's warmth in the short distance between us. I point my knees away from him, and he keeps his gaze on the fire, and I contemplate how this *friendship* will be a greater agony even than being strangers. Had I been sitting with a person I did not know, my head would not throb from the effort of not looking at them; my hands would not clench, hungry for their touch; and my heart would not be aching from the chill between us because it remembered the heat.

Arthur clears his throat. "Seward and I had tea with the Harkers today."

"Oh, how was Mina?" I ask longingly.

"Mrs. Harker tried to keep our spirits high, but she misses you a great deal. Even after Seward failed to hypnotize me, she begged him to try the technique on her, but her husband objected. He didn't like the idea of her being in a trance, even with him near."

"That sounds like Jonathan. Protective beyond all reason."

"And why shouldn't he be? Her safety is naturally his chief concern." Arthur stretches his legs toward the fire. One of his feet is inches from my own, and it takes immense willpower to keep my shoe from sliding forward to meet his. "He told us about your visit and how he guessed that you are leaving England, though you could not tell him. It physically pained you to speak of it, he said." Our heads swivel toward each other, magnets no longer fighting their natural pull. Arthur's eyes are full of a tenderness he cannot hide, though he looks away before I can savor it.

"I am all right," I say quietly. "I even made a friend, an elderly German baroness. I miss London dearly, but it *was* exciting to leave. I've never gone anywhere without Mina or Mamma." I push on, frantic to ward off the awkward silence. "The baroness and I rode the train with Nell, a young American woman, who laughed when I observed that her accent was not of Texas. She said we English think all Americans are cowboys." A faint smile touches my lips. "I miss all of you at home, and I'm glad to have someone to talk to when the missing grows too heavy."

Arthur's warm hand suddenly finds mine, a relief akin to stepping out of the rain toward a roaring fireplace. I look down at his fingers and think of the first time they had held mine at a dance on an autumn night. How I had dreamed of them for weeks afterward, imagining what I wanted them to do to me in the dark.

He pulls away, clasping his hands together until the knuckles turn white. "I'm happy you have travel companions. I know you cannot tell us where you are bound, but can you say where you are? I should like to know. And Mrs. Harker would, too," he adds hastily.

I hesitate, then decide it is worth trying. It would not reveal anything about Vlad, nor would it endanger me further with Dr. Van Helsing and Quincey, who already suspect that they have seen me. "I am on a ferry leaving Dover," I say as the image of pale cliffs and the crashing sea blooms in my mind. "The storm forbade our voyage last night, so I stayed at the hotel in town. That, too, was exciting. There were so many different people, and the man at the desk told the baroness that they often had famous guests there. One was a singer, I think."

I talk for almost a quarter of an hour, spinning out even the smallest details of my short trip for Arthur's amusement, and he soaks in every word I say. When I fall silent at last and dare to glance in his direction, I am surprised to see a small, distracted smile playing on his lips.

"What is it? Have I bored you to tears?" I ask.

He shakes his head. "No. It's just . . . you have a way with painting images of the things you've seen and the people you've met. I feel as though I had gone with you."

The whisper escapes me before I can restrain it. "I wish to God that you had."

The look in his hazel eyes is somehow both searing and soft, and I am aflame with the frustration of sitting so near yet not being in contact with him. It feels wrong. Again, Arthur is the first to turn away, staring determinedly up at a painting of deer by a pond. His lips tremble as he searches for something to say. "Even if none of us can go with you, we are always thinking of you and how we might help. Mr. Harker said you advised us to share all information and to withhold nothing from one another, for our own safety—"

"And I hold to that advice," I say, grateful that Jonathan Harker listened to me.

"We have been hard at work. Or rather, Mrs. Harker has."

"How so?"

"Dr. Van Helsing gave her an assignment." Arthur gets up to retrieve a bundle of paper tied with blue ribbon. He hesitates before taking a seat on the settee beside me, his warmth washing over me once more as he hands the pages to me. "He asked her to transcribe her husband's journal, and she has been typing every spare moment she has."

The texture of the paper feels familiar, and I realize it is the same kind that Jonathan Harker uses. Last night, the unbound pages of his journal had been scattered all over his office, but the sheets I hold contain neatly typed print, not handwriting. The first entry is dated in May of this year. *I boarded the train from Munich after a rather disappointing breakfast at the hotel. I look forward to a decent meal in Vienna, perhaps one worthy enough to bring the recipe home to Mina. It would be almost as enjoyable as traveling with my dear one . . .*

"Mr. Harker purchased a special typewriter that makes several copies at once," Arthur explains. "Much of his journal was written in shorthand, all lines and dashes and squiggles, and his wife is translating it for us. She expects to finish the task soon."

"Yes, Jonathan taught her stenography years ago." I flip through the pages, scanning the earliest details of the fateful journey that brought Vlad into my life.

Forever drawn to powerful kingdoms and shifting empires, Vlad had decided to settle next in England. He had written to several

London lawyers to purchase a property, and Mr. Hawkins had sent Jonathan Harker, his most trusted protégé, to handle the transaction. Thus Mina had given up her beloved, Jonathan had walked straight into a trap, and Vlad had bent all of his thoughts on coming to England . . . and through the mists, to me.

Dr. Van Helsing is beginning to put two and two together. He has linked my symptoms—bite wounds, loss of blood, pallor, and weakness—with what Jonathan endured in the castle, and when the journal is completely transcribed, he will know for certain. He has also seen Vlad for himself, transforming from man to bat as he left my room. It will not take him long to realize that the monster who seduced me can not only shape-shift into an animal, but also disguise his age.

That is why he and Quincey Morris are pursuing me. They believe that I will lead them right to Vlad's lair, and they intend to finish us off . . . or perish in the attempt.

"Lucy, you're shivering," Arthur says softly. He places a hand on each of my shoulders and rubs my arms, then half rises. "Wait here, and I'll get you a blanket—"

"No," I say, clinging to his hand. "Don't go."

He sits back down, closer this time. Our legs are touching, and one of his arms is still wrapped around me. We are nose to nose, eye to eye, and I hear his heart accelerate as I breathe in his comforting, familiar scent of cigars and pine. Slowly, I lift my hand to his face, stroking my fingertip over his left cheek, where an errant eyelash rests.

"Lucy," he whispers, his breath stirring my hair.

I hold up my finger. "Make a wish."

His eyes do not leave mine as he purses his lips, sending a gentle puff of air over my skin to blow the eyelash away. His leg presses harder against mine, and his arm pulls me a bit closer as I burn with the need to taste his mouth. We never had our wedding night, and here in this dream, we could explore each other the way I dreamed we would—the laces of my dress tearing beneath his fingers, tongues dancing, the legs of the settee creaking a slow and languorous rhythm as we move together. *It is only a dream, and no one need know what we do here.*

The words, unbidden, jolt me out of the dream.

Arthur stands up, looking down at me in horror. "Lucy? Lucy!" I hear him cry, his voice growing ever fainter as I plummet through the mist, going . . . where? Not to the ferry tossing on the English Channel, but to the inside of a dark and luxurious carriage upholstered in burgundy velvet. The curtains are not drawn, but tied back with golden rope, revealing a stormy evening sky, turbulent and furious, and trees bracing themselves against the violent wind.

I am on a plush seat with a cranberry-colored throw over my lap for warmth.

Vlad sits opposite me, legs crossed, one white hand resting upon his knee. There is no sign of the bent, grey old man he had been when Jonathan was at his castle. I see only strength and vitality that fill the space with a charged energy. He looks as he always has to me: an elegant, well-dressed man of forty, with dark wavy hair, a long straight nose, and a thin mouth in a pale aristocratic face. He is big and broad and takes up almost the entire seat, but where his size might be ungainly in some men, he has an effortless, preternatural grace even in stillness.

He looks at me with eyes like the sea, dark and fathomless with the promise of untold secrets . . . or my death by drowning. And God help me, I sense my fragmented soul trying to stitch itself together under that gaze, desperate to please him and to be whole again so that I will not provoke his distaste. I feel the urge to be everything to this man—wife, lover, and confidante. His slave, for blood, for pleasure, for whatever he requires.

But there is a part of me, too, that holds back. That remembers. That knows his magnetic pull is a way to control me, a lowly pawn on his game board, lured into forfeiting my soul for an existence I did not understand because he did not see fit to tell me the truth. I have never been worthy to him. I will never mean anything to him, no matter what he claims.

Vlad watches me cycle through surprise, longing, sadness, and finally hatred, and a smile touches his cruel mouth. "Hello, Lucy," he says.

CHAPTER SEVEN

I hold his gaze, struggling between unbearable yearning and equally unbearable loathing. After a long moment, he lifts a thick, dark brow. "I have never known you to be so reticent. Has something happened on the journey?" he asks, his rich voice like the held notes of a cello. His perfect English is shaded with many different accents, French and German among them. He sighs when I remain silent. "You know I can find out the answer, whether or not you respond. I am being courteous by asking you. So if you have somehow lost the power of speech, well . . ."

Pinpricks of pain erupt over my scalp like a helmet of needles, signaling his invasion into my thoughts. I grit my teeth and push them out, imagining their sharp tips breaking in two. "You told me I am part of you now," I say coldly. "You can see and hear everything, so there is no need to plunder my mind like a greedy child delving for sweets."

Vlad laughs. "She speaks! There is the bride on whom I dote." He runs his long fingers over the velvet seat beside him. His hand is bare now that he has given me his garnet set in brass, and his eyes move to the gem on my finger with satisfaction. "I'm glad to see that you are still wearing my ring. How will people know you are mine otherwise?"

"I have told you many times that I belong only to myself."

"Yet you haven't told Nell Wright-Davies that." He winks. "Fear not. I won't begrudge you a bit of fun, not when you have so faithfully promised never to expose me."

I clench my fists. "Only to avoid the pain of feeling like I am being ripped apart."

"And not when you will soon be put carefully away," he goes on as though I have not spoken. "Like a piece of fine china to be stored with my other valuables, safe and sound. All of my porcelain together in my castle." He pauses. "Though I suppose one of you is rather more like priceless black jet, but no matter . . . the metaphor still serves."

I think of Thabisa, the dark-skinned bride who the baroness told me possessed a beautiful singing voice. "And I'm certain she loves being compared to an inanimate object as much as I do," I say wearily. "What do you want with me, Vlad?"

"Nothing. I miss you and wish to know how you are." His face is so earnest that any stranger witnessing our conversation would believe him to be an adoring husband. Though I know how adept he is at mimicking human emotion—he has had five centuries to practice, after all—it is still difficult to remember when his eyes hold such devotion. "You may have forgotten those nights we shared in Whitby, but I still think fondly of them. And of you."

I look away. "Stop it."

"Don't you remember how you sought me in the mist? How I held you in the garden of statues, and danced with you in the ballroom of starlight and roses?" Vlad's baritone is low and soft, and his gaze is like a gentle kiss on my neck. "Remember when I carried you to our bench in the shadows, to keep your feet dry from the rain? I came to you in a storm like this one. I rode the wind across the sea to find you. To be with you."

I want to believe that I know him too well now to fall for this. Affection is a weapon he wields as deftly as malice, and I am no longer the innocent girl he seduced. Yet my faithless body still hungers—not for *him*, but for care and understanding, and he knows it. He knows I am a soul adrift, yearning and solitary. All my life I have searched for someone who would see and accept everything I am, and he had tricked me into thinking that person was him.

"Lucy," he says, his voice caressing my name. "Will you not come here to me?"

"No." I speak calmly, but I am tense and shaking. The space that separates us is both too great and too little all at once. I refuse to look at him, so as not to plunge into the hypnotic ocean of his eyes again. Swimming back out of the waves grows more and more difficult each time.

"Why not?" he asks, and he has the gall to sound hurt.

I run my trembling hand over my eyes. "Save this farce for someone else. Surely there is some other woman in London, young and beautiful and stupid, for you to entrap."

"Plenty of them. But right now, I want you." I hear a tremor of emotion in his voice, and some dark ribbon tied beneath my heart unspools. "I want to relive our moonlit evenings. We can have them again, Lucy. I will always bring you back to me, here in this place only we two know. Between the waking and the dreaming, and the living and the dead."

I clench my jaw. "You tricked me. You shamed and mocked and exiled me, and I will never forget your cruelty when I thought you were my friend."

"I *am* your friend. Won't you rest your weary head on my shoulder as you once did?"

An image appears in my mind, so vivid it is almost as though my consciousness has split yet again, this time sending me to a cliff on a windswept summer night blanketed with stars. A man and a woman sit on a bench beneath a willow tree, its drooping branches framing their dark romance. I ache to be that woman again—not so I can sit under Vlad's arm and feel his cold lips in my hair, but for the chance to run back down the cliffs to my warm bed with Mina sleeping in it, behind a locked door and a threshold he cannot cross. Could I do it? Would I *want* to?

"Let me be," I plead. "Is it not enough that I am obeying your orders and will soon be locked away in your castle, out of sight and out of mind? Why must you torture me?" I hate the way my voice breaks, but I cannot help it. "You have already caught me in your snare. There is no need to toy with me or pretend that you care anything at all for me."

"But I *do* care for you. We are kindred souls, and there is no one I can talk to like this. You know everything I am, and yet you wanted to be with me. Be *like* me. Come," he says, reaching for me in the darkness. "Find your way back to me again."

I sit in rigid stillness, fighting the urge to scream and pound my fists upon the windows. He is a maddening, fickle weather vane and he always has been—forever seeking a better wind, yet turning back to face me just when I think I am finally free of him.

He sighs again. "Once more, I am being courteous by asking you."

"And once more, I refuse."

"Come here." These words are imbued with some compelling power that wraps around my limbs like wire. I feel my resisting body fly straight into the cradle of his arms, landing in his lap with my arms around his shoulders. He brushes a kiss against my neck as he tugs out the pins securing my chignon. "I prefer your hair down," he says, running his hand through the dark silk waves. His ice-cold fingers stroke my scalp, and my traitorous body shivers with pleasure. "It always smells like flowers, like the white gardenias you wore the night of our wedding."

"My loved ones buried me with those flowers," I say stiffly. "And there was no wedding, only a sick orgy full of people you ensorcelled to satisfy your lust."

He presses his smile against my ear, sending tingles down my spine. "What could be wrong with that? You enjoyed yourself. It was the last time you fed, wasn't it? *Truly* fed."

I try to remove my arms from his shoulders, but they tighten against my will, pressing my breasts harder against his jacket. His hand squeezes my hip, hard enough to leave a bruise.

"Animal blood is all very well," he says lazily, pulling away to look at me. "It will dull your hunger for a while. But a word of warning, Lucy: we are vampires, and humans are our *true* prey. Ignoring your need will only drive you to insanity and . . . erratic behavior."

"What do you mean?"

Vlad shrugs. "I just don't want you walking down a street and turning it into a massacre when you can no longer control your hunger. That is all." Our faces are so close that we almost share breath, the air leaving his nose to enter my own, like new life bestowed upon me yet again. I cannot help thinking of Arthur and of how close his mouth was to mine only moments ago, and a jolt of desire runs through me as Vlad leans forward to kiss the corner of my mouth. "This advice is true of *all* kinds of hunger. Not just bloodlust," he adds knowingly, the rumble of his deep voice vibrating through his chest into me. I gasp when his freezing lips find my neck again, licking the very spot where he had once bitten me.

As a human, I had been full of wanting, forever inappropriate for a chaste young lady of my station. Society prefers me neatly pinned and trussed, content to fold my hands and wait to be pursued. And when some man, any man, has won me at last, I should lie back and think of green pastures while he has his way with me. The perfect woman of the age.

Hearing that thought, Vlad gives a soft laugh. We both know I have never been a perfect woman—that I would prefer to be the hunter, whether my object had broad shoulders or delicate soft skin. I picture Arthur's hazel eyes burning in the darkness of his drawing room as he bent over me on the settee. I imagine golden hair tumbling over my face and full breasts spilling from an unlaced corset. It has been too long since I felt this steady, breathless climb toward pleasure.

Vlad smiles. "You missed me, too," he says as his hand makes its slow ascent under my skirts, the coldness of his touch driving me into a rising frenzy.

And I think, *If I am a pawn in his game, why not make him one in mine? Why not use him to satisfy my needs in exactly the way he uses me?* And just as these thoughts intrude upon my mind, Arthur's face appears, whispering, "I would have us be friends." My heart gives a pang of despair, but I quickly push the memory away and turn around in Vlad's lap, pressing my back against his chest as he pushes aside my layers of clothing. I fold my legs and kneel on the edge of the seat, facing away from him, as he wraps an arm around my waist.

I moan when his greedy palm finds my breast—but that does not mean I care about him.

I lift my skirt, the air cool on my bare skin—but that does not mean he is anything to me.

I lower myself, drenched and slick and stretching to fit his fearsome girth—but that does not mean I will forgive him for what he has done to me.

"You're right," he whispers into my hair. "I don't deserve forgiveness. So punish me."

I brace my hands on his knees and sit down hard, taking him in even deeper. Then I raise myself back up a few inches, savoring the icy granite length of him before plunging back down again, rough and ferocious. This time, we both cry out.

"We ought to be quiet. We are on a busy street, after all." Laughing, he reaches for one of the windows and opens it slightly, revealing stone buildings, lit lamps, and people hurrying past with umbrellas. Three ladies stand twenty feet away as a gentleman holds an umbrella over them, sheltering them from the downpour. Their words carry easily to me, debating which shop to visit next as the gentleman impatiently glances up and down the street. It is too dark for them to see us inside the carriage, but they would certainly hear us if we left the window open.

Vlad smiles against my nape. "We wouldn't want to shock them, would we? Not with the sounds I can draw from you." His hand under my skirt finds the point of connection between us and I let out a groan, thankfully quieted by the rain.

I lean back to whisper into his ear. "I can keep quiet when I wish. It is you we should be concerned about." And then I grip his knees and rise up just high enough to feel the edge of him before plummeting, impaling myself hard and fast. A wicked smile forms on my lips when I hear him moan a curse. Over and over, I lift up for a long teasing moment before forcing myself back down upon his icy length. I do not hold back. My rhythm is rough and steady, merciless and cruel in its intensity, and Vlad buries his face into my hair to muffle his cries as I ride him, my body sore but able to take more and more of him with each movement.

A high female voice carries toward us. "Perhaps you could ask the people in that carriage. They may know where the shop is."

We hear a deeper voice protesting before footsteps approach our window. The gentleman peers inside, disgruntled, squinting into the darkness. "Hello? Is anyone in there?" he asks.

I freeze, trying not to pant.

"Yes, there most certainly is," Vlad says, miraculously calm even on the edge of laughter.

"I am sorry to disturb you, but do you know where Mrs. Ridgeway is? The milliner?" The man continues to narrow his eyes, which focus at last on Vlad's face without seeming to see me.

"Why, yes," Vlad says. "It is on the next street over, with a bright blue door."

"Thank you, sir." The man touches the brim of his hat, and suddenly, his gaze finds my own. I see the exact moment he realizes that I am not sitting opposite from Vlad, but *on* Vlad, and I cannot help giving him a dazzling smile. He backs away, his face bright red. He says a few hurried words to the ladies and rushes them away down the street.

Vlad and I are both laughing now, and in this moment, I can almost pretend that we have never been anything other than what we were on the Whitby cliffs—friends, confidantes, *kindred souls.* He hears this thought and strokes my hair before making as though to lift me off him.

"I am not finished yet," I say through my teeth, then slam the window shut before ruthlessly completing what I have begun. I am sure passersby can hear us even through the glass, but I do not care. I savor every ringing cry from my throat and every responding groan from his, and only when I am satisfied do I climb off and return to my seat. I am damp and breathing hard and satiated—but I do not feel happy with myself. It turns out that using someone without entangling my emotions and guilt into the bargain is not as easy as Vlad makes it seem.

"I've forgotten how charming your holier-than-thou attitude can be," he says in an airy tone. He has already put himself to rights and looks as crisp and polished as ever. "You were only answering your body's needs, Lucy. There is no shame in that."

"I know there isn't," I snap. "But I answered them with *you*, and of that I *am* ashamed."

He rolls his eyes and straightens his cravat, then knocks three times on the ceiling of the carriage. No driver answers, but the wheels begin to pull us down the street. As buildings speed by, blurred by the rain and mist, Vlad asks, "Why did you leave the box behind?"

"What box?"

"The box of earth I left in your tomb so that you could rest as I do. It was a generous gift, if I say so myself." He arches a brow. "Seeing as I only brought thirty to distribute around England, to ensure that I would have a sanctuary no matter where I went."

"Thank you. It *was* generous," I say, knowing it is what he expects to hear. I bend to fix my stockings, priming my mind against his invasion of my thoughts. Keeping secret my ability to walk in the sun may yet serve me somehow. "But I can make do with coverings and curtains. I may despise you," I add, knowing that a lie sounds truer when laced with honesty, "but I will not take something so valuable from you, not when you had them shipped at such great expense."

He is quiet, and I wonder if I have overplayed my hand. But then he says, with genuine warmth, "How sweet you are to me. And considerate of my comfort and safety."

"Yes, for you do not deserve it in the least," I say sourly.

"Ah, Lucy, I really have missed you. I suppose that is why I've gone to see her so often."

I look up. "Who?"

"Partly why, anyway," Vlad goes on, ignoring me. "She is a great deal like you, though I had my doubts. You seem bolder and less afraid of opening your mind to new thoughts. But I am beginning to see that she, too, is brave in her own way. That remarkable Mina of yours," he adds, his grin widening. "The last time I saw her, she got rid of me in such a polite way that—"

"The last time you saw her?" I repeat, fear spreading in my chest like ice.

Vlad frowns. "You know I hate being interrupted."

"Where did you see her?" I demand. "Surely she did not invite you inside?"

He stares at me until I fall silent, knowing I will not get answers until I do. "As I was saying, Mina is like you. She is forceful and direct, but in such a pretty way that I am never offended. I can see why you love her so much, that rosy, ripe Mina Murray. Mina *Harker*, that is," he corrects himself, smiling. "Now that she is married to my dashing young lawyer."

I bite back my questions, knowing he will withhold the answers if I dare to ask them.

Vlad gives me a nod of approval as a reward for my restraint. "I visit her once or twice a week and stay on the doorstep. She is proper and will not invite me in so late in the evening, not even when her husband is awake. Too bad. I should have liked to see Jonathan again."

And to taunt Jonathan with his strange familiarity, no doubt.

My anxiety fades a bit. Mina is holding fast to her promise to me. She did not understand why I insisted on her never inviting strangers into her home, but keeps her vow regardless.

"Always she is eager to be rid of me," Vlad says, his mouth curving. "She does not know why this foreign count, once so enamored by her lost friend Lucy, visits even after Lucy's death. Perhaps he could be— Oh!" he gasps. "Might he be falling for *Mina*, a happily married woman, instead? The horror! No, it would not be appropriate to invite him in, not with Jonathan there."

"Vlad," I say, urgent and desperate, "let them be. They have done nothing to you."

"But why? They are so very entertaining," he says with the air of humoring a wayward child. The carriage stops and he climbs out, reaching for my hand. "Come and see for yourself."

The rain batters me as I leave the carriage, but the cold and the wet do not bother me as much as they might have, had I been human. I look along the tree-lined street, which is far quieter than the one we had just left. Stately residences surround us, and when I gaze at the building in front of us, I recognize the windows, for I stood in that very hall last night.

We have arrived at Mina and Jonathan's home.

CHAPTER EIGHT

"What are we doing here?" I ask, tense and rigid as Vlad approaches the residence, moving not to the door but the window. The mist parts around me as I follow him and peer inside the Harkers' home. I see the hall, now familiar with its walls papered in green, a vase of lavender, and the ornate mirror in which I had seen my unblemished human reflection. I had almost forgotten how devastating it was to wake up from the dream and peer into a looking glass, both fearful and hopeful, only to realize that my nightmarish, blood-splattered shadow self had returned.

Vlad walks around the side of the building. We pass more windows, through which I see a spacious, well-appointed kitchen in which an older, kind-faced woman is bustling around, steeping tea and laying cakes on a small platter. Beside the kitchen is a handsome dining room with tasteful paintings on the walls and old but serviceable furnishings.

"They must have inherited this place from Mr. Hawkins," I say absently. "The lawyer who raised Jonathan as his own son and left everything to him when he died."

"Your friend made a fortunate marriage indeed. Ah! Here they are." Vlad stops in front of a window toward the back of the house, facing a little garden with two cherub statues.

I frown, not liking the voyeurism no matter how badly I want to see my friend. He lets out an exasperated sigh. "They will not notice us. I have made certain of that," he says as the mist rises with a movement of his fingers. When I stand motionless, he makes another impatient gesture, and I feel my body fly toward him through the fog, landing in front of the window. I start to snap at him for moving me like a doll, but what I see inside the house stops my words entirely.

The sitting room of Mina and Jonathan's home is brightly lit and cheerful, with a roaring fire in the hearth to stave off the chill of the October rain. An oil painting of a river at twilight hangs above the mantel, and all around the room, the furnishings echo the soft blues and greys of the art and give the space a charming harmony. It clearly has Mina's touch, for I am certain that an old, unromantic bachelor like Mr. Hawkins would never have thought to adorn his London home—used only when on business in the city—with pretty porcelain figurines on the mantel, plush cream cushions on the sofas, or the pot of vivid geraniums on the windowsill.

Jonathan Harker sits in a chair by the fire, looking even thinner and more gaunt with a woolen throw on his lap. The silver in his hair is more noticeable, and he still looks ill, but his eyes are bright as he looks at his wife, who is getting up from the desk across the room.

Tears sting my eyes at the sight of Mina. My beautiful friend wears a high-necked white lace blouse and a blue-grey skirt that skims the floor, with her hair swept into a lovely knot at her nape. Tiny pearls glimmer at her ears as she adjusts the pillow behind Jonathan's back. He reaches for her hand, and she entwines her fingers with his, their gazes soft as they talk.

I press my fist to my chest, right over the heart that no longer beats and yet can ache so deeply. Their love is palpable even through the glass. It is as inevitable as breathing, the way she tucks his hair behind his ear or the gentle kiss he bestows upon her fingers.

Vlad watches me, enjoying my pain and jealousy. "Well-matched, aren't they?" he asks, then rolls his eyes. "Stop weeping. Not because they might hear it, but because it irritates me."

I ignore him, watching Mina speak to her husband. They look across the room at the typewriter on the desk, which is covered by as much paper as Jonathan's study was, though in neat, organized piles. I catch sight of a map pinned to the wall. The servant I saw earlier enters the room, handing Mina a tea tray with a curtsy. They exchange a few words before the woman leaves and Mina begins pouring Jonathan his tea and cutting slices of Victoria cake.

"What a scene of domestic bliss. It would be a shame to interrupt them, would it not? But I may just do so anyway." Vlad tilts his head in mock thoughtfulness. "I've only ever seen Mrs. Harker at night, but she looks even lovelier in the light. She is a creature of the day, with that sun-gold hair and eyes like the sky. She reminds me so much of . . ." His voice has become soft and wandering, as though he is speaking to himself. I know that neither bride at the castle fits this description, and so I wait, wondering who he will mention. Wondering if I am meant to be jealous. "Well, better to let the dead lie in peace," he murmurs.

I glance at him sharply, but the touch of melancholy on his cold, stern features slips back into a cruel smile as he turns toward me.

"I would like to see if she is as lovely up close," he says. "Shall I knock, Lucy, and see?"

My chest tightens. "What is this game you are playing?" I demand. "Why do you plague Mina when there are so many other women in London?"

He laughs. "How selfish you are. You would sooner inflict me upon a stranger than have me speak to this woman you love so ardently. That is why you amuse me. Only ever looking out for your own concerns, just like me," he adds with an affectionate chuck of my chin.

I jerk away. "I am *nothing* like you. Let Mina and Jonathan be. Why torment them?"

But he is already walking around to the front, and I hurry after him, panicked.

"If you toy with Mina and visit her so often," I say, trying another tactic, "they will grow suspicious of you. It is sheer arrogance, showing yourself so often—"

Vlad goes up to the door and lifts the brass knocker, letting it fall hard against the wood. The mist surrounds me, sweeping its chill breath over my hair and skirts, and when the door opens and the Harkers' servant appears, she seems to see only him.

"Why, good afternoon, Count," she says, surprised. "What brings you here?"

"I am sorry to disturb you, Mrs. Traver." Everything about Vlad has changed in an instant. His voice is full of sheepish humility, and his words are tinged with a pronounced foreign accent. He wears a mild expression, chin tucked slightly and broad shoulders stooped as his long white hands fiddle with the buttons of his jacket. With this subtle adjustment in face, speech, and posture, he transforms from a cold, mocking monster into a shy, harmless gentleman. "But I believe I dropped my pocket watch here when I came to call a few nights ago. It must have slipped out of my coat. I wondered if you or the Harkers ever found it on your doorstep?"

The woman glances downward as though the watch might be at their feet. "I have not seen it, sir, but I will ask Mrs. Harker. Perhaps she found it and put it somewhere safe. Will you wait out here a moment?" She retreats inside and pushes the door shut, and though I know Mina and Jonathan have surely warned her not to invite anyone in, I still let out a small sigh of relief.

Vlad smirks at the closed door, which opens again promptly. "Ah, Mrs. Harker!"

The top of Mina's head comes up only to his chest, so she is forced to look up at him. Her figure is appealingly soft and rounded, and up close, I see grief in the shadows around her eyes and the peeling of her lips. She looks small and delicate, and yet she directs her gaze with such force upon Vlad that I know her strength and intelligence cannot be lost on him.

"Hello, Count," she says, her tone cool, calm, and even. "Mrs. Traver tells me you've returned for your watch. I found it when I stepped out yesterday. Here it is."

Vlad presses a hand to his chest in a pantomime of relief. "Thank goodness. It belonged to my father. It was a gift from my mother and one of his most cherished possessions. I was afraid it had been lost forever, this symbol of their enduring love. Thank you, Mrs. Harker. Thank you kindly." His gratitude is so convincing that even I would be fooled if I did not know better.

Mina's eyes soften, and when she smiles, every inch of my body is starving for her. Ten steps and I could be in her arms and she in mine. My hunger to hold her is unbearable. I move forward and reach out, but I touch only empty air. Desperately, I try again, and again I fail.

"Mina!" I plead, my voice trembling.

Neither of them pays me any mind.

"I am glad to have kept it safe for you, then," Mina is telling Vlad.

"Fortunate is the man who has anything in your safekeeping," he says quietly, with great feeling. "You are a lady of integrity. One knows that he can leave much in your care, even something as fragile and precious as his own heart."

Mina's smile fades into shock at the unmistakable meaning in his voice.

He laughs and nods at the pocket watch. "Silly of me, I know, to think of an object as my own heart. But it feels so much like a piece of my dear parents and their love story."

Relief washes over her face. "I see. I am sorry for your loss." She holds the watch out to him. Slowly, he closes his long cold fingers around both the watch and her hand.

"Thank you," he murmurs, looking deep into the summer sky of her eyes, and pulls her toward him ever so gently. Dazed, Mina stumbles, and his free hand is immediately on her waist while hers finds his solid chest. His head bends down to hers, caring and protective. Their faces are inches apart, sharing breath as he and I did in the carriage. The memory floods over me like a scene inside my own mind: a woman moving atop a man in the darkness, her skirts hoisted, and her face turned upward in breathless ecstasy. But the hair that tumbles down her back is not black, like mine—it is golden like wheat, and the man buries his smile in its soft mass. *Vlad*, she moans, and then stretches her hand out to someone sitting opposite them. A slight, dark-haired woman, who leans forward eagerly to kiss her lips. *Lucy*.

"I could have both of you in that carriage with me," Vlad whispers, his words like dark music. I do not know whether he is speaking them aloud or only in my mind, but my whole body shakes with unease and furious desire. "And you could have each other."

Suddenly, the door opens wider, and Jonathan appears, his tall body dwarfing Mina's as he stares at his wife's hand nestled in Vlad's. The seductive vision trance ends, and I return to the Harkers' doorstep, feeling as frightened as Mina now looks. Vlad lets go, and she steps back, pressing against Jonathan, who puts a hand on her shoulder as he studies Vlad. I can easily guess his thoughts: *Why has this man come? What does he want with Mina? And where, oh where, have I seen him before?*

It is the first time he has encountered Vlad since the castle. He has never seen his captor in this younger form. If only he knew he was looking into the eyes of an agent of the devil, a monster who would snap his head off without a second thought. I want to scream a warning, but I know he and Mina will not see me through the mist with which Vlad has covered me.

"Mr. Harker, I presume. A pleasure." Vlad bows and holds up the gold watch. "I dropped this the other night when I called upon your wife, and she is kindly returning it to me."

Jonathan remains silent.

"Surely she has told you that I am the count who made her acquaintance this summer in Whitby. And also," Vlad adds gruffly, "that of dear Lucy . . . that is, the late Miss Westenra. I am sorry to be improper, but Lucy meant a great deal to . . ." He turns away abruptly, as though in abject pain, and his gaze meets mine with a dark twinkle of malice.

"I see. My wife, too, is grieving Lucy's absence . . . ah, loss," Jonathan corrects himself. It was a mere slip of the tongue, but I am suddenly fearful beyond all measure that Vlad will learn that I have visited Jonathan and Arthur in the mist, and that—like anything which gives me hope or pleasure—he will find a way to end it. He never expressly forbade me from seeing them, but I sense that I must keep this as faithful a secret as the fact that vampirism manifests differently in me. These are the only cards I have to play in his twisted game, the rules of which are known only to him, and I must protect them with everything I have.

Mina draws herself up. "Lord Godalming, too, is in mourning for Lucy," she says pointedly. "You met him at that ball in Whitby, Count, when he was still Mr. Holmwood."

"Yes, I remember—" Vlad begins.

"Under happier circumstances, he would be Lucy's husband right now," she interrupts him. Jonathan squeezes her shoulder in warning, but she barrels onward. "He has a far greater claim on her than you do, and more right to grieve over her death. Forgive me, Count, but you seem to place too much weight on your brief friendship with her."

"Mina," Jonathan says with quiet reproof. "I am sure the count means well."

"Be that as it may," she goes on, her eyes blazing up at Vlad, "surely he can see that it does no good to come calling so often. Sir, I know that you liked Lucy very much and had a special regard for her, but you must reconcile that on your own."

"No, Mrs. Harker. It is *I* who must apologize. I only came to retrieve my watch, but I can see that my calls distress you and that I am unwelcome." Vlad's tone is distant and polite, as befitting a gentleman both offended and embarrassed, but I can feel the underlying amusement in his words. He likes a challenge, and Mina is certainly that.

Jonathan shifts his weight. "Count, my wife did not mean—"

"On the contrary, I think she *did* mean every word." Vlad bows. "I will go, and you need not see me again. I will be in London less frequently, at any rate, as the work on my property is complete. Goodbye." He strides away, his shoulder brushing mine as he heads toward the street.

"Dearest, you offended him," Jonathan whispers to Mina.

"I know," she says miserably. "Wait, Count, please!" Vlad turns around mid-stride. "I am sorry to have spoken with so little tact, and I hope you will be very happy at Carfax."

A small smile touches Vlad's lips. "You remember the name of my new house."

"Yes." Her answering smile is sad. "Carfax, meaning a crossroads. The place where four roads meet. And I also remember that it is in Purfleet." She looks up at Jonathan. "The count has purchased the property adjacent to Jack's, my dear."

Jonathan goes still. His eyes move from her to Vlad, whose smile widens. "Purfleet," he repeats. "The property adjacent to Jack's."

"Is something wrong?" Mina asks, looking between them.

Her husband rubs his forehead, agitated. "No, nothing. . . . What a strange coincidence."

Mina frowns. "Coincidence?"

This is it, I think, as my palms go clammy with dread and anticipation. *This is the moment when they will realize.*

But Vlad's manner is perfectly at ease and natural. "I do find myself at a bit of a crossroads. But I think the time has come for me to choose a road ahead." He looks down at his watch and then back at the Harkers, his voice breaking ever so slightly. "I wish you both every happiness. Your love is an inspiration, and I will think of it in my darker, more lonesome hours."

He can already see that Mina's heart is soft, much more so than my own, and at the emotion in his voice, she steps forward and offers her hand again. "Grief has made me curt," she says gently. "I am sorry to have caused you pain when you only wish to be a friend."

"You could never cause anyone pain. I know it." His voice is achingly tender, and I am stunned to see his eyes glistening with tears, for Vlad has never cried before me. He strokes the side of her hand with his thumb, just out of Jonathan's line of sight, before releasing it. It is how he seduced me, once, with kind words and subtle gestures of love and care. Mina stands frozen, her hand suspended in midair, as Vlad mutters, "Goodbye," and turns away, hurrying back to his carriage like a man struggling to hide his tears.

The clouded confusion in Mina's eyes frightens me. I step in front of her, willing her to see me, hear me, *feel* me if nothing else. "Mina, please," I beg. "Do not fall for his tricks."

But she turns away without seeing me.

"What did he say to you?" Jonathan asks as they go back inside.

"I *had* to tell him to go away. I had to—" The door closes, cutting off her words.

I stand like a dog left out in the rain, forlorn at the loss of her face and her voice.

"Well, I certainly did right to silence you," Vlad says coldly. I turn to see him behind me in the mist, his stare like the arctic sea. "I thought I told you never to expose me. And here you are, trying to turn Mrs. Harker against me and ruin my fun."

"Your *fun*?" I sputter. "She is a woman! Not a toy!"

"Oh, but you're wrong. All of you are mere toys. Don't be jealous. You had me all to yourself in the carriage, but sometimes we must share. And I meant what I told you." In the blink of an eye, he closes the distance between us, and it is now *my* hand in his freezing grip. I wince as he tightens his hold and leans forward to whisper in my ear. "I could have both of you any time I wished. Would you like that, Lucy? An eternity with Mina?"

Beneath his mocking tone, I hear the gravity of his intent. I saw it, too, in the way he had looked at her. I was once the object of his obsession, after all. Vlad has always been interested in Mina. She is no blushing girl ready to faint into his arms and never has been. She loves one man and one man alone and will not step outside the bounds of her marriage or what society expects of her. Not willingly. Of course such an obstacle would intrigue him—I have seen evidence of it in the past, in his being spurred on by my rejection, in knowing full well that pushing him away makes him want me more. But I had never thought his attraction to Mina anything more than a passing fancy for a beautiful, unattainable woman.

Now, I know he means to turn her, too—or at least taste her blood, as he did mine.

"They will put the pieces together," I say through clenched teeth, as coils of fear crawl in my belly. "They will know that it was *you* in the mountains, *you* who tortured and imprisoned Jonathan, *you* who tricked and killed me. They will find out."

He does not speak, but the look on his face is answer enough. I fall backward at the revelation, my mind reeling. This is all a part of his diversion: his growing desire for Mina, her reluctance to succumb to him, his single-minded pursuit of her. He does not worry about calling so often because he *knows* they will realize who and what he is. Humans always do.

Vlad is forever on the run, constantly fleeing from this country to that. He shamed me once for not predicting his nomadic existence as a disadvantage of immortality. It does not matter to him that Mina and Jonathan and Dr. Van Helsing will succeed in their investigation. He *wants* them to succeed. It is a tantalizing game of cat and mouse, alternately swapping roles with his hunters and challenging himself to contaminate Mina—to *win*, in that way—before all is over.

The selfishness of it, the conceit, takes my breath away.

"What else should I expect," I seethe, "from a man with everlasting life, but greed and arrogance? Nothing means anything to you. Whatever falls from your lips is a disgusting lie."

"It's a pity Mina does not sleepwalk," he says with quiet, venomous delight. "It is much easier to trap a bird that spreads its dark wings, as you did, than a turtledove in her nest. But no matter. I will find a different tactic with this one. One way or another, I will have Mina. I love women who interest me . . . but I do not need to tell *you* that, do I?"

"Do not *ever* come near her!" I scream. "I will find you, Vlad! I will stop you. I will warn them. I will do everything in my power to protect her—" My words are cut off in a squeak as he seizes my arm, grasping so tightly that a bone pops and tears spring to my eyes.

"You are *never* to expose me. I took measures to ensure you never will, but this is a little reminder, my dear." He angles his grip and the bone cracks again, louder this time. I fall to my knees, weeping. My broken arm will heal almost immediately, I know, but the memory will not go away so soon. "My plans will unfold as *I* command, not you. Mina is no longer yours to protect. If you interfere, you will feel pain a thousandfold greater than this. Do you hear me?" He flings my arm back distastefully, and I hug it tight, crying. He nudges me in the ribs with the toe of his boot when I do not answer. "Do you hear me?" he asks again, each word a drop of poison.

"Yes, I hear you," I choke out.

"You'll be locked away soon enough." He gives my ribs another punch with his boot and strides away, climbing into his carriage. It leaves without me, dissolving into the heavy mist.

And then I am pulled back to the ferry, with the English Channel tossing beneath me.

CHAPTER NINE

Later that evening, I stand on deck, gazing into nothingness as my veil whips in the frigid gust. The sharp bite of the wind sent most people straight to their cabins after dinner, and there is hardly another soul here aside from one or two coming out for air before hurrying back inside.

"Lucy, you're here. I half expected you not to come," says a low, amused voice. Nell strides toward me, wrapped in thick furs against the chill, though I can see the sparkle of sapphires around her milky throat. It hurts to look at her, for she resembles Mina even more in the shadows, and perhaps that is why my voice comes out cooler than I had intended.

"Where is Charles? I thought he would escort you here like a prisoner."

Nell raises an eyebrow. "He does not share my enthusiasm for a stroll before bed. Of course, I neglected to mention you would join me. Are you worried he might be jealous?"

"He already is." I turn back to the restless waves. The ferry rocks as though it is a mere toy propelled by a child's hand, and though the movement has sickened many passengers, it affects neither Nell nor me. "He can hardly avoid it when you seek me out so obviously."

Nell leans on the railing an arm's length away, the wind carrying her honeysuckle scent to me. "You were the one who began our acquaintance first, don't forget," she says lightly. "Your gaze through the window of my train compartment was full of fire and intent. You looked like you would break down the door for me."

"That was only when I thought you were Mina."

She laughs, unbothered. "How cool and aloof you are tonight. Won't you even lift your veil for me? If I didn't know better, I would think you were trying to build a wall between us."

"I am trying to keep you out of trouble."

"I only want to know you better, Lucy. It's not a crime to make a friend, is it?"

I grit my teeth, still smarting from Arthur telling me he now wishes only to be friends. "Is that what you want me to be? A *friend*?"

"What else?" Nell lifts her chin so that the lamplight gleams down the line of her throat. I recognize a fellow master of coquetry, for it is a trick I myself have employed in many a ballroom. But then she shivers and pulls her furs tighter. "Come, let us be in motion. Shall we walk the length of the deck? It's as cold as the fingers of death out here. . . . Dear me, how poetic! I must write that in my journal later, when I take down every lurid detail of our meeting."

"Do you keep a journal?" I ask as we stroll past piles of rope and rubber life preservers. A crewman hurries by, doffing his cap politely.

"I do. I always thought if I could somehow escape the noose of matrimony that I would work for a newspaper. Can't you see me as an intrepid reporter? Why, you have given a jolt, Lucy. Are you shocked? Ladies *can* be reporters, too, you know—"

"I am not shocked. It is only that . . . well, my friend Mina has also kept a journal for years because *she* thought she might like to be a reporter."

"I really ought to meet this Mina of yours someday," Nell says cheerfully. "She and I sound as alike as two pennies."

I swallow past the ache in my throat. "In some small ways, perhaps, but not at your cores."

"Tell me more about her."

We reach the end of the deck and loop back around the other side. We pass a bundled-up couple talking contentedly with their arms around each other, oblivious to us and the cold. They look so in love that I am forced to turn away, pained by the sight of their simple human joy. "Mina was as vital to my life as my own breath," I say. "She was there for every tragedy and every triumph as my sister, friend, and confidante. She knew and loved me better than almost anyone in this world . . . even if she didn't quite understand me."

"Why the past tense?" Nell asks, and when I do not answer, she goes on chattering. "*My* Mina was a schoolmate named Evie Brown. I served as bridesmaid at her wedding. Her *principal* bridesmaid, and how her sisters despised me for it! But the person who knows and loves me best is my older brother, Edward, who lives in Boston and is happily married to his work."

"And what is his work?"

Her eyes twinkle. "Death," she says in a dramatic stage whisper.

I raise my eyebrows. "He is a hired assassin, then?"

"A doctor. He teaches at the medical school and carries out experiments on corpses. Nothing so compelling as reanimating a modern Prometheus, sadly! Rather, he is studying the process of decay and what happens to the body after we die. He spends his nights in a dark laboratory, sawing away at the dead and trying to discover the secret to eternal life."

I cannot help smiling under my veil at the irony of her introducing such a topic to me. "And how does he get on with finding the key to immortality?"

"He hasn't found anything except the scorn of his colleagues. They all think he's off his rocker. But then Ed is a genius, and a genius cannot hope to be understood by the masses."

"You admire him. I can hear it in your voice."

She shrugs. "He is brilliant and a pioneer in his field. It takes great courage to pursue an unpleasant topic like death, and to stare it in the face as he does." She speaks in such a casual, offhanded way that I feel certain human Lucy would have been hard-pressed to fight her infatuation with this singular young American. In fact, vampire Lucy is struggling to do so.

We pause by the railing, and she looks at me for a long, charged moment, her eyes intent.

"You don't seem frightened or disturbed by death at all," I say.

"Why should I be? We all die." Slowly, deliberately, she comes closer. Her sweet scent and warmth are invigorating in the icy air. The spot where we stand is wreathed in shadows, nestled between pools of lamplight, and I can see only the tantalizing outline of her features: the flutter of her long pale lashes, the tip of her nose, the indent just above her full lips. "I would not speak so carelessly of death to anyone but you, Lucy. People would think I was as mad as Ed, but I sense that you understand. You and I don't hide from unappealing truths, do we?"

I hear Vlad's voice echo in my mind: *Kindred souls*. I try to push him out, but he sticks like tar, soiling the edges of my consciousness.

And so I do the only thing I can to distract myself.

I lift my veil and look into Nell's beautiful face—both strange and familiar all at once—and then I lean forward and kiss her. I find her mouth ready and willing, her lips honey-sweet as they move urgently on mine. The smell of her perfume mixed with her blood, reminiscent of cloves and roaring with desire for me, is overwhelming. Her soft tongue slides back and forth across my bottom lip, and I let out a gasp as my fangs suddenly snap down, piercing my gums.

I push Nell away so hard that she stumbles against the railing and cries out in pain and surprise. "We cannot do this," I say roughly. "Go back to your husband and forget me."

She stares at me, hurt and angry, her blood screaming with her turbulent emotions, and I press my hands over my ears as though that might somehow suppress my undeniable hunger. I am *ravenous*, a mere breath away from seizing her, clasping her to me, and finding out if her blood tastes the way it smells. She is a bird caught in my net, heartbreakingly fragile and easy to destroy. She is a means to an end, an answer to a question, a disposable version of Mina I might use to sate my lust and then throw away. I breathe, trying to calm myself as she shrieks at me.

"How dare you toy with me!" Nell shouts. "You're a coward, Lucy Westenra. You're so afraid of finding happiness that you would willingly throw it away with both hands."

"What happiness could there be?" I demand. The taste of my own blood slipping down my fangs only increases my appetite. "I am a stranger, and you are married."

"*You* kissed *me*! You want me just as much as I want you!"

I bend over at the waist, heaving. I have not fed on human blood in so long—*too* long—and I must fight my instinct to kill with everything that is in me. Nell moves toward me. She is walking up to the mouth of hell and does not even know it. "Stay where you are," I command, my voice almost guttural with desperation. "Do not come any closer, Nell!"

"My marriage to Charles is a joke," she says bitterly. "I have felt more in my short time with you than I *ever* have with him, and if you beckoned, I would come running." The roar of her blood slows, but still my skin prickles with need. I want her pressed against me, helpless and weak with lust as I mold my wicked mouth to her throat. My hands form tight fists, the nails pressing hard into my palms. "But you must decide what *you* want. You are divided—"

"Go away! Leave me, Nell, *please*," I beg, knowing that one more second of smelling her will undo me completely. Thankfully, she heeds my command. The fragrance of honeysuckle and cloves fades as her footsteps move away . . . but it is quickly replaced by the scent of someone else's blood, sharper and tangier than hers, with an undertone of copper and amber.

"Miss? Are you all right?"

I am still bent at the waist, panting. I feel a strong hand on my shoulder as a man pulls me into a pool of light several feet away. He smells like soap and sweat, and when I look at him, I recognize the crewman who had walked past Nell and me earlier. He is young, not yet thirty, with dark stubble along his chin and neck where a big, beautiful blue vein pulses. I stumble forward, weak with unsated lust and hunger, and when his arms instinctively go around me, I think of Vlad moving over me in the darkness of my room, of Arthur locking me in his passionate embrace, and of Nell, so like Mina, neither of whom I can have.

"I cannot do this," I whisper.

"How can I help you, miss?" The crewman's eyes move to my ungloved hand pressed against his chest, Vlad's ring glinting in the light. "Madam, that is."

A vampire needs blood, Vlad whispers. *You are like a human drowning herself needlessly, depriving herself of the air she needs.*

"Stop it," I moan, and the crewman frowns.

Feed, Lucy, Vlad says, a smile creeping into his voice. *I give you my permission.*

It is a command, one I could not ignore even at full strength. So I straighten in the man's arms and call to the mist, summoning a thin serpent of fog that blankets the man's face as I say, sweet and low, "I feel a bit faint," and lean my head over the steady drumming of his heart.

"Not to worry, madam," he stammers as though he can hardly believe his luck. Beautiful women swooning in his arms must be few and far between in his line of work, and the mist is clouding his mind, turning this into a vivid dream. It will be a memorable one for him.

I will make certain of it.

Feed, Lucy, Vlad whispers once more.

In one swift and powerful movement, I pull the crewman into the shadows and sink my fangs into the bulging vein in his throat. His blood gushes into my mouth like nectar, steaming in the night air, as he groans with as much relief as I feel. My lips kiss his rough neck as I suck, and my body trembles deliciously with the feeding, the warm heat of well-being flooding every limb. I could drink every drop he has to offer. I could drain him dry.

No, I think. *I will not kill this man. . . . I must not.*

Each time I had bitten a human in the past, I failed to stop emptying their veins. But something about the cold air and the crashing waves clears my head and prevents me from losing myself, and I am able to wrench my fangs out of his throat after a minute or two. I am not fully sated, but no longer am I ravenous, and the crewman is still alive, though half asleep in my grasp.

He is twice my size, but I lift him easily and lean him against a doorway. "Lie down in the warmth," I whisper into his ear. "I will not have you die out here." Dazed, he staggers away to sleep off his stupor. I clean my mouth as I melt back into the cold and the darkness and gaze at the unseen horizon with relief. I have done it. I have resisted killing.

The man will recover fully, even if he suffers the fatigue, confusion, and thirst I myself endured once. He will avert his eyes if he crosses my path, ashamed by his disturbing, erotic dream of me, and he will make up a story to explain his strange wounds—rats or insects, perhaps.

Still, I am plagued by uneasiness, for I know who is hunting me . . . and who will be most intrigued if they hear about this crewman's mysterious ailment.

Almost unconsciously, my hands lift the mist, dimming and obscuring the lights of the ferry. Van Helsing knows I am bound for Calais, but at least I can prevent him from taking over our vessel unawares like some ruthless pirate. When I am finished, I feel as drained as if *I* were the victim and not the vampire—though another kind of hunger is raging within me. My mind floods with images of climbing atop Vlad in the carriage—as much as I hate myself for it—and memories of lying in bed with Arthur or kissing Mina that one forbidden day. The ache of desire tugs at me as I stumble up to my cabin . . . only to find that the corridor is not empty.

Nell Wright-Davies stands between her door and my own in some would-be perverse purgatory, her body tense with expectation. She turns when she hears my footsteps. "Lucy," she breathes, each syllable of my name drenched in yearning.

And then we are a tangle of lips and tongues and teeth, kissing as though starving for each other and pressed so tightly that we almost inhabit the same space. "We cannot do this," I mumble against her mouth. "Not here, not now. Your husband—"

"Oh, hang Charles!" She grasps me so violently that our mouths collide, and I taste salt and iron in her kiss. Her blood carries notes of sun-warmed fruit, every bit as delicious as I have fantasized, and I give a silent prayer of thanks that I sated my hunger with the crewman. Now, I can simply savor every drop I slowly suck from her cut lip. I do not need to enter my vampiric state to have her utterly and completely in my power. I want her sprawled before me and yielding everything to me—*being* everything to me.

"Lucy," she moans again as I push her into my cabin and lock the door. We struggle against each other in the shadows as I unfurl her clothing like unwrapping a gift. When I kiss her naked shoulder and she throws her head back, I catch sight of my reflection in the looking glass, grim and horrific, and quickly throw a shawl over it.

A mirror has no business seeing what we do, I think as I push Nell onto the narrow bed and nudge her legs apart.

"Lucy," she says, almost weeping, when I get on my knees and bend my head over her, my wicked, ravenous mouth once more taking what it craves.

Outside, the mist blankets the ferry like a bridal veil . . . or a funeral shroud.

CHAPTER TEN

"Another delay," the baroness says, gazing moodily out the window. "Even the captain seems out of sorts. We would have reached Calais in five hours in good weather, not two days!"

"Such is the life of a sailor," I say. "He could not have predicted this storm."

"Or this mist! I wonder that the crew can see anything at all."

My friend and I are at lunch in the dining room, though neither of us is very hungry. The ferry journeyed all night at a snail's pace, and this morning, the captain announced that we would not reach Calais until tomorrow due to reduced visibility. Many passengers complained, but I sighed with relief, knowing this unpredictable timing will make it more challenging for Dr. Van Helsing to find me. *Go back to London*, I think. *Give myself up and protect Jonathan and Mina.*

Following the captain's address, I heard him mutter to a crewman, "It worries me, this strange mist. It covers only the rear of our boat and none of the others that have passed, as though we alone are haunted by the fog . . ."

"You do not seem concerned," the baroness says, breaking into my thoughts. She studies me as she sips her steaming cup of tea. "Dare I suggest you seem pleased?"

"You know where I am bound to go and why. There is time enough to enter captivity."

"Mrs. Wright-Davies also seems cheerful about this extra day on board," she teases, then sobers. "I warned you about playing with fire, but I can't help feeling glad at the same time. There is so little happiness in life not to seize it when it appears. I wish I had done the same."

I look back at her, at the creases around her eyes that hint at a past love of laughter, the sadness in the shape of her mouth, and the wisps of white hair framing her face. How quickly she has endeared herself to me, this lady who sees all that I am yet does not judge me for it.

Two crewmen pass our table, looking worried as they talk in low voices, and she murmurs, "They must be disturbed by the delay."

"More so by the mysterious illness of one of their number," I say, my acute hearing catching the words she cannot. I look down at my ageless hands, ashamed. "I fed last night. I drank only a little, but he is still sick and abed. It is unavoidable, what I am. I often wonder at your befriending something like me. Nell, at least, has no idea that I am a monster—"

The baroness gives me a stern look. "Befriending *someone* like you, not *something*. You still have a heart, whether it beats or not. You speak feelingly for the ones you love and feel guilt for those you have hurt. Monsters don't feel or love or regret." She takes my hand in her own frail, paper-skinned one. "You made a choice without fully understanding it, and nothing can be done now. You cannot turn back time, undo your deeds, or bring back the lives you have taken."

"Then what can I do?" I ask softly.

"Look to the future, daughter. Do you mind if I call you daughter? I never had one, you see." Her smile is almost shy, and there is such tenderness and gentle understanding in her eyes that it brings tears to my own. Somehow, the spirit of my own mother seems to have found a new home in this woman she had never even met.

"I would like that," I say, wiping my cheek. "And you are right. I must look to the future and learn how to survive without killing anyone else. I have to try."

"Hong and Thabisa hated their existences," she says. "I knew it even as a child. Yet they chose to make the best of it and live in such a way that negated any past harm they had done."

I think of Vlad's restless, perpetual wandering. Despite his limitless time and freedom, he has yet to find meaning in immortality. I am terrified by the prospect of such an empty, lonely life, forever chasing and being chased and never making anything of the endless years ahead. "I am eager to meet those women. They will help me, I know. I do not want to squander this life, but learn how to accept it and to live in such a way that you would praise *me* as you do them."

"I believe you will," the baroness says. "God knows how I sympathize with you. Had I been offered the same chance at twenty, I might have been tempted myself."

"It is odd, sometimes, to think that I will never age as you will. It feels wrong. Unfair."

She laughs. "I am content. The sweetness of life, for me, is in knowing there will be a final day, which brings meaning to each hour I have left. If I were in the peak of health, like you, an extra century would be a boon. But no, I am ready and willing to go when my time comes."

A headache pulses at my temples. The soup does not appeal to me in the least, not after tasting human blood last night. Early this morning, I crept into the kitchens to steal some raw steaks, the thought of which makes my gums prickle with anticipation. "Please excuse me," I say, rising from my seat. "Immortality awaits this monster."

"Not a monster," the baroness says quietly. "Remember?"

But when I step into the waiting arms of the mist and return to my cabin and the oozing steaks, there can be no word more suitable for me than *monster*. For as I feed, I fantasize about the salt and iron on my tongue last night, the skin of a warm human throat, and the veins that had burst in my mouth, and all I can think is *Monster, monster, monster*.

Later that evening, in the shadows of my bed, I ask, "Would you want to live forever?"

Nell turns her head on the pillow, eyes heavy-lidded and face flushed from our exertions. Her golden hair pools around us like light in the darkness. "What put that odd question into your mind? I suppose it depends on the manner in which I will spend eternity. If I can be young and beautiful and with you endlessly, then yes. I would want to live forever."

"Wouldn't that bore you after a few centuries?"

She snuggles closer to me, her soft breasts pressing into my arm. "Bore me? Being young and dazzling and achingly in love? Of course not."

"But what else would you do?" I persist. "With the endless time you would have?"

"You sound so serious and disapproving. Why can't youth and beauty and *you* be enough for me? We could buy lovely clothes, eat fine food, and see the wonders of the world. And trust me," she adds throatily, kissing my neck, "I would make sure you never got bored."

I turn away, wondering what I hope to achieve from this pointless infatuation. Proof that I am still human enough to feel desire? A hollow distraction from what I have become? Or perhaps a bit of weak comfort in seeking a version of Mina I *can* have?

"You're displeased with me," Nell says, watching me. "You don't like my answer. Look at me, Lucy. What did I say wrong? I was only being honest with you."

Wordlessly, I stare into her face, so like Mina's. My dear friend would have given a very different response. She would have thought it over seriously before answering. She would have pledged to spend eternity doing good, fighting hunger, and absorbing others' griefs and sorrows instead of choosing a wasteful, frivolous existence. Mina would be of service to others, not long for admiration as Nell does. And in a moment of rare self-reflection, I wonder if people have always seen *me* the way I see Nell: vain, coquettish, and greedy for the spotlight.

Nell sits up in bed, the sheet slipping from her naked body. "You *are* annoyed with me. What do you want me to say instead? I will say anything, do anything, to please you."

"I am not annoyed—"

"You are," she frets. "Talk to me! You are forever keeping me at a distance. You know everything about me, but I know nothing about *you*. Who you were, what Arthur was like—"

My head snaps up. "What?"

"Arthur. Your husband." Nell gives a short, bitter laugh. "You talk in your sleep. Last night, and also tonight. Both times, you spoke to Arthur and told him you loved him. He is gone and *I* am here, and yet you insist on keeping us apart when we are soulmates—"

"Soulmates?" I repeat in disbelief.

"Kindred souls!"

It is the very phrase Vlad uses, and it is too much. Abruptly, I get up, suddenly exhausted by her presence. "We should retire for the night," I say, sighing. "Go back to your cabin, Nell. I'm sure Charles is worried after you returned so late last evening from your *long walk*."

"Don't push me away!" Nell says fiercely. "You are only afraid of what you feel for me."

"What I feel for you is affection, nothing more. This can go no further. You are married, and if you knew the truth about me, you would not want to be with me." I turn my face to the wall, averting my eyes from her pain. "Go back to your cabin."

"What truth? What do I not know?" When I remain silent, she yanks on her dressing gown, nearly tearing it in the process. "I see. None of this means anything to you. If you could know the hope you've given me . . . the light you've been through the bleak prospect of my marriage to Charles—" She covers her face and lets out a choked sob.

I try to touch her, but she jerks away violently. "Mina loved me," I say quietly, "but when I . . . changed, I thought her love had turned into hate. It would kill me to go through that again."

"You won't let me decide for myself," Nell says angrily. "You tell that ugly old woman everything, but you won't tell me. You're a selfish coward, and I wish I'd never met you. I don't ever want to see you again." She leaves, slamming my cabin door behind her.

I sink back onto my rumpled bed, holding my head in my hands. I have made so many mistakes, and Nell is yet another one. But she, too, is someone else I must give up.

I get dressed and go out on deck. It is still cold, but the sea is calmer—we have made it safely through the storm. I gaze broodingly toward the land we will reach at sunrise. France awaits me, and beyond that, the castle that will be my home forevermore, as Vlad commands.

My hands clench on the railing. My existence should be up to *me*. It *will* be up to me. If I can summon the courage to seize immortality, then surely I can be brave enough to learn about what I am, what I can do, and how to use it against Vlad—the man I once hoped would be my friend and mentor, the man I had foolishly thought cared for me. But it was never going to be respect with him, or love, or tenderness. Not the way it would have been with Arthur.

"You talk in your sleep," Nell had said. "You spoke to Arthur and told him you loved him."

I sit wearily in one of the deck chairs, thinking of every familiar detail about Arthur: his walnut hair, the curve of his lips, the cheek that hides his dimple. Remembering just the tilt of his head makes my throat close up with longing. I had given him up readily, this gentle man who had wept as he asked me to marry him and had held me on the very last night of my life.

"Arthur," I whisper, a tear freezing on my face as I close my eyes against the mist.

And then suddenly, the sky and the sea and the ferry disappear and I am in the drawing room of Ring once more. Both the room and Arthur's face are warmer, brighter, as we run toward each other and my feet leave the floor as he grabs me in his tight embrace. There is no sense of time passing or of anyone else in the world—just us breathing together, arms around each other like sailors clinging to a storm-ridden mast. Vlad only holds me with possession, but here I am surrounded by a love that asks for nothing in return—only to give me peace.

A moment later, Arthur lets go, his face flushed. "You left so quickly when I saw you last. One moment you were there, and then you faded. When I woke up and told Seward I had seen you, he was ecstatic. He vowed to try hypnotizing me again, and here I am . . . with you."

His eyes seem larger and his cheeks more hollow. "Are you eating enough?" I ask him.

We sit together on the settee, and a drowsy old black spaniel lifts its head, gazing at him with liquid, intelligent eyes. "Flossy does not think so," Arthur says, caressing the dog's greying head. He sighs. "It feels wrong for Mother and me to eat without Father sitting at the head of the table. Like the foundation has been torn out from under us, or the world has been reshaped only for her and for me, and we are puzzled as to how everyone else can simply go on."

I squeeze his hand. "Grief is an old friend of mine," I say. "I used to dream nightly that Papa was alive and I only had to find him to be with him again. I walked that cliff's edge for so long, in love with the idea of falling . . . but now I know there is nothing there. They are gone and we are here, and they would want us to *live*. There is no sense in clinging to the dead."

He gives a soft laugh. "I remember a girl who once told me of her obsession with death."

"Yes, and she was silly and naïve and confused her reluctance to live an unwanted life with giving it up entirely. She fell straight into a trap." I watch him pet his dog, scratching behind her silky black ears. "I always hoped to be with you and Mina somehow, foolish as that was."

"You could not have known. No one blames you, except—" He sits bolt upright. "Has your boat reached France? Are the ferries running in this awful storm?"

"We will arrive by morning."

He turns to face me urgently. "I should not tell you this. Van Helsing would be angry—"

"He and Quincey are following me, bent upon my destruction. I know," I say calmly, and he goes pale when I describe my near-encounter with the two men on the docks.

"They keep us abreast of their whereabouts, as Mr. Harker requested, but they have not replied to my telegrams since Dover," Arthur says, raking a hand through his hair in distress. "I sent ever so many, hoping to stop them in this misguided mission."

"Do not fear," I say. "This storm may lessen the chance of them finding me. They suspect I know their intentions, and they will expect me to run. To leave France at once."

"Won't you?" he asks, his jaw tight with anxiety.

"No. I may stay in Paris. Lose myself in the city, find a hotel, disappear into the crowd for a few days before going on to Germany."

When I had mentioned Nell's plan to stay at the Destin-Savoir, the baroness had suggested at once—with bone-deep exhaustion in her eyes—that we stay as well, to break up our long journeys. "I am weary of being in motion," she had said.

Despite his distress, a small smile touches Arthur's lips. "Hotels, cities, and crowds. Listen to you, so well-traveled already. I'm happy for you, Lucy. You would not have gone—" He does not finish, but I hear his unspoken words. "You would not have gone had you married me."

"Soon, I will be traveling myself. Mr. Harker and I are bound for Whitby," he says instead.

"Whitby?" I echo, startled. "Why on earth are you going there?"

Arthur studies me for a long moment. "Do you sleep in a box of earth? For your safety? Only answer if it will not hurt you. Mr. Harker told us it physically pained you to speak of your situation."

Indeed, even as elation rises in me—that devilishly clever Dr. Van Helsing has not wasted time; he begins to see all—my skin already tingles with the promise of pain. Vlad's spell, keeping the truth at bay. "I sleep in a bed," I say carefully. "I rest in one even during the day."

Arthur's eyes widen at this revelation. "At first, Van Helsing assumed you would rest in a tomb, a coffin, but then he changed his mind . . . something about the origin of the soil, and how only those who call it home may require its protection. Do you know, it was Mrs. Harker who brought the boxes to our attention. She combed through her diary and mentioned a foreign vessel arriving in Whitby with a cargo of thirty boxes. Van Helsing suggested—"

"Arthur, wait," I break in, suddenly afraid. I think of Vlad whispering and taunting in my mind. Information is a deft weapon in his hands, and if he can enter my thoughts at will, I must know as little as possible. "Tell me nothing more of this trip you and the Harkers will take."

He tightens his hand around mine. "I trust you, even if you do not trust yourself," he says evenly. "And I go with Mr. Harker alone. His wife will stay with Jack Seward."

"Why should she do that?" I demand, burning but forbidden to speak. My throat is tight with panic. *Jack Seward's property is adjacent to Carfax, and Vlad will be but a stone's throw away from Mina.* "Why can she not remain at home in London? She would have her servant—"

"We've taken precautions," he reassures me. "Seward's house is covered in holy water, garlic, and roses, as Van Helsing advised, particularly Mrs. Harker's room. She will be well and busy, what with transcribing Seward's diary now, too. He records it on his phonograph."

"Mina is taking down his diary as well?" I ask, confused. "Has he no assistant to help?"

The old black spaniel stands, agitated by my anxious tone, and hobbles over to be held by Arthur. She presses her silky head against his heart. "There, there, Floss," he says, low and gentle, then turns back to me. "There have been strange happenings at the asylum. Patients gone missing or behaving erratically. When some of them began to talk of drinking blood and seeing wings in the dark, Seward and Mrs. Harker wondered if there was some . . . connection."

I grit my teeth. An asylum full of people to control would be irresistible to Vlad indeed.

But now, there is hope. Now, my friends have linked Jonathan's ordeal to my own and are learning more about Vlad—enough to investigate Whitby, the beginning of my end, where I had sat dreaming on a moonlit cliff as a ship with black sails tore into harbor.

The dog begins to whine. "Flossy is a sensitive soul, aren't you, old girl? She loved my father, and now she's forever worrying about me. Hush now, stop your fretting, little one." Arthur rocks the old dog patiently, looking down at her with kind eyes, and I can see how he would be with a child. He would be a father like my papa, a man who scoffed at traditional roles, who paced up and down all night singing to his infant, and who felt like home to a daughter.

I see Arthur's future stretching out before me—his face aglow as a warm bundle is placed in his arms; him laughing as he runs, pursued by tiny feet; snow falling as he sits reading by the fire, a drowsy little head tucked against him—and it all breaks my heart. It is the life I had feared and willingly relinquished, and it is all Arthur has ever wanted. He wanted it with *me*.

He looks up then, and whatever he meant to say dies on his lips at what he sees in my eyes: unwavering, unflinching love I can no longer speak aloud. Not when we are an ocean apart. Not when I can never again give him what he had once yearned for.

"I wish to God I could have stayed and kept you all safe," I say, my voice trembling. "But I want you to follow Dr. Van Helsing's advice. Make use of everything you put in Jack Seward's house. They do not only protect. The boxes of earth—" My bones hum with the heat of agony and I am forced into helpless silence, but Arthur seems to have understood what I wished to say.

His brow is furrowed in thought. "All creatures need rest, Van Helsing says. This monster is no different. It sleeps in the boxes. But if they are destroyed or can no longer be used . . ." His head snaps up. "It cannot abide holy water and garlic. They pose a barrier not just for houses and rooms where dear ones sleep . . . but also boxes full of earth, closed against the sun."

"I could kiss you right now, Lord Godalming," I say fervently, ignoring the pain that is steadily intensifying in my skull. "As a friend, that is."

Arthur laughs, but I cannot enjoy the warm, beloved sound of it or the reappearance of his dimple. My head is prickling from the inside out, as though my mind has grown needles and is attempting to make holes in my scalp. "Damn you!" I cry. "I did not say anything!"

The drawing room flickers in and out of my vision. Everything goes hazy as though choked by fog. Flossy lets out a sharp bark as Arthur stands abruptly, ashen, reaching for me.

But I am gone.

A splitting headache racks my skull as my consciousness flits through the mist. I see corpses in the shadows with blank and staring eyes; great avenues of stone and lampposts glowing in the night; and then a rolling countryside beneath a bleak, starless stretch of sky.

And then I am standing before a great house in the dark, and somehow I know where I am even before the door opens and Vlad emerges. Once again, he has called me to him through the mist—but he does not look at me. He does not mock or berate me. He does not seem to register my presence at all as he watches a thin figure loping toward him in the darkness.

"Well, Renfield," he says. "What news?"

CHAPTER ELEVEN

My pain vanishes, and in its place, I feel delirious joy washing over me like the colors of a rainbow, the warmth of the sun on a spring afternoon, waves lapping at my feet. It is Vlad's happiness, I realize, as I watch him smile at the man now standing shoulder to shoulder with me—and yet Vlad still does not seem to see me. He often ignores me as a form of punishment, but this feels genuine and not purposeful. Somehow, he has summoned me without being aware of it.

"Master," the man says in a tremulous, high-pitched voice. He is in his early twenties, with dark hair hanging in long greasy hanks over his sharp white face. He drops to his knees and crawls over to lean his head against Vlad's knee with an expression of utter devotion that chills me. It is not unlike the way Flossy had looked at Arthur. "Oh, Master! I cannot go back there. Will you let me stay here with you? I can sleep on the floor. I will be good!"

Vlad holds his hands out of the man's grasping reach, frowning. "Renfield, have you done what I asked of you? You will not be rewarded otherwise."

"Oh, a reward!" the young man says longingly. "How about a spider? Eggs and flies and webs and lives. Sun and moon and far and soon, up and down. Forever and forever and forever." His words, spoken in the wild rhythm of a child's made-up song, end in a shrill giggle. "I am a flea and a flea is me, and I want a cat. Will you give me a cat?"

"Only if you did what I asked," Vlad says. "Only if you are very good indeed."

I watch in horror as Renfield shakes with unhinged laughter. "Yes, I have been good! Do not make me go back there to *him*." I follow his gaze to a building on the adjacent property, its windows glowing with light. "He is not like you, you, you. He will not give me a cat, that doctor with the coat and the frown and the cold, cold, cold silver needles." He shudders, even as one sly hand moves searchingly up Vlad's thigh. He laughs again when Vlad slaps it away.

I stare at Renfield in horror, noting his stained ankle-length nightshirt. This, then, is one of the asylum patients whose odd behavior has alerted both Jack Seward and Mina. Knowing what I know of the regimented, disciplined Dr. Seward, his hospital must be both organized and secure. Schedules, timetables, locked doors to keep both the staff and the patients safe . . . but what is a locked door to Vlad? It would have been simple for him to enter, to invade, to infect.

"You have not answered my question," Vlad says with a touch of impatience in his calm baritone. "Have you done what I asked of you?"

"Yes, Master, I have."

"All is ready for me? And the doctor is out?"

The young man nods. "The doctor is out. I will show you! Follow me." He scrambles to his feet, desperate to please. In the dim light, his eyes are vague and unsettling, darting about as though unable to focus as he stumbles through the mist. Vlad follows him, gaze glittering with triumph, and I drift after them unnoticed. At one point, Renfield pounces on something hidden in the grass and Vlad barks,

"Leave it!" before prodding him onward. I peer at the ground to see a fat earthworm, blind and slimy, burrowing into the ground.

Like Carfax, the asylum is a stately manor house, and through the bright windows I see uniformed staff carrying trays and striding down corridors. To the east, about half a mile down the road, is a much smaller red brick house, tidy, charming, and covered in climbing green ivy.

Not so long ago, Dr. Seward had hoped to bring me to this very home as his wife, and now I am following Vlad and Renfield to the garden behind it. I can barely make out the shapes of leafy shrubs and a tiny bubbling fountain, for the mist seems heavier there than anywhere else. Great clouds of it billow along the grass with unnerving, predatorial speed. My apprehension rises with each step, and when I see the pale figure on a stone bench, I know why the fog is here.

Mina stretches across the bench with her head thrown back, her hair cascading in ripples of sunshine gold. Not much skin can be seen beneath the high neck and long sleeves of her prim nightgown, but there is something shockingly intimate about her posture: parted lips; breasts swelling with each excited breath; knees open, with a foot touching the grass on either side.

I clutch my own throat in longing, despair, and terror—for it is the very pose in which I had lain in the churchyard the night I gave Vlad all of me.

"I won her trust," Renfield says, reedy and breathless. "She wanted to visit the doctor's patients and give them cheer during her stay here, and when I told her I liked her face, she came back every day to ask how I was. She has a kind heart."

Vlad strokes a cold finger down the length of Mina's alabaster throat.

"They filled her bedroom with everything you hate. But I drew her right out of it, I did. Knocked on her door as soon as the doctor left on his fool's errand." Renfield pitches his voice higher, sweeter, somehow managing to sound frighteningly like Mina. "'Renfield, how did you get out? Renfield, please wait!' I led her here like you wanted me to, Master."

"Well done," Vlad says. "You may return to your cell."

The young man's hopeful smile fades. "B-but, Master, why? I thought—"

"Go, and do not let anyone see you. I can't have them raising the alarm when I am so close to my prize, can I?" Vlad turns his back, his finger finding the strong, determined pulse in Mina's throat, and after a moment, Renfield gives a sullen nod and scurries back to the hospital.

"Mina, wake up, my beauty," Vlad says gently, and my mouth goes dry at his tone, as soft and smooth as silk. He had used it only for me once upon a time.

Her eyes flutter open. "Count?" she asks, confused. "Where are we? I was asleep, and I heard a knock. It was that poor soul, Robert Renfield. Where is he? Is he all right?"

"He is safe. Think only of yourself now, my darling. Think only of me."

Mina looks at him with sharp, clear intensity. But her features slacken when Vlad raises the mist and sits beside her, positioning her head against his shoulder. I want to scream, but I have no voice—not by any power of his, but by my own horror and trauma, for they are sitting just as we once had on the cliffs. It is too soon for me to see this. Too heartbreakingly familiar.

"Mina, don't you care for me at all?" Vlad's soft voice is one meant only for a lover, to tell her she is the only one in the world who can touch his heart. The perfect woman of the age. "I think of nothing but you, day and night. When we are apart, you fill my every dream."

"I cannot," she whispers. "I am married."

"What can Jonathan offer you that compares to this?" He kisses the top of her head, and she closes her eyes, her face so peaceful it makes my heart clench. "You are safe with me, my sweet one, and no evil will touch you whilst I am here. Let me prove that you belong with me." He tilts her face up to his, mere inches apart. "Kiss me. One kiss is all I ask."

Alertness suddenly returns to her eyes and she sits up straight. "No," she says, firm and clear, and I want to weep with pride at her strength. She has done what I could not. "I will not."

"Then let *me* kiss you." He lifts the mist, and I can feel Mina fighting with all her might beneath the trance. Vlad's cruelest power is to separate a victim's mental and physical self, and it is all the more disturbing to watch, having been subjected to it myself.

His lips meet hers, soft and sweet, not asking for more. I know too well this illusion of gentlemanly courtesy, of letting Mina feel like she is in control when she is not. When he pulls away, she whimpers and kisses him again, succumbing to the mist and his turbulent eyes.

I am frozen where I stand as he takes her kiss greedily, then trails his mouth along her jaw to breathe a kiss upon her neck. And then I see the glint of his long, sharp white teeth.

"No!" I roar, finding my voice at last. I plunge forward, parting the mist like a tidal wave. It rattles the windows of Dr. Seward's house as I seize Vlad and send him flying against the fountain, cracking it in half. He recovers almost at once, rising and touching the gushing cut upon his brow. For the first time tonight, he looks at me, and stabbing, violent, punishing pain radiates across my entire body. It feels like invisible insects digging sharp pincers into my nerves and burrowing into the marrow of my bones. I crumple to the ground in silent agony.

Voices and running feet. The dizzying sway of torchlight searching in the dark.

"Hello! Who's there?"

"Get Renfield back in his cell. Double the guard."

"You three, come with me!"

The pain suddenly stops and I retch onto the grass, bile burning my tongue. I turn to see Vlad transform into a great grey wolf just as Jack Seward and his assistants enter the garden, brandishing guns and torches, sweeping the light around without seeing either Vlad or me.

Jack runs toward Mina. "Mrs. Harker! Are you all right?"

She touches the spot on her neck where Vlad kissed her, and when she moves her hand, I am utterly relieved to see unmarked skin. I have intervened in time to save her. "I'm fine," she says as the doctor helps her up. "I dreamed Renfield escaped and led me out here . . ."

"It was no dream, I'm afraid," Jack says grimly.

But it is all I have time to hear before Vlad seizes my dress with his wolf teeth, yanking so hard that I lose my footing. He catches me on his back, and I have only seconds to grasp the dirty, mangy scruff of his neck before he is loping away, carrying me off into the night.

He flings me down, hard, in a dark and empty field. I lie in the damp grass, panting, as he changes back to his human form, large and menacing and bleeding profusely from his forehead. He approaches me slowly, his face masked in the shadows, but I know what the glitter in his eyes promises. Within seconds, the sensation of crawling, stabbing insects returns, intensifying into the excruciating tensing of every muscle in my body at once. It is not pain, but outright *torture*.

"Why," Vlad says, his quiet voice unmistakable even under my screams of anguish, "are you here? I did not call to you. I did not give you permission."

The muscles in my legs feel like knotted rope. I try to grab my burning thighs, but my fingers are cramping, stuck straight out and useless. And then I feel a horrifying pressure beneath my fingernails, as though they are about to pop off my skin like scales from a fish.

"I asked why you are here. How did you know my plan?"

Tears roll down my face. "Please stop." After a long moment, the torment ends and I curl up into a ball, limp and shaking, my breath coming short and ragged. My throat feels raw as he stands over me, waiting for an answer. "I didn't know your plan. I was resting, and somehow I came to the asylum. I could feel how happy you were. Triumphant. I don't know anything else."

"You don't know anything else," he repeats, slow and mocking.

"Why would I come to you intentionally?" I ask, incensed. "Why would I want to see you?" My cheek and jaw are suddenly on fire, for he has struck me across the face with his fist.

"Watch how you talk to me. You are my creature, Lucy, and I do not tolerate disrespect."

"The only creature here is *you*," I spit.

He gives me another vicious punch, and I lie still and stunned. The vampire venom will heal me, but it does nothing for the memory of torment. My bones, muscles, and skin will recall this agony long after tonight. Vlad kneels beside me and I tense, expecting more blows.

Instead, he lays a gentle hand on my head. "Must I always school you in etiquette? You used to be so gentle and sweet and eager to please. So respectful and attentive—"

"That was before I knew you were worth less than the dirt in your boxes."

"What did I just say about manners?" Vlad asks quietly. "Wouldn't it be a shame if I tore your fangs right out of your mouth? I wonder if they will grow back? Or how long it will take you to waste away from starvation? What do you say, my dear? Shall we find out?" His fingers curl around a hank of my hair, gentle, but a warning nonetheless. "I think I have been too lenient with you. It is long past time for this lesson, but better late than never. Follow me."

I feel my bruised and bleeding body lift off the ground and float after him as he strides away. My skull feels near to bursting with pain and fury as we approach a small building, a kind of shed situated behind Carfax. Beyond it, I see the lights of Dr. Seward's home and hospital and feel a tug of longing for Mina. But I cannot run; I cannot escape. My body is not my own as it drifts in Vlad's wake like a boneless puppet pulled by strings.

When Vlad unlocks the door, a great clanking of chains sounds out in the still night air. Imprisoned in the shed are three people, disheveled and covered in blood and waste. The stench of vomit and urine mixed with the sweet aroma of rotting meat emanates from them as they strain against the shackles securing them to the walls and floor. I see dried blood around their wrists and ankles, and one woman's arm has been bitten down to the bone, torn muscle dangling like ribbons from her elbow—and from her mouth, indicating that *she* injured herself. But was she trying to escape . . . or feed on something, anything?

I know at once, from their pallor, that these people are vampires—or as close as can be.

"Master," says the young woman with the half-eaten arm, in a seductive purr that sends chills down my spine. Her long red hair is coming loose from its knot. "You've come back."

"Master," echoes the middle-aged woman, blond, full-figured, and fighting her chains so hard that the walls of the shed shake. "Feed us, Master. Give us something to eat."

"And if you will not," says the redhead, flashing sharp white teeth, "we will just have to eat you instead, won't we?" Vlad allows her to seize him by the jacket and pull him close for a long, deep kiss despite the shredded flesh adorning her mouth. Her greedy hand slips down to his groin as she hooks a leg around him. "Fill me with you. I am so empty—"

Not to be outdone, the older woman grabs his hand and plants it on one of her large breasts, bare beneath the torn fabric of her dress. "I go first. You've had your turn."

My heart shatters at yet another too familiar scene. Vlad's venom is swimming inside these women's veins, stripping their skin of color, racking their bodies with illness, and heightening not only their hunger but also their lust to an unbearable pitch. I remember being deathly sick after being bitten, yet fighting both Dr. Van Helsing and Dr. Seward when they stopped me from getting to the tube of my blood or answering the hunger between my legs with my hand.

As the women wail and claw and grab at Vlad, I realize they are wearing the same clothes: a long-sleeved dress of serviceable, cheap grey cotton; a once-white apron that covers their entire front; and a belt from which various items still dangle, including jangling keys, pencils, a silver watch, and even a whistle for the older lady, who also wears a small white cap on her head.

They are nurses, I realize. They *were* nurses at Dr. Seward's hospital.

And the man grinning at me in the corner—gaunt, elderly, eyes so pale they look white—must have been a patient, for he wears a nightdress similar to Renfield's. "Come here, pretty," he invites me, lurching forward, and I take a step back in the doorway.

"It was lonely at Carfax, waiting for Mina," Vlad tells me as the nurses squabble over him. "So I asked a few friends over. They are not full vampires yet, as they haven't had a chance to make their first kills. But I've bitten them each multiple times, and they are nearly drained, so they are close enough for my purposes. Aren't you, my beauties?"

I note the victims' laborious breathing and the deep hollows beneath their eyes. They are weak, exhausted, hovering at the crossroads between vampirism and death.

"I was saving them for a rainy day, but I can sacrifice them for our lesson," Vlad says, looking thoughtfully at me. "Did you know, Lucy, that you can still die? The thing you once longed for and hoped to avoid at all costs, indecisive as you are, is still here haunting you. A vampire, a lesser one created by me, can most certainly die. Not lingering on, not wandering through the mist. A *true* death. Wiped out of existence. Can you imagine that, Lucy?"

"Lucy," the victims chant, attracted by his repetition of my name. "Lucy, Lucy, Lucy."

My eyes close to a barrage of images behind my lids: Arthur sobbing over my body once again; heavy clots of dirt raining onto my coffin, wiping it from existence; Mina twitching under Vlad's big body as he steals every drop of life from her; and Vlad himself, sitting on a dais like a dissipated king as girl after girl takes her turn in his lap, a never-ending, eternal parade of *perfect women*, while I and every other bride he has ever created, every other starry-eyed maiden he has ever tricked and poisoned and seduced, fades from his memory.

I have never been anything more than a drop in the ocean to him. For this, I have given up my life. I have sacrificed it all for absolutely nothing.

"Lucy," Vlad says, and I open my stinging eyes just in time to see him plunge his fist directly into the redhead's chest. Bones crackle like firewood. Her muscles squelch beneath his searching fingers, splattering huge wet drops that look black in the darkness, before she falls away from him, limp limbs and blank gaze. In Vlad's hand is her heart, a mass of brown-black tissue that smells so strongly of decay that I lean against the wall and gag.

Quick as a flash, the older nurse seizes the heart from Vlad and sinks her teeth into it. I look away, retching, as the wet smacking sounds of her mouth fill the shed.

"Lucy," Vlad says again.

"Lucy," echoes the elderly patient, gleeful.

I try to press my face to the wall, but some powerful force turns my head back to see the nurse still chewing on the heart. Vlad makes sure I am watching before he takes one of the sharp pencils from her belt and stabs it with unholy force into her chest, over and over and over, until her breast is pocked with holes like oozing Swiss cheese. "I prefer a stake," he says as the pencil breaks and he takes another to continue skewering her. "But we will make do."

The nurse crumples to the ground, and the heart rolls to my feet. I kick it away, weeping.

"What's wrong, Lucy?" Vlad asks tenderly. "Didn't you give your heart to me on the cliffs above the sea? No? Perhaps you would rather pretend you had given your head instead." He walks over to the patient and wipes his gore-drenched fingers on the old man's nightdress. And then, without preamble, he pops the man's head from his shoulders with a great wet crunching sound, like chopping a rotten rain-soaked log. The body stands for a moment before tumbling, and I can see the top of the spine shining white where the head had just been.

I collapse, sick with dread. Tonight, I will meet my end as these people just have, and I will never see Arthur and Mina again. It has all been for nothing. Vlad comes to stand before me, and I hate myself for cowering at his feet. This is not the way Lucy Westenra should die.

And so I sit up straight. I take a deep breath. And I tilt my head back to look into the eyes of the man who will kill me, defiant and full of rage to the last, and I wait for my end.

"Do you see now?" Vlad says. "All the ways in which I can kill you?"

"Get it over with," I snarl. "But know that I will haunt you from beyond the grave."

"Ghosts don't exist." He laughs and lowers himself to face me, tapping my nose with mocking affection. "I was merely demonstrating. How can I kill you tonight when you have just proven how powerfully connected you are to me? More than anyone else has ever been? No. I've summoned you through the mist many times before, but this evening, I seem to have done so simply by *feeling*. You were drawn to my emotions, like a true kindred soul."

"I have never been your kindred soul and never will be," I say coldly. "We are enemies."

"Enemies! And should I be afraid of you, as my enemy?" He grabs my throat, tight enough to stop my breath. "Mina is no longer your concern. She belongs in this game I play with these so-called hunters who think themselves worthy opponents to me. They amuse me. I want to see what happens. I want to know how the story ends without you spoiling my fun."

"I may not speak of you without pain," I croak. "I may be your creature. But my love for Mina is greater than any hold you have over me, and I will protect her until my final day."

Vlad studies me, cold and impersonal. "You don't deserve to be killed, not after derailing my plan. Not when I have found the perfect woman of the age, only to be thwarted by you. If I kill you now, it would look like forgiveness. Weakness, by another name. No, it won't be that easy. I am going to make sure I punish you *adequately*. Have no fear," he adds, "you will still reach my castle in one piece. At least, I think you will, knowing that intractable will of yours."

"Nothing you can do to me is worse than what you've already done. I am not afraid."

"Oh, but I think you *are*. Even if you would rather die than admit it." He stands and offers me a hand, but I ignore it. "What's this? You once longed so for my touch."

"From this day onward, I will long for you no more," I say flatly. "I will never seek your regard or approval or care for you ever again. There is now nothing between us but enmity."

Vlad sighs and steps around me. "Then goodbye," he says matter-of-factly. "I wish you an unforgettable journey to my home in the mountains. And if you ever find yourself wandering through the mist to me again without my permission, you will leave immediately. Stand in my way just once more, and Mina will know the same pain you have just endured."

With that, he vanishes into the night, leaving me alone with the remains of his bloodshed.

CHAPTER TWELVE

"Land at last!" the baroness proclaims as we move down the walkway toward the docks.

Calais is a welcome sight despite the grey morning sky and a cloying fog that shrouds the harbor. Rows of boats line the shore as passengers disembark and form a teeming crowd. The air tastes like salt and smoke and tar. It is a new beginning, even if it does not include freedom. It never will for me, not if Vlad has anything to say about it.

The old woman squeezes my arm. "Cheer up, dear. You will have another chance to mend your rift with Mrs. Wright-Davies in Paris." After seeing how Nell had ignored me at breakfast, she thinks our quarrel is the cause of my dark mood, and I do not disabuse her of that notion.

As we proceed, I hear a man comment on a nearby battered-looking ferry to the captain, who says disapprovingly, "It would have been in good condition had its crew not risked life and limb to get here in that storm. They departed Dover half a day after we did, yet arrived last night! One of the passengers must have paid quite a sum to expedite the trip."

Unease slithers down my spine. Perhaps it is only the weight of worrying about Mina, but I veil my face as I step down, cursing myself for not having done it earlier, and scan the crowd . . . but for what? Am I searching for dark skin, a strong jaw, or the piercing narrow eyes of a trained physician? Am I listening for a certain cadence of speech, authoritative and tinged with Dutch, or a drawling American accent? My skin crawls as though someone is breathing on my nape. *I am being watched*, I think, sick with anxiety. *I have been watched since the moment I arrived.*

The feeling does not subside even when the baroness and I hide away in a compartment on the train to Paris. It is not like the ferry, where there had been no possibility of a newcomer. Here, I startle whenever a shadow passes our door or a male voice speaks in the corridor. *Curse you, Vlad*, I think bitterly. *Curse you for showing me, as cruelly as possible, that death stalks me even now . . . that the fall I had once longed for still lingers inches from my feet.* One misstep, one second of distraction, and it will all have been for nothing.

Only when the train reaches the city do I let myself breathe. I even laugh as I lift my veil to look out the window, for one glimpse is enough to convince me that I have done right in choosing immortality. To live forever would be to see all the beauties of the world, and Paris—with its buildings gleaming in the autumn rain, river reflecting the sky, and the patina of history, art, and fashion gracing every corner—is a marvel I never dared dream I would see.

The baroness is pale when she awakens from her nap. The journey is seeping her of her strength, bit by bit, and I know that when we say goodbye, I will never see her again, this kind, iron-willed woman who has stepped into my beloved mamma's place for a short time.

I am so focused on caring for her as we exit the train—helping to smooth her dress and letting her lean upon my arm—that I almost forget my anxiety. But as a conductor helps her down to the platform and I follow, my acute senses register something odd . . . something *wrong*.

I taste iron in my mouth, though I have not drunk a drop of blood.

I feel cool air brush my face, which I have again forgotten to veil.

I smell a strangely familiar combination of mint, clean linen, and gunpowder.

I see a pistol flash as its owner points the barrel directly at my heart.

I hear his finger squeeze the trigger.

In the split second before the bullet hits me, I claw at the billowing train smoke and turn it into mist. It is not enough to shield me, but it deflects the path of the projectile, sending it not to my heart but to my left shoulder. I gasp as the burning, red-hot bite of pain grips me.

"Lucy!" the baroness cries.

Startled shouts ring out. Footsteps pound on the platform.

Quincey Morris's dark brown eyes lock on mine. The grim determination in them is not what frightens me most, but the grief and the loss I also see there. He is a man driven not by hatred, but by the love he had once held for me, and that makes him an even more dangerous adversary—his solemn belief that to destroy me would be to save me.

He hates me now. The thought appears with such clarity as I act on instinct and wrap the thickening mist around myself, the baroness, and our belongings and sweep us to the other side of the platform, unseen, as onlookers and train conductors alike frantically search the spot we have just vacated. Two policemen rush to the scene, attracted by the commotion.

"Oh, Lucy!" the baroness gasps, wrapping her scarf tightly around my bleeding shoulder.

But I am focused on Quincey and Dr. Van Helsing, who are being interrogated by the police. Quincey's head swivels, searching for me, his face twisted with panic and fury.

"I take full responsibility," the doctor explains to the policemen in French. "It was I who pointed out the thief to my companion. He only wished to protect a lady from being robbed."

"It does not matter," says a short, stern policeman. "He could have killed someone."

"Please, sir." Dr. Van Helsing uses his most jovial tone, and though his back is turned, I sense the disarming smile that accompanies it. I know the tactic well. People with heritages like ours quickly learn how to deflect and defuse in European circles. "My friend is an American. You know how they are with guns. Shoot first, ask questions later! Thankfully, no one was hurt."

"But I thought I saw a woman—" an onlooker protests.

"Why would an injured woman run?" Dr. Van Helsing asks patiently.

As the policemen exchange glances, Quincey grabs the doctor's elbow, and I hear him hiss, "I got her. I *know* I got her, and she is still here somewhere."

The baroness touches my arm. "Lucy, we should get you to a doctor—"

"No doctor. There is no infection worse than the one I already carry." Gritting my teeth, I remove the scarf and dig my fingers into my wound, pinching out the bullet with a wet sucking sound. Already, the gash is closing like a seam being sewn up and the pain has receded to a dull ache. I wipe my hands on the scarf, turn it inside out, and wrap it around myself. "There! I'm right as rain." My tone is light, but I am trembling, reeling from my brush with death. Had my instincts failed me, Quincey's bullet would now be sitting in my heart and not my hand.

"Who were they?" the baroness asks as we hurry out and hail the first carriage we see.

"They were once my friends. But nowhere on this earth will I be safe from them now."

We are silent as the carriage passes stately buildings and elegantly dressed people strolling down the avenue. And then the old woman asks, "Will you be traveling on to Germany? It isn't safe for you to remain here, Lucy."

"No," I say, after a moment of deliberation. "I will stay with you at the Destin-Savoir, at least for a few days. But the reservation will need to be under your name."

"Of course." She looks almost grey with worry as she takes my hand in her fragile one. "I will take care of you, my dear. My daughter."

I bring her fingers to my lips. "We will take care of each other. Have no fear. Paris is a large city, and I can easily disappear among so many strangers. Though I doubt I will be able to attend that masquerade ball now," I add with forced cheer.

"No, indeed, that would not be wise." Her eyes are on my shoulder. I lift the scarf to reveal bloodstained but otherwise unblemished skin, as though no one had ever shot me at all.

"*Unwise* is just the word," I agree, though I feel a twinge of melancholy at turning down the opportunity to dance and flirt and enjoy myself. How many parties will I ever attend again once I am imprisoned in that castle in the mountains? But as I envision a candlelit space full of people in fancy dress, twirling and sipping champagne, I think of fluttering fans sending waves of blood-scented air straight into my nostrils. I imagine the smell of skin and sweat and all of the veins pulsing around me. "You and I can have supper together in our rooms instead."

The baroness touches my cheek, her eyes full of gentle understanding. "That sounds delightful, my child. I look forward to it.

That night, I am brushing my hair in my chamber, which adjoins the baroness's by way of a shared sitting room, when I sense a presence in the corner behind me. It is a sickening, unnatural feeling, like opening my sewing basket to find eyes watching me from inside—the sensation of an observer where logically there should not be one—but I know exactly who it is. I force myself not to turn around, and to remain calm and continue combing my hair.

"This fairy tale is a bit backward," Vlad says. "Cinderella ought to go to the ball."

"Cinderella wished to escape her existence," I say with my back still turned to him. "I do not have that privilege. I must remain what I am forever, therefore I will do whatever is necessary for my own well-being and that of others."

"How sad and tedious for you."

"Why does it matter to you whether I go or not? My happiness is no concern of yours."

"Is it not?"

Nettled, I lower my hairbrush and turn to see his face only inches away from mine. His low, soft baritone sounded as though it were coming from the far corner of the room, but he has been kneeling behind me the whole time. He laughs when I jerk away in surprise. "Of course I care about your happiness," he says. "You are my bride. You are a part of me, and what gives me enjoyment must surely do the same for you. We both love parties, you and I."

I try to move away, but I seem to be frozen where I sit. "I do not wish to go to the ball."

"It was your fearless heart that first drew you to me. Your courage to tread where others would never dare dream. I thought turning you into a vampire would make you more yourself, but now I worry it has done the opposite. Where is that brave, dauntless Lucy I used to know?"

"I avoid temptation so that I do not expose you, as you have forbidden me to do."

Vlad lazily wraps my hair around his fingers. "I'm not sure I like you thinking you're better than me. You believe that I am addled by greed and arrogance and that I have wasted my existence, whilst you intend to make something different of yourself. Is that not true?"

"There's nothing wrong with wanting something better from my immortality."

"What, then? Will you spend eternity weeping and wailing over weak humans? Washing their feet, laying flowers on their graves, and feeding hungry children? Don't be so foolish."

"Foolish? Me? When you are the one who spends your life playing sadistic games?"

His smile does not falter. "Be careful not to forget yourself, my dear. You belong to me."

"And yet I have told you again and again," I say calmly, "that I belong only to myself."

"You will learn. Like all of the others who came before you, you will find that you are as beholden to your nature as I am. Vampirism controls you. *I* control you, my dear, and I will prove it. I think it's time for another lesson." My stomach twists at the promise in his words as his grip tightens, pulling my hair taut at the roots. "You consider yourself to be above my games, but do you want to know what I think? I think you ought to go to the ball. In fact, I *command* you to go. Buy a dress, make yourself beautiful, and obey every single word I say. Do you understand me?"

An uncontrollable, full-body shiver takes over my limbs. I am rigid as his cold words sink into my bones, and my mouth opens, not of my free will. "Yes, Vlad, I understand."

"You will go to the ball?"

"Yes, Vlad, I will go to the ball," I hear myself say, even as I scream and rage inside. I bow my head, hating everything: the ease with which he can control me, my inability to rebel, and the tears that spring to my eyes. "You take such delight in tormenting me."

His expression is gentle and compassionate, utterly chilling on the face of a monster. "You brought this upon yourself, Lucy," he says kindly, letting go of my hair to stroke my cheek with the back of one ice-cold hand. "These are merely the consequences of daring to steal immortality. But for now, goodbye. I have an important engagement I cannot miss."

"Vlad, wait," I say desperately, almost begging, as he gets up to leave. "I do not wish to go to the ball or to hurt anyone. Command me to do something, *anything* else—"

But his body dissolves like mist, leaving me alone and quivering with fury and despair.

On the evening of the masquerade, the baroness sits on the chaise in my room, watching me style my hair. She did not comment when I told her I had changed my mind about attending and still has not spoken one critical word, though I see her unease in her tight jaw and clenched hands. Still, she tries to keep up a cheerful banter. "A bit of music will do me good," she says. "I like to watch people dance. I was never skilled at it myself, but I imagine you are quite adept."

"No self-respecting daughter of Audrey Westenra could fail at the social graces," I say, glancing at her in her black silk gown and long gloves. Her thin white hair has been caught up with two diamond pins that make her eyes sparkle, and she has opted to forego a mask. "How lovely you are. Everyone who looks at you tonight will think you are the height of elegance."

"None of them will be looking at *me*, not when I am with you." The old woman looks directly into my eyes. "Are you certain a ballroom will not be too much for you, Lucy?"

The hairpin I am placing into my chignon suddenly snaps in half. I drop the pieces on the vanity, affecting carelessness, and pick up another pin. "A ballroom has never been too much for me," I say, though my gut wrenches at the fear and disappointment in her gaze. I am sure that reneging on my vow not to attend seems thoughtless and flighty. Perhaps she no longer thinks me as worthy as the two women she met at the foot of Vlad's mountain so many long years ago.

I turn back to the mirror, for staring at my own horrific reflection—the whorls of blood splattered over my skin and the whites of my eyes looking even more vibrant against my pale dress—is better than facing the judgment in the baroness's face. *But what does it matter what anyone thinks of me*, I ask myself miserably, *if I myself know how foolish and dangerous this decision is?* Hundreds of people will be at risk, no matter how many animal steaks I feed upon in advance, and I—though a wolf among lambs—will be exposed in such a setting, what with Dr. Van Helsing and Quincey Morris ruthlessly hunting me.

The theme of tonight's masquerade is Anges et Démons, and though I ought to dress as the demon I am, the demon Vlad is making me be, I have opted to go as an angel, knowing that many of the women will be dressed as such and I will be better able to hide among them.

This morning, I purchased the simplest gown I could find in Paris, crafted out of a soft cream satin that complements the golden tints of my skin and the darkness of my hair and eyes. The dress is modest, with a high ruffled chiffon neck and a full skirt that trails behind me as I walk, like a glistening stream of water. It has no sleeves, leaving my arms bare from shoulder to fingertip, and I wear no gloves. A pair of large snowy wings, made with real swan feathers, is affixed to the back of the gown, and I have twisted my hair into a demure knot at my nape. Aside from my rings, my only jewelry is a pair of small pearl ear drops, a birthday gift from Mamma.

It is obscene, how virtuous I look, and I am sick with terror at what Vlad might make me do tonight. But perhaps being surrounded by such temptation will be torment enough in his eyes.

"Will it not be overpowering for you?" the baroness asks.

"I will be well. I have to be." I know she can hear my quiet desperation, and when she comes to stand behind me, her expression holds not only worry, but pity. "Shall we go down?"

I slip on my ornate mask of white lace and swan feathers, which covers my entire face but for my eyes and red lips, and ties behind my head with cream silk ribbons. I offer the old lady my arm, and she takes it as we leave my room to descend the grand staircase together.

The Destin-Savoir is more gaudy than tasteful, sprawling on the corner of one of Paris's most fashionable streets like an overdressed strumpet amid the disapproving elegance of the older buildings. The manager had proudly told us that a Swedish hotelier and his American millionaire wife had built the place in record time, wanting to make their mark on Paris before the new century. Every part of the building is gilded to within an inch of its life: stone cherubs beam down from the soaring ceilings; rosy seashells carved from Italian marble tile the walls; chandeliers dripping in diamonds and gold leaf bathe the halls in warm, ebullient light; and rugs of rich Persian red and sumptuous royal blue cushion our footsteps, so that despite the great crowd gathering for the party, there is an almost reverent hush over the proceedings.

"What a shameful clash of styles," I hear someone mutter. "Is it rococo or baroque or something else altogether? Yet somehow, one can't take one's eyes off of it."

Panic seizes my gut as we enter the lobby. Such a gathering would overwhelm any human, but to a vampire, it is close to unbearable. I have been practicing narrowing my focus and closing off my senses so that hearing and smelling everything within a five-mile radius will not drive me insane, but tonight will be the ultimate trial of my nerves.

My eyes are assaulted by color: jewel-toned silks, garish masks glittering with beads and sequins, and manic candlelight on cut-glass champagne flutes. Everywhere, *everywhere* is the smell of blood, salty and rank and sweet, mingling in my nostrils with perfume, soap, and sweat, like a cross between a gluttonous feast and a butcher's shop.

I am electrified with excitement—not just that of attending a splendid party, but also that of a hunter anticipating a feast. *I can control it*, I repeat to myself. I know I have a steady head and an iron will, no matter how much Vlad mocks and belittles me.

The instant he crosses my mind, I wish he had not, for with the memory of him comes disgust, despair, and renewed terror, and it is overpowering when coupled with the sensory barrage around me. The baroness tightens her hand on my arm and asks, "Lucy, are you all right?" It does not help matters. Everyone always insists on underestimating me.

"Come along," I say a bit brusquely. I lead her into the ballroom, where the orchestra is striking up the first of many glittering waltzes. It is much darker in here, lit only by thousands of candles that give the space an intimate and romantic air. My body relaxes somewhat. After all, a ballroom has always been my favorite battleground. How many hearts have I conquered with a flash of my fan and a fleeting, dangerous touch of naked skin? I am home wherever there are lilting violins and shimmering dresses. "Let us find a place to sit down."

"I see some chairs there," the baroness says, pointing at the back wall of the room, as far as we can get from the dance floor and the crush of people.

I nod, ignoring the pressure building at the base of my skull like the start of a splitting headache. We push through the wall of dancers. I hold my breath in the way a child covers her eyes with her hands, for it does nothing to make either me invisible or the party go away. The room grows even warmer as people begin to waltz, and the thick, unctuous fragrance of blood and meat is even more buoyant in the heated air, rising to meet me from every corner.

Enjoy yourself, Lucy, Vlad whispers. *What will you choose to do with immortality?*

The pressure in my head intensifies. I breathe in and out, searching for my fangs with the tip of my tongue and relieved that they have not emerged. The baroness glances at me, and I try to smile reassuringly, but the stretching of my mouth only worsens the tightness in my head.

We pass noisy Americans shouting conversations at the top of their lungs. I know before I see her that Nell is among them, for her honeysuckle perfume is unmistakable. Her husband is in a simple suit with a perfunctory scrap of black silk over his eyes, while she wears a ballgown with peacock colors that shift hypnotically in the light. Teal feathers adorn her bare shoulders, flowing gold hair, and the mask over her eyes, which spark at me with both hurt and longing.

I do not stop as I escort the baroness to a set of red-and-gold chairs, many of which are filled by other elderly ladies. They watch me settle her beside a dreadful brass table carved with dragons in some half-hearted and almost certainly insensitive nod to chinoiserie.

"Shall I bring you a glass of water?" I ask with a pang of guilt as she sinks into her chair, exhausted by the speed with which we walked. She shakes her head, trying to catch her breath.

One of the elderly ladies gives me an approving smile. "What an attentive daughter you are. And your simple gown is a relief from all of these outrageous costumes. Look at that young chit over there! Practically falling out of the top of her dress."

"You look modest and angelic," one of her friends agrees. "A vision in white."

I bow and smile, even as the pain in my skull vibrates in my jaws. "You are very kind."

Heads turn, taking in my slender figure and swan feather wings, and a bold man—tall and svelte with a confident stride—approaches.

Beneath his neatly tied cravat, his blood smells like mahogany and dark honey, as tempting as a glass of French wine. And as good as an invitation.

His brown eyes gleam at me. “May I have the honor of this dance, miss?”

I look coyly at him over my shoulder, but the baroness tugs at my hand, forcing me to bend down. “You told me you took care to feed earlier tonight.”

“I did.”

“You finished all the steaks?” she persists. “Every single one?”

“Of course,” I say, irritated, as the muscles in my neck sing with pain.

“Then why are you as taut as a bowstring?”

Behind us, the man clears his throat, and I, too, am losing my patience. I lean closer to her ear. “Because I am a weapon, Baroness,” I murmur. “As you should know by now.”

“Oh, go on and let her dance!” one of the old ladies tells her. “Girls have to grow up and be noticed sometime, you know. Let the young people enjoy themselves, and we will keep you company. Won’t we?” Her friends titter and smirk, fluttering their fans.

The baroness ignores them. “Let’s leave. For both our sakes and that of everyone here.” Her voice is brisk and assertive. It is a command, and that is what makes my decision for me.

I snap my hand smartly out of hers. “You may do as you please, but I am my own creature tonight.” Our spectators gasp and laugh, and one elderly lady actually applauds at what she thinks is a girl defying her strict mother. I place my hand in the man’s glove, enjoying his admiration as he leads me into the rushing whirlwind of dancers.

The waltz is one in which the dancers switch partners at the end of every thirty-second musical phrase. It is exhilarating to watch, like witnessing the workings of a finely made clock, each pair snapping into place and moving apart to make way for a new pairing . . . but to actually participate is even more exciting. My partner and I slip into a gap between couples and meld into the dance as easily as breathing. Clearly, he is as well-trained as I am.

"Lord Anthony Varga," he says. He is dressed in autumnal colors, with a well-cut jacket and waistcoat of deepest plum and a mask of rich October gold. His eyes alternately shine bronze and chestnut in the candlelight, as inviting as the delightful honey smell of his blood. I ignore my own rising hunger, which I can and *will* resist. "May I know your name?"

"Is there a point?" I ask archly. "We will soon switch partners and never meet again."

"*Never* is a strong word; one I do not wish to use when it comes to you."

"In thirty seconds, you will be saying the same thing to another woman."

"What other woman? I see only you in the whole of this ballroom."

I laugh, trying to enjoy the familiarity of flirtation. But ravenous need grips my body. I *know* I fed enough earlier, so this is not hunger, but greed—the avarice of a child who craves candy after a filling supper. This ballroom bursts with blood I have never tasted, blood like hot liquor and salty broth and sticky molasses, blood that smells like roses and clover and musk, blood from America and Europe and Africa and the Far East, where my family's roots lie.

You will never feed enough when you drink animal blood. Vlad's whisper flutters in my mind like a death's head moth. *It is a poor substitute, like water when you need wine.*

Leave me be, I think furiously, trying to push him out of my head.

Show me you can control yourself, he murmurs. *Prove it to me.*

Lord Anthony lifts my hand above my head, and I twirl to the music, delighted by the simultaneous swirling of other gowns around me. The spin ends tantalizingly, with my back pressed to his front and his arm wrapped around my waist. When I turn my head to meet his burning eyes, he lowers his lips to my naked shoulder. It is a daring breach of propriety, but he must have sensed I would not protest. This close to me, his blood is even more intoxicating.

Taste him, Vlad whispers. *See if his blood is as sweet as it smells.*

My gums pinch with pain as my fangs descend. Lord Anthony spins me to face him, my breasts pressed to his jacket, and slowly, dreamily, I lift my head to look into his eyes.

Just one little taste, Vlad says. *It won't hurt him and no one will see.*

No, I think. *Don't make me do this.*

But I am weak with hunger and lust. And before I know it, I am slipping my fingers into the crisp linen of Lord Anthony's cravat. His eyes widen, but then his gaze becomes unfocused and drowsy as I breathe against his ear. "My name is Lucy." And as his strong heartbeat thrums against my breastbone, I tug aside the cravat and put my lips to his throat.

It takes all of my self-restraint not to sink my teeth in. Instead, I graze him just enough to draw a few drops of blood. He groans, and I feel his arousal as I lick him clean, sliding my tongue across his neck before patting the cravat back in place. "Disappointing. It's not like honey at all."

In the deepest recesses of my mind, Vlad laughs.

And before Lord Anthony's trance ends, I am already slipping into the arms of my next partner. This one is old enough to be my father, with a face as lined as that of the baroness, but that doesn't stop him from raking my body with his eyes. "Well, aren't you a beauty?" His breath is rank, and his blood moves like slow, stodgy syrup in his veins.

It might surprise you, Vlad says. *Why not give him a try?*

I don't want to.

Play the game, Lucy. I want you to sample all the flavors this masquerade has to offer.

My fangs ache, aroused by the excitement and desire in the room. I cannot resist, not with Vlad urging me on. I look into my partner's eyes, and as soon as he enters his trance, I graze his throat with my teeth. His blood, surprisingly, is sharp on the tongue and crisp like apples.

Vlad laughs. *You cannot fight your own nature. Do not stop until the waltz is over.*

His command takes hold of me, and as the dance goes on and on, I drink from men both tall and short, fat and thin, pale and dark, plain and handsome. A drop here, a drop there. Blood that tastes of almonds, berries, and hickory smoke. Blood that is salty and sweet, bitter and bland—all of it soothes the pressure in my head and gives me a burst of delicious, exhilarating energy.

And then my next partner appears, and I know I have been too foolish, too distracted. I should have detected him at once with that smell of mint and gunpowder, and now it is too late.

"Good evening, ma'am," Quincey Morris says. His broad, handsome, unmasked face looks hard at me, as though seeing right through the feathers and lace. "How do you do?"

I press my lips together in a tight smile, praying that my mouth is clean of blood. If I speak, he will almost certainly see my fangs, even in the dim light.

But he will not accept my silence. "Are you enjoying the ball?"

"Yes, thank you," I say, barely opening my mouth as I adopt the baroness's thick German accent. "I like very much this music."

"You are not a native of Paris?"

"No, I am of Frankfurt. I . . . visit a friend."

His shoulders relax, and I give a silent prayer of thanks that my accent is authentic enough to fool him. "I've never been to Frankfurt, but I hear it's a marvelous city." He scans the crowd as he speaks, and I follow his gaze to Dr. Van Helsing. The physician stands on the perimeter of the dance floor, intently watching the couple beside us. The woman is my height, with black hair and a white gown—a description that could match most of the ladies here tonight—and she also wears a pair of pale wings like my own. The only overt difference between us is our masks: hers is of a bright, showy gold velvet. Quincey's eyes also move to her, appraising.

We will switch partners soon, I think, trying to stay calm. *Trick him and disappear.*

"You are not of Paris, sir," I say, light and friendly.

"No, I'm from America. I work on a ranch."

"You are a . . . cowboy?"

"That's right. I'm not always in elegant company like this, nor dancing with such a lovely partner," he adds, gallant even while hunting the undead.

"I do not know cowboys dance so fine. You ride horses, no?"

Through the crowd, I see Dr. Van Helsing's eyes leave the other woman to find *me*. My spine tingles as he tilts his head, thoughtful.

My mind races. I had assumed he and Quincey would haunt the train station, watching every departure in order to intercept my escape. But somehow, the doctor guessed I would stay in Paris. He must have ruled out the hospitals, knowing I could not draw attention to myself, no matter how badly injured. He calculated that I would seek a hotel—the larger, the better—and this ball must have seemed perfect for a vampire who is hiding in plain sight. Who needs sustenance to heal. Who was once a girl who had loved to dance.

What have you done to me, Vlad? I think, panicking, but for once, there is no response.

I wonder if the men saw me tasting my partners' blood, but Quincey would not be dancing so calmly with me if they had.

"They have ladies in America, too, you know," Quincey is saying, and I try to focus on him even as the doctor's eyes bore into me. "Some of them taught me how to waltz."

Out of the corner of my eye, I see the doctor move toward us. "And what other dances do you know?" I ask desperately. "The mazurka, perhaps?"

Quincey raises his eyebrows. "The mazurka?"

"Yes," I say as Dr. Van Helsing hovers at the periphery of my vision. My sharp hearing picks up his "Excuse me, please" as he slips between two couples. Quincey's fingers seem to be closing around mine, and his hand on my waist is like a vise. I am numb, numb all over, even as I force a carefree laugh. "Yes, the mazurka. Did you not say to me once . . . ?"

It is then I realize my mistake.

Months ago, at Mina's engagement party, Quincey and I had danced for the first time, and he had joked that for me, he would dance the mazurka, let alone the waltz. That must have lingered in my mind until now, prompted forth by this similar conversation with the same man.

Déjà vu, the French call it, translating literally to "already seen."

"Quincey!" I hear Dr. Van Helsing call through the crowd. "Stay where you are!"

But the cowboy is not looking at him. He is staring at me. His eyes land on the spot on my shoulder where a bullet wound should be, and though he does not speak, I see the shape of my name upon his lips. I hear his heartbeat accelerate, followed by a quick intake of breath, and I feel the air move even before he reaches for his guns. He hardly has time to touch them before I am calling to the mist and dissolving into its chill embrace. The dancers shiver at the sudden fog, but they continue waltzing blithely, perhaps believing it to be engineered by the hotel to give the masquerade an air of haunted romance.

I sweep the mist over the woman who resembles me, and she and her partner slow their steps, their expressions growing vague and dreamy. Quickly, I switch our masks, giving her my white lace-and-feather one while I tie her gold velvet over my own face. I detach my wings and affix them to her partner instead. Neither of them blinks as I whisper, "Leave the hotel. Take a winding path out of this room." And when the mist dissipates, I am on the opposite side of the dance floor behind a man in a garish court jester's costume. I laugh, almost dizzy with relief as I watch the scene I have just vacated: the couple obediently slipping in and out of the crowd; Quincey in hot pursuit, pushing aside dancers, one of whom pushes him back and shouts indignantly; and Dr. Van Helsing crouching low to the floor, trying to avoid skirts and legs as he follows the woman he believes to be me.

My shoulders shake with mirth and jubilation and awe at my own ability to evade. The doctor is no match for me, whatever he may think. I am drunk with hysteria, with exhilaration over these ungodly powers I have seized for myself. I press my hands over my face, laughing and laughing as Quincey and Dr. Van Helsing run out of the ballroom after their false target.

"Excuse me, miss. Do you care to dance?" says a low voice with a South Asian accent.

The court jester is gazing at me. He is a broad man with dusky brown skin and beautiful, long-lashed dark eyes beneath his red-and-yellow striped mask.

I know it is folly to stay—I ought to say no, find the baroness, and get myself back up to my room before Quincey and the doctor return from their fool's errand. And yet the waltz is coming to an end, everyone is seeking their final partner, and this man standing before me has blood that smells more delicious than any I have tasted tonight, smoky and peppery with a hint of sweetness. This could be my last opportunity. My last dance before my long imprisonment.

This time, it is not Vlad urging me on but my own self giving in to temptation.

"Yes," I say, stepping into the man's arms. His neck is both easy to reach and covered in layers of black frills. I look into the depths of his eyes, and he goes slack in my embrace, falling into the trance as I lick the rich, savory saltiness of his skin. He shivers with delight as my teeth cut a small, sharp line in his throat. His blood slips into my mouth, and it tastes exactly as it smells, spicy, thrilling on the tongue, and utterly delectable. It is like being given a slice of heavenly, mouth-watering chocolate cake, but only being allowed a single taste before I must push it away to sit tantalizingly before me upon the table. One taste is not enough.

I tense, waiting for Vlad to ridicule me, but still he is silent.

Just one drop more, I decide. I let my fang widen the cut ever so slightly, and more of the man's delightful blood coats my tongue, rich and warm.

When the music ends, it is almost as though Vlad's command, Vlad's spell, ends with it. My hunger and headache are gone, sated, and in their place is an empty, hopeless well of shame, revulsion, and self-hatred. When I lift my head, I see Nell Wright-Davies standing nearby, her eyes welling with tears, and I know she has seen my lips on my partner's neck.

"How could you?" she asks, her voice high and piercing in the silence between waltzes, and curious heads swivel in her direction. She looks heartbroken, not horrified.

"Nell," I say warningly.

As the violins begin playing a new piece, Nell turns and runs away from me, almost tripping on her long peacock skirts as she takes off through the crowd.

In the darkness, surely she did not see what I was doing. I tell myself that she is only upset because she believes I am beginning a new tryst, kissing the neck of my new lover.

But I have to be sure beyond the shadow of a doubt.

Cursing Vlad and damning my own weakness, I hurry through the ballroom after her, ignoring the stares and whispers that trail in our wake.

CHAPTER THIRTEEN

On the far side of the ballroom, I see smaller antechambers for private functions, each with a set of double doors. Nell stumbles into one and tries to shut me out, but I am too strong, and she storms inside with her gloved hands fisted. Teal feathers from her hair and gown litter the floor as she snatches off her mask and flings it away, revealing a face stained with tears.

Quickly, I close the doors. "Nell, please don't make a scene."

"Stay away from me!" Her voice thick with weeping, she runs to the opposite wall where a set of gold-and-cream chairs and tables are stacked. "How could you make me care for you and break my heart like this? Oh, why didn't you take the next train out of here?"

"Because Charles ordered me to stay away from you and I can't resist a challenge."

Nell puts her trembling hands over her face. "I never meant anything to you, did I? I was just another nobody in your long string of lovers, easily used and thrown away."

Sighing, I remove the gold velvet mask. "Of course you meant something to me. Our time together made me happy, truly. It reminded me of better days and of who I used to be. But what I told you on the ferry is true: you should not be with me. If I let you get too close—"

"Then I might hurt you like *Mina* did," Nell says, spitting the beloved name.

"Leave her out of this," I say evenly. "She has nothing to do with you and me."

"She has *everything* to do with you and me!" With her cheeks blazing and shoulders heaving, she looks so different from Mina that I wonder how I could ever have mistaken them. Lightning sparks from her eyes as she glares at me. "You wouldn't have even looked at me had I not resembled her! The only reason I caught your eye is because you thought I was her at first!"

"Please calm down—"

"All you wanted from me was another chance with *her*. It was all a lie and—" She falters and stares at the front of my gown. "What is that? Are you hurt?"

I look down to see red-brown drops splattered on my white satin bodice. "It looks like face paint from one of my partners' costumes," I lie, inwardly cursing my carelessness. "Some of them are dressed so absurdly tonight. Did you see the man with—"

Nell shakes her head. "That's blood, Lucy. I know blood when I see it."

"Don't be ridiculous."

"Did something injure you?" She seizes my hand, and the feel of her soft, warm fingers is so disorienting that I do not realize she is leading me to the floor-to-ceiling mirror adorning the antechamber wall. "Come over here and look for yourself . . ."

In the mirror stand two lovers, one dark and one fair, but only one has a reflection that shows her as she is. Nell's confusion turns into shock as she drops my hand, looking from me to the glass and back, over and over and over. For a long moment, we are silent as she processes the odd phenomenon of me standing beside her with only a few drops of blood on my gown, and me in the mirror covered in dripping gore that pulses over my skin like living organisms.

My mind races. I could summon the mist. I could put her into a trance. I could persuade her that this is only a nightmare borne of her frustrated longing for me.

Slowly, her eyes never leaving my reflection, Nell takes a step away from me. "What are you?" she asks, her face as white as my gown. "What *are* you?"

"Nell," I say, but then we hear people shouting from the ballroom.

A premonition snakes down my spine as I hurry to open one of the doors, just in time to see an odd group move past: four revelers in costume, struggling under the weight of a limp body. "Careful with his arm!" one of the men cries. The person they carry wears a court jester's costume, striped with red and yellow and adorned with black frills at the neck. My hand finds my throat as I recognize my latest partner, he of the beautiful brown skin and spicy blood. His head lolls, giving me a glimpse of his drawn, unmasked face as he is carried out to the hotel lobby.

Surely I did not drink enough to hurt him, let alone kill him by accident . . . did I? But then again, his blood had tasted so delicious. Perhaps I forgot myself. Perhaps, in my jubilation at escaping my hunters, I took too much from him.

"What happened?" I hear a woman ask.

"He fainted, I think," someone answers. "It is revoltingly hot in here . . ."

Dr. Van Helsing and Quincey will know. They will not be fooled long by my decoy, and they will return to look for me, and though I am strong and fast, with powers they have not, I know I shall never be free of them. The doctor will follow me to the ends of the earth.

I must find a way to be rid of Nell and escape. I must go to Germany *tonight*.

I begin to close the door when I see another man struggling through the crowd. "Make way!" he shouts as he drags a grey-haired gentleman alongside him. With a jolt, I recognize the older man as my partner of the sour breath and crisp apple blood. He is conscious, at least, but just barely, leaning on his companion and moaning as he holds a hand over his throat.

Panic stabs my abdomen. I thought I was being so careful and so clever, and here are two partygoers sickened by me. I have exposed what I am, and Vlad will punish me, conveniently forgetting that it was he who had first put me in this situation.

I had nothing to do with it, Vlad whispers. *It was you who could not deny your nature.*

I have been so foolishly arrogant. How soon before my other partners faint or notice their wounds or realize they had all danced with the same woman? And Lord Anthony even knows my name—but perhaps none of them will remember me. I *hope* they will not.

"Lucy, what's happening?" Nell asks.

I turn, pondering what to do with her before I control the other damage I have done, when the door opens and Charles enters, his milk-white face a mask of wrath when he sees us together.

"What are you doing in here with my wife?" he spits. "I told you to stay away from her!"

"Charles, keep your voice down," I say, looking at the still-open door.

He stares at me in disbelief. "Are we friends that you can use my name so familiarly? Well, then, *Lucy*, hear this. If I ever see you with my wife again, I will call the authorities." A nervous young staff member appears in the doorway, and Charles rounds on him eagerly. "You there! Escort this woman out of the hotel immediately."

"But why, monsieur?" the young man asks, looking hopelessly out of his depth.

"Because she is a demon of unspeakable lust who is poisoning my wife with her kisses! Yes," Charles adds, stomping toward Nell. "I know what you have been doing, my dear. I'm not the simpleton you think I am. You have been mooning over her our entire wedding journey!" He gives her arm a vicious twist, and she cries out, tears streaming down her cheeks.

The pain in my head returns with a vengeance. I do not even wait to react. In one fluid motion, I pull the staff member into the room, shut the door, and detach Charles from Nell, sending the man flying across the room into the stack of tables and chairs. He crashes into them and lies motionless beside a pile of broken wooden legs, too dazed to utter a sound.

"Lucy?" Nell breathes. "How did you do that? How are you strong enough to . . ."

"M-madam," the staff member sputters, gaping at me.

My head throbs as I look into their aghast faces. I must contain this mess at once. I know I cannot let any of them leave this room and reveal what I am. Shame, horror, despair, regret—all of it knifes through me. I promised I would not hurt another soul, and here I am, contemplating.

"What are you?" Nell is shrieking. "How can you throw a man like that? And have the reflection you do?" She points to the mirror, where the three of them are arranged like a dramatic tableau of victims on a theatrical stage and I am the monster looming over them.

The door opens again, and the baroness hurries inside, looking pale. Seizing his chance, the staff member tries to push past her and exit, but I am by his side before he has time to blink. He crumples to his knees, weeping, when I pull him back inside and stand guard before the door.

He knows you will never let him leave this room alive, Vlad says, soft and malevolent.

I will not kill him!

You will do what is necessary to save yourself. Clean up your mess, or I promise you . . .

What? I ask defiantly. *I'm not afraid of the pain you cause me.*

Vlad laughs. *Pain? I was thinking of Mina.*

The baroness looks uneasily at the others: the staff member crying on the floor, Charles leaning heavily against a table, and Nell shivering where she stands. "Lucy, at least three people have fainted," she tells me. "The staff believe some strange illness is going around, perhaps having to do with the wine or food, and guests are leaving. Take me back to my room, please."

See the way they look at you? Vlad breathes. *They all want you dead, even the old lady.*

It should be only a vicious lie, but I cannot help believing him when I see the frustration and disappointment in the baroness's eyes. She thought I was so strong, so *good*. But she was wrong, and now she knows I am weak-willed. Mindless. Violent. I will never be like the women in the castle, loath to harm a soul. I am just like Vlad.

She is sick and dying, he breathes. *She is at the end of her life, and you are only at the beginning of yours. She hates you, Lucy, even if she will never admit it.*

"Lucy?" the baroness asks, her eyes narrowing. "Did you hear what I said?"

Listen to me, Lucy. Listen to me.

Vlad's words sink into every corner of my soul. I feel my mind slacken as though some invisible rope tethering me to reality and to my own self has let go. When I speak, it is as though my voice comes from someone else's body. "There's no point in lying anymore," I say distantly. "They know . . . or at least suspect that something is very, very wrong with me."

The old woman's gaze shifts behind me. "Look out!"

I whirl to see Charles flying at me with the sharp end of a broken chair leg, aiming for my heart. I take his wrist as easily as picking up a pen. I would have done so even if he had been at full strength and uninjured. I bend his hand backward, reveling in his pain as he had done mere moments ago to Nell. "Were you trying to kill me, you pathetic little man?" I ask.

"She-devil!" he roars. His heart thunders like the drums of war, and the smell of his blood is oddly attractive, considering how he himself repels me. It smells clean and starched, like linen drying in pure mountain air, and I think if I pressed my face to his throat, I might smell lavender. His free arm flails, trying to scratch my face. I twist his hand harder and hear his bones snap.

"Lucy!" the baroness utters as though she has been punched in the stomach.

"Stop hurting him!" Nell cries.

In my mind, Vlad is laughing. *He deserves it. I think you ought to end him, Lucy.*

No! I want to scream, but my mouth is no longer my own. I feel as though a cold and invisible hand is gripping my throat. "You would defend this sorry excuse for a husband? After all he has said and done to you?" I ask Nell.

With her blue eyes burning, calm and righteous, she looks disconcertingly like Mina again. "Don't you *dare* speak of him to me, you soulless monster," she says.

There it is. *Monster*.

It was what Mina had called me in the heat of the moment, in the throes of her fear that night in the churchyard when she and the others had found me feeding on a child—or so they wrongly believed. *Monster*. The word stabs through my mind and what is left of my heart.

They hate you, Vlad says. *They would kill you if they had a chance. Why do you hesitate?*

Through the pain and rage echoing in my skull, I feel like I am floating. I am weightless, detached, a mere observer watching a play unfold. The antechamber with its mirrors and lights is the stage, and the actors have gathered to perform their roles with dramatic flourish: the cowering staff member; the old dowager, speechless with horror; the newlyweds, united at last in fear; and the slender, dark-haired woman standing in a growing cloud of grey mist, looking like a bride or an angel in her snowy white gown and wings.

The memory of the churchyard flashes before my eyes. The moon glimmering down from a star-dusted sky, shining its eerie light over London. The wind, chill with the breath of autumn. Gravestones and mausoleums watching like sentinels as I kneel on the grass in a wedding gown, facing people who had once loved me but now stare at me like I am a plague to be eradicated. *Monster! Monster!* The brutal word, spoken in my own beloved Mina's voice, spears my heart.

They want you dead, Vlad whispers. *Everyone wants you dead.*

The memory vanishes, and I am back in Paris. The shrill of violins, the swirl of gowns.

Blood in my mouth.

I do not know how there came to be so much of it coating my tongue, but someone is screaming. When I leave my reverie and return to my body, I realize that Charles Wright-Davies is clasped in my arms like a lover and that my fangs are sunk deep into his fleshy throat. It is *his* screaming I hear as every drop of his life drains away, tasting as clean and sweet as I had thought it would. Somewhere in my rational mind, I recognize that I am doing everything to ensure that he feels as much pain as I can give. Nell, the baroness, and the staff member are all on the floor, clustered together, swooning and wailing as I drop Charles's lifeless body like a used rag. With a surge of adrenaline, the staff member makes one last attempt to run for the doors.

The pain and lightness in my head are gone. My mind is clear as the voice of reason tells me that the innocent young man only came in here to help. But he will call for assistance. He is still a threat, and I am too far gone, too deep in Vlad's ensorcellment to resist the urge to kill.

It is your nature, after all, Vlad says reasonably.

In one heartbeat, I am emptying the young man of every drop he ever had as he gazes up in terror and longing at my beautiful, blood-stained face. I let him crumple in a heap by the doors.

Good, Vlad says, and his approval reminds me of the night and the sea and the cliffs.

I turn to see two women huddling on the floor. One of them has wet herself; the acrid smell of her urine rises over the scent of blood. I realize I have forgotten who they are, these two people whose hearts are the only ones still beating in this room filled with death.

The young, blond woman is babbling ceaselessly. "You *tricked* me! You cast a spell on me. How could anyone ever truly love you? You put me in a trance, you—"

"Lucy," the old woman murmurs, and I wonder how she knows my name. Her heart beats so weakly that it sounds more like the fluttering of a dying moth's wings. "Stop this madness. Stop it at once, or I will stop you. Listen to me . . ."

Yet another command. Me, an invincible and immortal goddess, and still everyone seeks to subject me to their will. It is as Vlad said. They all want to destroy me.

The question echoes over and over in my head: "How could anyone ever truly love you?"

Monster, monster, monster.

The blond woman's babbling turns into screaming as I rip out her throat and drink her blood—honeysuckle and caramel—and drop her, letting her head bounce on the hard floor.

Good, Lucy! Vlad says.

I stare down at the old woman whose name I cannot recall. I do not remember meeting her, but somehow her eyes know me. She does not cry. She does not beg. She only looks up at me calmly, her face lined with the creases and laugh lines of a life well lived, and her lips move. She says my name again. How is it that she knows my name, this fragile human with her heart like the last dry leaf that slips off a tree, never to return once it falls to the ground?

"Remember who you are, Lucy," she says as gently as a mother. "If you cannot remember who I am, at least remember yourself. Don't lose your own self."

She is nothing to me. None of them are. They are all sniveling, lowly creatures.

They are food.

But through the sound of Vlad's low, pleased laughter, I hear that other, weaker voice again. *No*, it says, growing stronger with each word. *No, this is not who I am! This is not what I want to do with my immortality. I want to do better. I want to be better.*

"Lucy," the elderly woman says, looking into my eyes without fear. "I befriended you for your heart. You still have one. You can feel and love and regret. Who you were is who you still are, and I see it. I see all of it. Don't ever forget that."

Her words stir another memory, hazy like a ray of sunlight. *Yes, sunlight*, I think abruptly. *There was sunlight in the compartment.* I see it shining through the window on my companion's face—*this* woman's face. We sat together on a train, and her eyes crinkled in a smile at me, the same smile she gave me on a ship cradled in fog as she looked at me the way that Mamma had once, so full of love and reassurance . . . and *trust*.

Mamma. Papa. I had been a daughter once, hadn't I? I had been cherished and beloved. *Do you mind if I call you daughter?* This woman had asked that not long ago. Slowly, I feel that unseen rope that tethered me to reality, to *myself*, grow taut and pull me back to safety.

"Baroness," I whisper, my lips trembling.

Her eyes shine with tears. "Come back. Lucy, my daughter, come back to me." I hear her heart slowing. The blood it pumps is like mud, crawling feebly through her veins. "We spoke of immortality, you and I. Do you remember?" Her voice is brittle, but motherly. So like Mamma, who had loved me and who had been so much like me a long time ago.

I nod, unable to speak.

"You have been given eternal life," she says, each word growing more and more labored. "You told me you did not wish to squander it, but to make something good of it."

My chest heaves with silent sobs. "I am, really and truly, a monster."

Her cracked lips stretch. "Not a monster. Remember, Lucy?" My name is the last word she will ever utter. It emerges on the final breath she will take in this world as her head falls back onto the floor, silent and still. Her eyes stare sightlessly upward at the ceiling.

It is like seeing Mamma die all over again. I remember her collapsing, senseless and gone, after watching—on the last night of my human life—as I gave up my mortality to Vlad.

This old woman is the baroness. I remember that now. The baroness who had known two others like me, who had believed that I would make the most of my existence, and who had asked if she might call me *daughter* because she had never had one. I come back to myself, fully. There is no voice in my mind but my own as I fall to my knees, sobbing, "Mother, Mother." I do not know for whom I grieve: the mother I lost or the mother I found on my journey.

I cradle the baroness in my arms, rocking her as I weep in a way I had never thought to do again. Blearily, I take in the scene of devastation I have caused. Four lifeless bodies, three of them cruelly, violently drained of blood. Four innocent people who had only wanted to save themselves—or save *me*. I have done this. I have allowed Vlad to coerce me into this.

"Vlad!" I scream. "Vlad, I hate you! Do you hear me? Are you still there? I hate you!"

I hear him give a soft laugh, but it is not mocking. This laughter is tender and inviting, and in my head is a vision of Mina gazing up at Vlad, her face full of wonder. After bullying and manipulating me into the catastrophe at the ball tonight, he is now applying salt to my wounds by allowing me a glimpse of where he is—in a dark room, a breath away from Mina, whose unfocused gaze is fixed upon him as though no one else exists.

"Vlad!" I roar, but the vision dissolves and I come back to a room filled with the dead. In the mirror, my reflection looks even ghastlier. Anyone unlucky enough to enter might be struck dead by the mere sight of me. The baroness looks like a doll in my arms, limp and breakable.

Charles lies on his back, his head flung to one side. Nell is on her stomach, her throat a bouquet of gore and her arms stretched out, as full of yearning in death as she had been in life. The staff member is crumpled between them, his face still a mask of terror. In the ballroom, I hear people leaving to seek other merriment in the dark streets of Paris. They talk and laugh as though nothing at all is amiss—as though the entire world has not just ended for me in this room.

I have behaved like a monster.

And if I allow Vlad to hold power over me, I can never trust myself again.

I used to think that immortality by his side would be a blessing—a life of discovery and adventure with him to guide, comfort, and teach me to make my mark on the world. I dreamed of exploring continents and oceans with him as my protector, my mentor, and my friend.

Instead, I have locked myself into an eternity in which he can control even my thoughts. He has never cared for me, no matter what I believed. A person who wished me well would be kind and patient and encourage me—not force me toward my darkest instincts to punish or prove a point. Someone who rules by fear, control, and violence is an enemy.

Vlad is my enemy. My foe, my oppressor.

The realization calms me somehow. Any confusion, longing, or regret I had felt for him fades into the cold and quiet rage now blazing in my chest.

I rise shakily to my feet and call the mist. One by one, the bodies stand up. Their eyes are clouded as they enter the world of fog to begin their task of wandering forevermore as lost, empty shells of the people they had been. I watch, my shoulders trembling with sobs, as the baroness disappears, followed by the others, never to return to the light again.

I have subjected them all to this.

"No," I say aloud, clenching my jaw. "*Vlad* has subjected them to this."

I may have no choice but to obey his command and retreat to his castle. But there, I will allow his other brides, Hong and Thabisa, to help and instruct me. I will learn everything I can about my strengths and his weaknesses. I will make him pay for his deeds.

And one day, I vow, Vlad will die by my hand.

But before that day comes, I must protect Mina. If I can somehow keep her from him and derail his plans for her yet again, it will be my small revenge for tonight—with interest to come.

I wrap myself in a cloak of mist and hurry up to my room, forcing myself into a state of absolute calm as I lie down on my bed. I never knew what clarity anger could give me, but I feel sharper and more alert than I have in some time. I close my mind to the wreckage I have caused downstairs, to Nell's brutal words, and to the baroness wandering away through the fog. I allow my awareness to drift, and everything fades: my hotel room, the baroness's empty chamber next door, the lights of Paris, and the moon sparkling on the Seine.

I raise the mist and seek Vlad in my consciousness with crystalline precision. If he can access my unguarded mind, then I may be able to reach his. He is with Mina this very moment, and if I am not too late, I can use the element of surprise to force him away from her once more. I know he is drawn to my emotions, so I search patiently for his. He will be triumphant. He will be lustful, exultant, and hungry for her blood, just as he once had been for mine.

I am lying on the bed, but then I am also wandering with my hands reaching out through the mist as dim lights, dead faces, and strange scenes flicker in and out of view.

And then I am there.

The windows of Jack Seward's house blaze with light, and male voices shout in the dark. There is no moon, and though I do not recognize the men running over the grass, I know they are frantic, desperate, searching for something lost. They shine torches and call out a name.

But the object of their pursuit is stumbling past me, unseen by them.

It is a woman. She walks unsteadily into a pool of light, and I see a nightgown and long fair hair spilling down her back. Her movements are erratic, and she staggers forward with a hand pressed to her throat. When she lifts her fingers, I see blood staining her smooth skin.

"Mina," I croak. I want to scream her name, but I cannot seem to find my voice.

She is weeping quietly, whether from fear or pain, I do not know.

What I do know is that I am too late.

Vlad has bitten Mina, and there is no force on this earth, no pain in existence that will stop me from killing him with my bare hands.

CHAPTER FOURTEEN

Heartbroken, I reach for her wrist, pulling her closer to me . . . and realize that I do not know who this woman is. Her brown eyes are vague and unfocused, she has a short freckled nose and a pointed chin, and aside from her hair, she does not resemble Mina any more than I do. I let go of her, stunned, and she hobbles away in a daze without seeming to register my presence.

"Mrs. Harker! Mrs. Harker!" the men shout. They, too, have been fooled. My mind races. If they are pursuing the wrong woman in the dark, where, then, is the real Mina?

Unerringly, drawn by instinct, my eyes move to the upper windows of Jack's house. And then I am running across the threshold, unbound by the rule that would have forbidden Vlad to enter without invitation. Yet I know . . . I *sense* that he is here. Who invited him in?

I see a home left in sudden disarray. Chairs pushed back, tea still steaming on the table alongside half-eaten pastries, maps of eastern Europe and typed pages littering the tables. A phonograph sits on a shelf, and I recognize Jack's voice emerging from it, tinny and distorted: "The fifth of September. The patients seemed unsettled today as I went on my rounds . . ."

Quickly, soundlessly, I go upstairs to a narrow hall lined with pictures of Jack's family and look into empty room after empty room before arriving at a closed door. Quietly, I turn the knob and enter. Belongings are scattered all around the small bedroom—a man's suit jacket hangs askew on a chair, a woman's gloves are folded atop the bureau, and the dressing table is littered with brushes, jars, and bottles. A suitcase spills articles of men's clothing onto the rug.

Jonathan Harker, pale and sweating, sits on a stool that should face the dressing table but is turned outward instead. Desperate, high-pitched sounds escape him as he quivers from head to toe—not from fear, but from the exertion of trying to move while some force pins him in place.

Mina lies on the right side of the bed. The pillow beside hers still holds a dent from Jonathan's head. I surmise, as his wild eyes meet mine, that he was lured downstairs and coerced into issuing the invitation after the others had left to pursue the false Mina.

And there is Vlad, stroking Mina's hair. They look like a couple deeply in love, and neither of them seems to notice me. How many years have I yearned for her to look at me thus? How can a stranger march in and simply compel her adoration? How can this monster swagger across the world, taking and taking and never facing a single consequence?

Well, then. Let *me* be his consequence.

Not for nothing have I been given inhuman strength and speed. I grab Vlad by the shoulders and throw him headfirst into the hall. It is unforgivably stupid to antagonize a vampire so much older and stronger. I know he will kill me, but I don't care. It will be worth it to die, I think, as I force his head into the wall. Picture frames rain down, showering glass over us. One particularly large shard lands in his chest, but it is not deep enough for my taste. I am calm and detached as I pull the shard out with a wet, gurgling sound and hold it over Vlad's heart.

His hand wraps around my wrist. He wrenches the shard from me and stands. "Well, well, Lucy, so you have decided to join me. You and Mr. Harker will be a captive audience, I'm sure."

"No, Vlad. This quarrel is between us!"

"Quarrel? A quarrel implies an argument between two equals, and I am your master and you are my creature who must be punished."

"Then punish me. I tried to kill you just now. Punish me and leave everyone else alone."

He drags me back to the bedroom and shoves me into the dressing table. Jonathan looks up at me in mute anguish. "I am punishing you," Vlad says pleasantly. "Watch closely, mind."

"Get away from her!" I cry, but an unseen force prevents me from going after him. I scream and thrash, frozen where I stand, as he approaches Mina with the gait of a panther.

"Count?" she murmurs. "Why are you here? I think this must be a dream—"

"Then let it be a dream," he says softly, touching her face. "Let me kiss you as I know you have wanted me to since the day I came to retrieve my pocket watch. Do you remember?"

A frantic, high-pitched whistle escapes Jonathan's throat, barely audible over my own shouting. But Mina does not see or hear us as Vlad bends his head down to hers.

"Will you let me kiss you, my darling?" he asks. "Here, where no one can see?"

Though her face and body are relaxed, in her wide eyes, I can see Mina fighting. After a long moment of silent struggle, she says, "My lips belong only to my husband, and I will not give them to you. Not even in a dream."

Elation rises in me. "Fight him, Mina! Resist—" My jaw gives a heart-stopping crack, and this time, I howl in pain, not anger, as an invisible fist shatters the side of my face.

Vlad runs his fingers over Mina's neck, and her breath hitches. Her eyes flutter closed as he blows a soft breath from her cheek to her collarbone. "Then let me kiss your throat instead. I have thought of little else but you. Give me a respite in my grief and loneliness. Will you?"

The legs of the stool scratch the floor as Jonathan fights to get to his wife, and I ignore the all-encompassing pain in my jaw as I attempt to free myself.

But our attempts are ineffectual. This is a train on a track, and it has always been charging toward the destination of Vlad's choice ever since I first met him in dreams and he plundered my mind for thoughts of Mina. The perfect woman of the age, gentle and docile and modest. She is his land in a storm, she is soft earth yielding beneath his hungry, searching fingers.

She is his prize.

Mina does not speak, but something glows in the blue fire of her eyes. She *feels* for him, this strange and lonely man, and after all, this is only a dream—or so she believes. She lifts her chin, freeing her neck, and when Vlad's lips make contact, she lets out a long, low, soft moan. He presses a line of gentle kisses down to her shoulder, and she arches her spine.

I scream again as Jonathan weeps in silent despair.

Suddenly, Vlad looks straight at me. "This should bring back memories for you," he tells me, his eyes black pools ringed with scarlet, and then his fangs bury themselves in her neck.

My shattered jaw sings with pain as I shriek Mina's name. Beside me, Jonathan vomits, his body convulsing with distress, but I hardly notice. I am sobbing as Mina's hands scrabble uselessly at Vlad's back before she falls onto her pillow, face drained of color and eyes darting around the room as though searching for some answer, some sense to this awful ordeal.

"Jonathan!" she cries, reaching for him. And then she sees me. "L-Lucy? Is that you?"

I let out a heartrending sob. I want to tell her not to be afraid, that it will be all right, but my mind is already reeling away from that dark bedroom and back to my hotel in Paris. I bellow into a pillow, broken in both body and spirit, my injured jaw shrieking along with me.

Stop sniveling and get up, Vlad's cold voice echoes in my mind.

My body obeys at once, abrupt and jerky as a puppet. I weep and struggle, but my limbs are operating of their own accord, and in ten minutes, the room is put to rights, my luggage is packed, and I am dressed and veiled. Mechanically, I convey my belongings downstairs to hail a carriage to the train station, passing a few stragglers from the masquerade in garish costumes, just as the first faint rays of dawn begin to touch the sky.

Bones crack in my jaw, putting themselves back to rights, and by the time I purchase my ticket to Germany, my face has completely healed. My heart, on the other hand, is still a broken mess as I shut myself into a compartment and close the curtains. There is no comfort in solitude, for I should be sitting on this train with the baroness. I remember her frail body wandering off into the mist and burst into sobs anew, aching with a grief and a fury that can never be appeased.

The conductor will come in soon to punch my ticket, but after that, I will see no one else. I do not deserve to be in company; I cannot be trusted. I will tie my veil to the latch, imprisoning myself until I reach Germany and there, *there*, I will enter the exile I deserve.

But oh, Mina! I gnash my teeth as the image of Vlad biting her replays in my mind. I may not have known everything about vampirism, but I *chose* it, fearing the entrapment of marriage and motherhood and balking against the restrictions of society. But Mina, who was orphaned at a young age, has only ever longed for a husband and a home full of children. Becoming a monster, as she had once called me, would be the death of her joy. The death of everything she is.

I ball my hands into fists. I must not, I *shall* not give in to despair as Vlad expects me to. There must be some way to protect my friends, some manner in which I can fight.

But all through the day-long journey, I am at a loss, and by the time we arrive in Munich, there is no denying that circumstances are bleak. It is evening once more, and my body, stiff and puppet-like, steps onto the frigid station platform, crowded even at this time of night. A porter approaches, switching effortlessly from German to English as he offers to find me a carriage.

Only then do I realize that Vlad has not given me further instructions. I hesitate, watching as other people climb in and out of carriages around us. And then something catches my eye.

Parked across from the station in a patch of darkness, far from the other vehicles, is a massive black carriage with gleaming onyx windows and shining wheels. Two dim lamps on either side illuminate rich ebony wood, a shining gold door handle and steps, and a magnificent team of four sleek black horses. The animals' eyes glow deep ruby in the night, and somehow I know without a shadow of a doubt that *this* is to be my conveyance onward.

When I point it out, the porter wheels my luggage over and helps me secure it to the rack. He frowns up at the empty seat behind the horses, asking, "But where is your driver, madam?"

I look warily at the reins, wondering if I am meant to drive myself. Perhaps this is a form of torment in which I must drive aimlessly about, searching for a castle whose location is as yet a mystery to me. The horses toss their necks and stamp their hooves, restless and agitated. Two of them are frothing at the mouth, white bubbles bursting over their hot dark muzzles. They will not be easy to control, not for a small woman who has never driven a carriage in her life.

"I shall manage," I say, tipping the porter, who shrugs and returns to the station. And then I put my foot upon the step, preparing to climb into the driver's seat.

Not there, Vlad whispers.

"Where, then?" I ask. He does not answer, so I step down and open the ornate door to reveal the plush, black silk-lined interior of the carriage. Perhaps the horses know where to go and there is no need for a driver. But as soon as I begin to climb inside, I hear Vlad again.

Not there, either. Farther back still.

"Where?" I demand, closing the door harder than necessary. The horses whicker at the sound, and the wheels tremble as I walk to the rear of the carriage. There, I notice a length of strong black rope that has suddenly appeared, tied in an intricate knot to the luggage rack. A trickle of unease slips down my spine.

Tie your wrists to the carriage.

I gasp and begin to protest, but no words emerge. My body is not my own as my fingers nimbly heed Vlad's order. I watch in helpless horror as a series of complex knots I have never learned appears between my wrists. Soon, I am so tightly tethered that I cannot lift my arms.

Vlad laughs, low and venomous. *Did you think you had been adequately punished?*

When he speaks again, I hear his voice in the open air as clearly and distinctly as if he were standing next to me. "Die Toten reisen schnell," he pronounces, and though I do not understand German, the horses seem to, for they take off at a run.

I am jerked forward, and my chest hits the sharp edge of my trunk, hard. The ground is rough beneath my thin shoes, and I almost trip on a crack in the pavement. My wrists are bound so tightly that I must hurry to keep up as the horses go faster and faster. We pass other carriages, but no one seems to see us in the darkness. No one will help me tonight.

For half an hour, I stagger behind the carriage as we enter the countryside. Land and sky stretch all around us, giving the impression that we are entering a great void. The horses barrel along as though they know exactly where to go. I am immortal and do not need breath, yet my lungs heave with the memory of being human. I am now moving at a trot, increasing into a canter. I stumble, feel my forehead hit the luggage rack, and fight to remain upright, for I do not wish to find out—vampire or not—whether falling can tear my arms right out of their sockets.

Vlad, please, I beg, choking on my quickened breaths.

Enjoy your scenic journey to my castle, Lucy.

This, then, is my punishment. I will be made to run the whole way through Germany and Austria-Hungary and up to his castle, which—I remember with dread—sits atop the Mountains of Deep Winter. This ordeal will not kill me, for I have inhuman stamina, but I know I will feel it all. I will endure it all—the bone-deep cold, the bite of the rope on my tender skin, the stones and cracks and branches tearing at my shoes, too fragile for such activity. And as though that were not enough, a freezing rain begins to fall, plastering my hair and clothes to my skin.

Perhaps it will only be another hour, I tell myself. Perhaps he will decide that is enough.

That hope becomes a maddening, looping refrain in my mind. I think it as the dark shapes of hills and trees and valleys become a blur. I think it as the rain becomes a chilly mist that clings to my wet face. I think it as the stars wheel in the sky and dawn appears in the east.

I am half-mad with weariness and pain in my feet, now devoid of the shoes that fell off in tatters miles ago. My stomach rumbles at the smell of my own blood caked upon my heels.

Where is Dr. Van Helsing? Where are Quincey and his guns when I need them? If only I had not been so quick to stop his bullet from entering my heart in Paris.

As the light of morning touches the sky, the carriage slows down at last. The horses pull to the side of the road, and I collapse as someone unties my wrists and lifts me into the carriage, washing my bloody heels and applying a cooling salve. I lie in a swoon as two voices converse. I do not understand the language, but when they address me, it is in beautifully accented English.

"Have no fear, Lucy," says a woman in a rich contralto made for music. Her voice is so kind, it makes me want to weep. "You are among friends. Can you open your eyes for me?"

Wearily, I obey and am surprised to see that she looks no more than sixteen or seventeen. Her skin gleams ebony, her lips are full, and a halo of tight black curls frames her lovely, high-cheekboned face. Her figure is tall and queenly, with a strong build. Still, something about her liquid dark eyes, ancient and intelligent, belies a soul that has known centuries of life.

"Hello," she says, smiling as she tucks a blanket over me. "I am Thabisa."

The other woman lifts a cup of water to my dry, cracked lips. "And I am Hong. Poor girl, you must have been running since Munich." Her voice is high, and her consonants are soft around the edges. She looks about twenty and is small and slight, and with her oval face, olive skin, and long black silk hair, she could easily pass for my sister. When Thabisa asks her a question in their language, she utters a clipped word—a curse, I presume, from the heat behind it—and responds in English. "Who can say? Certainly he means for her to continue all the way to the mountains. Here, Lucy, eat this," she adds, her anger fading. "It will give you strength."

I open my mouth for a spoonful of steaming, salty broth that tastes of meat, carrots, a hint of garlic and onion, and . . . *blood.* A bit thin and bland, but it is blood nonetheless.

"Rabbit's blood," Hong says, seeing my surprise. "I often make it for Thabisa." Where her beautiful, dark-skinned companion is calm, she seems to radiate a burning, intense energy. She mutters oaths in another language as she feeds me, pausing only to pat my chin with a cloth.

Thabisa tucks a second blanket around my feet, and though she is still smiling, her ageless eyes are sad. "There is still so much human in you," she tells me. "I see her in your eyes, the girl you still are. We are all the girls we once were. They never die, do they?"

"Even if they wish they had," Hong says bitterly, as she takes the empty bowl away.

Suddenly, I realize that I am no longer in the carriage. We are in a comfortable chamber with high ceilings and a large fireplace that fills the space with heat and light. All the art and furniture seems to have come from different countries and eras, but instead of looking haphazard, everything I see has a pleasing harmony: the walls hung with landscapes, oil renderings of fruit and flowers, and tapestries in sunshine yellow and geranium red; branches of fresh pine on every surface, lending a picturesque fragrance; and low, soft chairs piled with pillows and throws. The sofa beneath me sits closest to the fire, and its cushions hug and support my bruised body.

"I am here," I say with tears of relief. I do not know how I imagined Vlad's castle to be, but it was not *this*. The room is warm, inviting, and attractive, furnished specifically for a lady's comfort, with herbs and bubbling pots and shelves full of old books. "I have arrived."

The women exchange glances. "You are on your way to us," Thabisa says in her rich voice like a rare viola. "You will be here soon, my friend, and we will eagerly await you."

"But I am here," I say again, bewildered. "I am meeting you both, am I not?"

"Yes, in a dream. But your journey will not last much longer." Thabisa takes my hand in her strong ones. "We will do everything we can to ease it for you. Do not lose hope."

Hong's eyes flash. "Or give him the satisfaction of seeing your despair."

Already, they and the room are fading from view. The fire darkens, and the woolen blankets slip from me, and I sit up, horrified, to find myself back in Vlad's carriage on the side of an empty, open road. Outside, the day has died, fading into another dark night.

No time to waste, Vlad whispers.

"No," I sob. "Please do not make me do it again. Please!"

But my body is already climbing out. My feet, healed and shiny, meet the sharp stones of the road. My hands lash themselves to the rack with merciless knots. And my legs take off as the horses launch into a powerful canter. Gashes reopen on my heels as I desperately try to keep up, the wind whipping my hair. All night, I run in the biting cold, leaving bloody footprints in my wake as the road ascends steeply. We climb through village after village, and curtains twitch at the windows as people look out. But no one helps me. Instead, they all make the sign of the cross or kiss amulets hanging from their necks and vanish back inside.

They know what I am. They recognize the carriage. Perhaps it is not uncommon to see a woman being dragged by four horses straight out of hell, up to the coldest, most forsaken peaks.

There is nothing at all on earth that can spare me this torment.

Do not lose hope. Do not let him see your despair.

This time, the whisper is from Hong and Thabisa. The other women, the other brides. My *sisters.* I bend all my thought toward them, toward their kindness and compassion for me, as I plunge ever upward and the first hues of sunrise bleed over the mountains.

CHAPTER FIFTEEN

I run for days on end. Every sunrise, I am given a reprieve and brought into the carriage, which becomes that lovely room where Thabisa tucks me in by the fire, Hong feeds me rabbit's blood broth, and I weep with both relief and apprehension, knowing that at sunset, when stars sweep across the frozen sky, I will be made to run once more. The horses will plod on through the ice and snow, though at a slower pace as we traverse the brutal face of the mountains.

I flit in and out of consciousness, unable to distinguish between dreams and reality.

So it is that one night, I am not surprised when the frost-blanketed forest transforms into the bookshelves, the crackling hearth, and the mahogany desk of Jonathan Harker's office. I stop in the doorway, swaying with exhaustion, too tired to wonder why I am here.

And then: "Lucy!" A pair of soft arms hugs me so hard it hurts. I smell lily soap and see eyes the color of the sky. "Why, Lucy, don't you recognize me? Lucy!" My knees give way, and I am helped into a chair by the fire, where she kneels at my feet, frantic and tearful.

"Mina, it's you," I breathe, and she falls sobbing into my arms, holding me so tightly I can scarcely draw breath. Fortunately, I do not need air to survive. I only need her.

At last, she pulls away, holding my face between her hands and looking hungrily at me. "I feel as though I haven't seen you in years. Where are you, Lucy? Are you ill?"

"I might ask the same of you," I say, alarmed by the sight of her in the firelight.

Mina looks like someone at death's door. Her skin is waxy and transparent, with purple shadows beneath her eyes, pale lips, and a constellation of faint blue veins across her nose. My hand moves to the collar of her robe, and when I lower it to reveal two sores—bright red weals in a circle of white—on the left side of her neck, I cannot help uttering a sob of my own.

She wipes my tears. "Don't fret, darling. I will recover. I don't sleep as deeply as I did before, but I don't mind. Arthur says that is why you couldn't reach us through the mist, because he and I are such heavy sleepers. But now, he has Jack's hypnosis and I . . ." She hesitates. "I can at last sleep lightly enough to reach you in my dreams."

My heart aches at the changes the venom has wrought in her, yet I cannot find it in me to be sad for long. Not when we are finally together. "Jack? Arthur?"

Mina laughs. "I refer to them familiarly because they are like brothers to Jonathan and me now. We have reunited in London." Her smile fades. "All of us but Dr. Van Helsing and Quincey, who write that they are bound for Germany. They crossed paths with you and guessed where you were going based on the accent you used. The doctor said something about psychology."

I utter a groan that is also a laugh. Trust Van Helsing to put even the smallest clue to use.

"The directions Jonathan gave them to the castle also confirmed that Germany was the next most likely step on your journey. He did his best, for he was blindfolded much of the way. He is certain you are being compelled to go to the count's lair. Yes, the *count*. I, at least, can speak freely of him to you," she adds grimly, "and there is nothing left to hide. He has tormented us all, you and me and Jonathan, and I promise you he will pay for it."

I sag into her arms in utter relief. "It doesn't feel real, not being alone in this anymore."

Mina kisses my cheek. "You are not alone, and never will be again. But you must stay vigilant, my dear. I truly believed that the doctor and Quincey wished to help you—"

"If they help me any harder, I will end up with a bullet in my chest," I say dryly.

She sighs, her pallor returning. "Arthur and I sent countless telegrams begging them not to hurt you. But you know how single-minded the doctor is. There is no stopping him, especially not now when we suspect the count is also on his way to the castle. Going home."

I jerk away from her, startled. "How do you know this?"

"You mentioned boxes of earth to Arthur," Mina says. "The exact cargo carried by the *Demeter* to Whitby this summer. And so he and Jonathan went to speak to the shipping agents, who remembered the strange boxes well. They were only too happy to reveal that the shipment had been distributed all over London." She gets up and goes over to the desk, holding up a sheaf of letters and telegrams. "Even while pursuing you, Dr. Van Helsing found time to do research. He wrote to us that anything pertaining to faith, any religion in the world, will most likely repulse the count, who needs the boxes in which to rest. So if we sprinkled holy water upon that cursed earth, it would effectively bar him from entering any of them."

I cannot help laughing, impressed. "And that is what you did?"

Mina gives me a small smile. "Oh, no. Holy water was not enough for the doctor. He urged us to use *fire*. Jonathan, Jack, and Arthur hunted down almost every box and burned it to ash. I begged to come, but my husband forbade it." She sighs. "It was our first serious argument. We had never even disagreed before that."

"He only wanted to keep you safe, my love."

"Perhaps," she says quietly, touching the side of her neck. "Or perhaps he believed I did not wish to help, but to *hinder*. Oh, Lucy, sometimes I have feelings that do not belong to me. I see and hear things in my mind that I should not. I feel connected to . . . to that monster. I know I am too strong-willed, too steadfast to become his follower. Yet I worry I can no longer be trusted, and I think Jonathan does, too. He watches me and it makes me feel self-conscious. Ashamed."

"You have nothing to be ashamed of," I say sternly. "You are not to blame."

"Perhaps he thinks I am helping the count—"

"Jonathan would *never* believe that of you!"

"How can he not? When I am not certain myself? When he and Arthur were in Whitby, I stayed with Jack in Purfleet. I visited his hospital and learned just how much he is helping the patients there. I even befriended a few of them. One of them, Renfield . . . ah, you know of him. He is too far gone, too enamored by the count to ever be reached again. Jack thinks the poor man may serve as a conduit, a sort of human gate—" She breaks off, shuddering.

I get up and take her beloved face between my hands. "It will *never* happen. Not to you and not to me. We belong only to ourselves, do you hear me?"

Mina leans her forehead against mine. "I can glimpse where *he* is sometimes," she whispers, as though afraid to be overheard. "I am sure he doesn't mean for me to. But I am determined to exploit it. I plan to memorize everything I see and become a useful spy for the group." She forces a sparkle of mischief into her words. "There is a purpose to everything, and if we are clever enough, we can turn it into something helpful."

I laugh at the steely glint in her eyes, one I know well. "There is the brisk, no-nonsense governess I recall, for whom there is no problem without a solution." A thought occurs to me. "You said the men burned *almost* every box of earth. How many are left?"

"Only one. Arthur tracked it to Dover. That is how we know the count is leaving. There is no safe place left in England, and he must flee home . . . where we will be waiting for him."

"What on earth do you mean?" I demand. "Surely you're not coming here?"

"You thought we would leave you to face him alone? Now that we know the truth?" She covers my lips, silencing my protests. "Arthur and Jack have already left England. They plan to be in Germany in a few days. I told them I can sense the count's apprehension, his need to speed the journey home. He will not take a lengthy voyage as he did to England. He will employ ships, trains, carriages." She speaks coolly, mechanically, and though I know too well how linked Vlad is to the people he infects, her knowledge chills me. "They plan to intercept him. They will pass through Germany to Austria-Hungary, where the river will take them directly to the castle."

"And you and Jonathan? Surely he would not allow you to enter such danger?"

Mina scoffs. "You think I will sit and twiddle my thumbs at home whilst the men hunt this demon who stole you from me? No. I am a woman of action! Jonathan and I leave in the morning. Even he could not argue against the usefulness of my knowledge. And," she adds, smiling, "my ability to read a train timetable, which I am afraid to say he still lacks."

But I do not laugh as she hoped I would. "That means the party is splitting up," I say, biting my lip. "There is safety in numbers, Mina. None of you knows what *he* can truly do—"

"No? Not even I, who was given *this*?" She touches her throat, and I bow my head. "It's the best chance we have to intercept him, not knowing which route he will take on land. If we miss him, we will go straight to the castle. Jonathan believes he can find it again. He remembers a few landmarks. Villages, parts of the forest, and that long winding river. We are coming to you, and we will end this. We will find vengeance for you, my Lucy, my light. I love you."

"I love you." I take her hand and kiss her palm. "I think endlessly of you. Every moment we are not together, you inhabit all the corners of my mind. Promise me you'll stay safe."

Mina does not promise. Instead, she wraps her arms around my neck. "How comfortable it is to have you with me," she says, sighing. "I wish you were truly here. Where are you now?"

In hell, where she belongs.

We break apart, both of us crying out as the sudden low, malicious baritone slices into our thoughts. Mina presses her hands to either side of her head as though trying to squeeze out Vlad's voice. He laughs, cold and malignant, and I look down to see my feet are covered in bright red blood and weeping wounds. Thorns and clots of dirt cling to my skin, and when I swivel my right ankle, I see that every single toenail has been torn clean off my foot, leaving gaping angry pockets of red where they had once been. In the joy of this dream and being with Mina, I had forgotten my exhaustion and my despair, but now they come rushing back in a tide of grief and dismay. I look up to meet Mina's horrified eyes, already fading from me.

"Lucy!" Her voice sounds as though it is coming from an insurmountable distance away.

When I blink, she is gone and I am once more plunging through the snow, yanked onward by my wrists as the carriage ascends the mountain. I look blearily up at the sky, praying for the salvation of dawn, but there is nothing but darkness.

Perhaps his castle is weeks away. Perhaps he is making me circle it uselessly. Perhaps I will never reach it alive, and my arms will burst out of their sockets and a hunter from one of the villages will take off my head with his crossbow or some bird of prey will devour my eyes like swollen berries, and I will never see Mina again. Never, never, never . . .

But just before these thoughts can take poisonous root in my mind, the rough black rope around my wrist disintegrates. I crumple to the ground as the horses pull to one side, revealing the great doors of an immense castle, sprawling like a grey stone dragon atop the snow-covered peaks. Blood spreads around my ravaged feet, staining the frost.

This is another one of Vlad's tricks, I think as I lie motionless on the freezing ground.

But then one of the heavy doors opens and two women hurry out, silhouetted by candlelight. I smell the burnt wood of a fireplace, clean linen, and the scent of flowers as they bend over me. I cannot make out their faces, only two pairs of dark eyes.

"It's all right, Lucy," I hear Thabisa say in her soft soothing voice. "It's all right now."

And then I sink into oblivion.

CHAPTER SIXTEEN

I slip in and out of consciousness. I am aware, vaguely, when Hong and Thabisa carry me through a maze of corridors that emanate bone-deep cold, and how the faint torchlight flickers in the draft that slips in through the ancient windows. I smell rust and decay, rodent nests in rotting furniture, and wax and charred wood as we pass paintings of long-ago faces. The cold and dark fade when we enter a wing of the castle I already know from dreams, which greets us with the cheerful crackling of a fire, the smell of flavorful stew, and bright vases spilling pine and holly.

The women lay me on a soft bed. They remove my stained dress, tend to my feet, and brush the tangles from my hair before tucking me in like a child. As I sink into my pillows, I hear Thabisa whisper in English, "Drink this," before pressing her wrist to my lips. A thin stream of her blood slips into my mouth, tasting of summer fruit and honey.

Sleep finds me quickly, but not before I see a strange vision in my head.

I am standing in the mist, which clears to reveal a low, narrow room of damp, worm-eaten wood. Amid the soggy lumber, coils of wet rope, and portholes streaked with salt, I see a young Thabisa looking out at the roiling sea. Her tight curly hair is longer, her dark eyes wider, and her face softer, more frail and vulnerable, and I realize that somehow, through the tasting of her blood, I have been granted this glimpse of her as a human girl.

Footsteps thunder across the deck above, cutting through the peal of bells and the clamor of men shouting. Thabisa glances nervously around, searching for a hiding place as the sun begins to set. My heart clenches with dread when she notices a long wooden box against the wall. She hurries toward it, her face tense with panic. But when she opens the lid, a man sits up on a bed of earth, the lengthening shadows obscuring his face but for his widening smile.

And then I succumb to slumber and see no more.

When I awaken, Hong sits beside me. Beyond her, I see more details of the bedroom they gave me: warm wood floors, rugs woven in the verdant shades of summer, a dressing table with a pewter basin, and intricate wall tapestries full of fantastical creatures. I see silver unicorns on green hills, dragons with batlike wings in a sky of azure blue, and mermaids frolicking in a grotto.

Hong follows my gaze. “Irina had a penchant for whimsy. She who lived here before any of us . . . but there will be plenty of time to explain. Drink now and regain your strength.” She offers her wrist, and I taste brine and salt and lemongrass in her blood.

Once again, a vision blossoms in my drowsy mind. I am shocked to see the familiar cliffs of Whitby, on which a man and a woman sit side by side on a bench, an obvious intimacy between them even though they do not touch. I recognize Vlad at once, grave and brooding and silent, but I jolt with surprise when I realize that his companion is not me. It is Hong, beautiful in the moonlight with her pale gold skin and long-lashed dark eyes.

She asks him a question in another language, but when he makes an impatient gesture, she repeats it, sulkily, in English. “Why have you brought me here of all places?”

"Because this is where I met *her*. Your successor, and Thabisa's as well." Vlad speaks with a soft, affectionate lilt. "I do not think I shall return to our mountains for some time, so you must entertain yourselves. You will not miss me too much, I hope?"

Hong's precise English is flat and emotionless. "No, we will certainly not."

His ease slips into displeasure, and he turns to face the sea. "I like England already. My body has not even reached its shores, but I have been wandering it in dreams whilst on board my ship. You will be happy, my dear, to hear that your successor is a worthy one."

Hong is silent, her mouth a thin, taut line.

"She is young and beautiful, of course. She would not have caught my fancy otherwise. But she is also quick and curious and very strong. I could feel her trying to fight my influence." Vlad laughs. "You know I like a woman with fire, and this one's bones burn with fury, yearning, and frustration. And her blood! Oh, if only you could smell it! You would know at once that she is of your homeland. Her ancestry is diluted, perhaps. But whenever she is near, I can see those sun-soaked trees, that blazing sky, plants blooming in the arms of the river."

And before sleep pulls me into its dark tide, I realize, startled, that he is talking about *me*.

The next time I wake up, sunlight is streaming in through the windows. Thabisa weaves at a loom nearby, piecing together what looks like a cape of many different colors. She sings quietly, perhaps an aria from an Italian opera, and her music is as glorious as her speaking voice promised it would be. She smiles when she sees me. "Good morning! How do you feel?"

"Wonderful," I say, surprised. My body feels renewed, and my feet are back to normal, smooth and unblemished. I sit up and stretch. "Thank you for helping me. Both of you."

Thabisa waves away my thanks and helps me out of bed. I stand firm and strong, my legs no longer shaky. "Do you feel well enough to eat? Hong has been cooking a feast for you."

"A feast?" I echo, moved by the kindness of these women.

She slips a robe over my shoulders and laughs, showing strong, straight teeth. "You are a good excuse to make all the delicacies she and I long for. Here, take my arm."

The great room looks even more cheerful by day with its overstuffed chairs, shining pots, and roaring fire. Hong stirs a delicious-smelling cauldron of soup. "Ah, good, you're awake." Thabisa and I take seats at the table as she dishes out the food.

I gasp, for I recognize the meal. White flour noodles float in a savory, meaty broth that smells as though it has simmered for days. I see swirls of marrow from the bones she used for cooking, bright green herbs, and cracked pepper amid chunks of delectable, thinly sliced beef. The aroma brings back Papa's gentle face and ringing laugh. He was always as eager as a little boy to try our cook's latest attempt at making the dishes of his grandmother's homeland.

My eyes fill with tears at the sight of my father's favorite meal, and Hong's mouth twitches, pleased by my reaction. "The true ingredients are hard to come by," she tells me. "I've had to make do, and I'm afraid it won't taste nearly as authentic, but please enjoy."

I hide a smile. Papa used to say that my great-grandmother—who had been very proud of her own cooking—had always had a self-effacing comment at the ready whenever praised. I take a huge spoonful, followed by another, and then another. Thabisa laughs, delighted by my appetite, and when I have emptied the bowl, Hong gets up and refills it at once.

"I did not imagine you would have such comfortable quarters," I say, admiring the room.

"Most of this place is cold and cheerless, but if you have to spend eternity in exile, it might as well be in pleasant surroundings." Hong speaks with a touch of dark humor. “There were many spectacular pieces scattered around the castle, and Thabisa and I brought here what we liked best. Everything you see was handpicked by us or the women who came before us.”

A childish painting catches my eye. It depicts two ladies, one with dark skin and the other with straight black hair. “That is the Baroness von Bassewitz’s gift!” I say, my heart soaring. “I do not know her maiden name, but she was called Elisabeth and her grandfather lived nearby.”

“How on earth do you know our young friend?” Thabisa asks, pleased and startled. She and Hong grow sober when I tell them, briefly, of the kind old woman’s death. “Well, I’m happy she lived a full and fairly long life, by human standards. She was such a winsome little girl.”

“How long have you both resided here?” I ask.

“I was brought in the late 1700s, and Thabisa came almost a century before that.” Hong gives a dry chuckle at my shock. “The years go by every bit as slowly as you would imagine. I admit, it is not the most terrible existence. We have each other and the run of the castle, and we hunt animals and buy what we need from the villages. But we cannot ever leave the mountain.” Her voice is calm, but her eyes burn more and more with each word.

Only when Thabisa gently touches her shoulder does Hong sit back in her chair and let out a long breath, calming herself. I can tell this is a familiar ritual for them: Hong seething, and Thabisa soothing. Their bond does not seem romantic, yet it is an intimacy that has clearly bloomed over time. Something true, grown out of darkness. Vlad could never have predicted it.

“We do not mention him often, but it is our choice and not a spell,” Thabisa says as though hearing his name cross my thoughts. “You may speak freely within these walls.”

Hong raises a brow. “You will find, Lucy, that our *husband* . . . or rather, our *jailor*, is not a favored topic. But this castle has become a true home to us. We have occupied and cared for it for so long that we have won its allegiance and are safe within its walls, even when it comes to our link with him. We can choose to keep him out of our thoughts. With a few exceptions."

We are all silent for a moment, lost in our own dark thoughts. "When you gave me your blood, I saw a glimpse of your pasts," I tell them. "You, Thabisa, encountered him on a ship. And you, Hong, were summoned by him into a dream of Whitby, where I had first met him. He called me a worthy successor to you. Me! After that initial period of romance, he only ever told me how stupid I am, and how my friend Mina is the perfect woman I will never be."

"When he met me, he told Thabisa he had found someone much stronger and braver than she was," Hong says. "And he constantly compared Irina to his human wife, who he claimed was a princess of more integrity than she could ever hope to be."

I laugh, low and bitter. "None of us ever measure up, do we? There is always someone more perfect. What a simpleton I have been. How could I have ever allowed him into my heart?"

"We all did," Thabisa says quietly before excusing herself and vanishing into her room.

Hong exhales. "Irina was like a mother to her. Thabisa grieves for her still, and only solitude can give her solace. I will explain when I show you the chapel, if you are not too tired."

I am only too happy to agree, and we step into the winding stone corridors of the castle. The place seems to have been designed to be as confusing as possible, and I mention it to Hong.

"It is designed to disorient any enemy who found his way inside. Or any victim," she adds, and I picture Jonathan Harker running through this labyrinth. What courage it must have taken to explore this trap of secrets and danger, all to return to his beloved Mina.

We pass through a banquet hall that must have once been grand. One wall is covered by a Renaissance hunting scene in which men on horseback bring down a stag. "I think," Hong says, gazing up at it, "you know by now that Thabisa and I drink only animal blood."

"How do you resist? Are you not tempted by the villages you visit?"

"We must resist. We cannot afford to invite a mob here, trapped as we are. He does, however, bring us a victim from time to time and forces us to feed." She scowls. "Human blood entices us. Of course it does. But we can satisfy our hunger through other means. It takes a very long time to build up the willpower, and each time we drink human blood, we must build it up anew." She glances at me. "You're a new vampire, and your instincts are more powerful. You will not be as adept at ignoring your craving for blood, but over time, you will find it easier."

"I want to be like you, and to live blamelessly," I say fiercely. "The people I have harmed haunt me, and though I can never be rid of them, I can at least avoid adding to their number."

Hong studies me. "Yes, I think you mean that, Lucy Westenra. We will teach you, as our sister. You and I look enough like family that it will not be difficult to imagine. I, like your great-grandmother, also belonged to the royal court of Vietnam . . . though I lived many generations before her." She leads me through an immense library that smells of damp books. "My bloodline afforded me privilege, but I was nothing more than a pawn in the hands of my male relatives."

I marvel at our shared heritage. It feels too providential, too much like destiny. But then again, everything in my short life seems to have pointed me here, to this moment and these women. "I may not be royal, but I know something of that."

Hong runs her hand over books in different languages. "Thabisa and I love to learn. It makes the time go by more quickly. We speak a new tongue every week, for they fade with disuse. I know twelve fluently, and Thabisa fourteen." She laughs. "The villagers love her for speaking like one of their own. The children give her gifts, bells and buttons and medallions meant to ward off our kind once, but are now mere trinkets. She is weaving them into a cloak."

We pass other rooms that must have once been sumptuous, including a hall with a great throne where Vlad and his ancestors must have held court during their lifetimes.

At last, we reach the chapel, all dark wood and stained glass that still shines even after years of neglect. There are no benches, only enormous tombs. The largest, a coffin of cracked black granite, glowers down from a dais where an altar should be. I would have known whose it was even if *Vlad*, followed by a succession of lofty titles, had not been etched into the stone.

Hong clenches her jaw, her body going rigid at the sight of it. "That is where he sleeps at home. And when he is here, Thabisa and I are forced to sleep in our tombs as well."

I examine a row of humbler tombs. They are unmarked, but I see signs of the people who had lain within: dead flowers and withered oak branches; a pair of old-fashioned shoes, strangely affecting, with a buckle that still shines; and a tarnished headpiece adorned with jewels.

I can sense which belong to Hong and Thabisa. The coffins hold each woman's essence: the breath of flowers for Hong, bursting gold and ruby beneath a tropical sun, while Thabisa's smells of the sea, of salt and mist and bloodstained sands. I glare at Vlad's ostentatious tomb, at the titles with which he honors himself while all the other names have been lost to time. Only he matters here, and everyone else is a mere accessory to be forgotten when no longer useful.

"This is what I wanted to show you." Hong indicates a coffin of earth-hued marble just below Vlad's tomb. It is etched with blooming roses and has been raised above the others on a low dais. It is the only other coffin to bear a name: *Irina*, followed by a list of titles nearly as impressive as Vlad's himself.

"Did he love her?" I ask, astonished by the grandeur of her resting place.

Hong's sharp laugh seems to deepen the cracks of Vlad's tomb. "No, I rather think he is displaying her as a trophy. She was forbidden to him in life, and when he became what he is now, he took her for his own out of spite." She hesitates. "I used to hate her, even though she died long before I came. So many nights did I wander through her abandoned bedroom, hoping to learn more about the woman who had captured his interest before he ever laid eyes upon me."

Beneath her anger, I feel something much harder to forget: heartache.

"He does that to a woman. Makes you feel that you are the center of his world, his jewel, his prize. He is an explorer, and you are his most important discovery." She shakes her head. "He promised I would be happy in his castle, and I *have* been happy. I wanted to leave Vietnam. My uncles married me off to a brute, and my mother let them do as they liked. I didn't matter to anyone. I was already planning my escape when he found me. French roots have choked the soil of my homeland for a long, long time. They infiltrated the court, and he was one of the most highly ranked. I felt special, *chosen*, when he sought me out and made his offer."

I watch her touch Irina's tomb, this relic of the woman Vlad had chosen first.

"No gift from him is ever free," Hong says quietly. "You cannot grow love with seeds of cruelty. It took me too much time to learn that. But yes, at long last, I can respect Irina and admire her kindness and devotion, through what Thabisa tells me."

"Qualities she retained even in misery." Thabisa enters the chapel. Her face is drawn and sad, but her head is held high. "I know you wish to spare me pain, my dear Hong, after I let my emotions overwhelm me. But this is my story to tell. I, who knew Irina well."

Hong may be filled with hatred for Vlad, but she loves Thabisa like family. I see it in the way she looks at her friend. I know this is her human self I see, someone gentle and loyal, with tenderness wrapped around her backbone of steel. She bows her head in respect to Thabisa and moves toward a tiny tomb that could only have been crafted for a child.

"I was only a girl when he brought me here. Not yet seventeen as a human and not many months old as a vampire." Thabisa laughs, unexpectedly, the sweet music cutting through the silence. "Irina and I were an odd pairing. She a pampered princess, white as snow, and I a girl of my people's proud blood. We had no common ground or language, yet she forever changed me. Come, Lucy. Walk with me." She lifts a graceful hand to summon a wintry mist that sweeps in through the windows, and together, we step into its embrace.

CHAPTER SEVENTEEN

A woman stands weeping in a tattered wedding gown. She is close to my own age and is much taller than I am, with a statuesque frame and a luminous face as pale as cream. She wears no adornment but a slim diadem, silver inlaid with sapphire, on her lustrous wheat-colored hair.

Thabisa and I are in the throne room of the castle. Outside the windows, night has fallen, and Vlad sits imperiously on the throne as the woman pleads in a language I do not recognize.

"This is only a memory," Thabisa says when I tense at the sight of Vlad. "I had just come to the castle. I was eavesdropping in the rafters but did not understand a word of Russian. All I knew was his penchant for cruelty was not exclusive to me. I was not alone in being forced to bend my knee, open my legs, or empty my veins without question, like an obedient little bride."

I watch Irina crumple before a silent, emotionless Vlad. "What is she asking of him?"

"My freedom. His keeping me like a trophy did not sit well with her." Thabisa's voice is almost inaudible. "First, the Portuguese came. Then the Dutch. We were overrun by European settlers and their diseases. Theft, famine, and rape, and now smallpox, measles, and influenza on the burning shores of the land I loved but could no longer call home. I had to leave South Africa. I had no one left alive. Any surviving relatives were seized, and I thought if I could hide on some boat headed for Europe, I might find them one day and make a new home elsewhere."

I gasp. "The vision I saw of you on the ship—"

"It was his ship," Thabisa says flatly. "I stowed away, thinking it would be my salvation. But I found my damnation instead." She turns back to the scene before us with wet eyes. "Irina always had a gentle heart that longed for a child, and he mocked her for being weak."

"Weak?" I scoff. "And yet there she is before him, pleading her case and not giving in."

The mist replaces this memory with another. The windows of the women's wing are open to the summer air, and Irina toasts bread in a pan as a young Thabisa struggles to play the violin. The girl's bow slips, making a scratching noise against the strings. But she perseveres, and in a moment, she is able to play a few notes as Irina beams approvingly at her. But the older woman's smile vanishes when a boy of two or three lets out a high-pitched squeal, having burnt his hand attempting to reach for the hot bread. She snatches him up, kissing and soothing him.

"Her son's name was Petyr," Thabisa says.

"Was he adopted?" I ask, shocked when she shakes her head. "But vampires must forsake their human lives, no? We die to become what we are. I assumed that we could not—"

"*He* cannot have children. The infection is stronger in him and forbids it, but it is weaker in us. Normally, it would favor its own survival above all and thus kill a baby. But Irina believed drinking only animal blood weakens the venom somehow, making pregnancy possible. She discovered this after a miscarriage or two, for she rarely slept alone when he was gone."

I watch Irina coo to her son, processing this. Never in my human life had I ever wanted a child of my own. But I am as amused as I am unsettled by the irony of my having chosen this existence in order to escape motherhood—yet still being haunted by its possibility. It pursues me still, just as death does. "Irina had a man? A human, from one of the villages?" I ask.

Thabisa nods. "It was her only solace. We brides are unbearably attractive to children, and it was Irina's torment, as a woman who had been forced into the life of a monster, not a mother." She purses her full lips. "He often toyed with her by starving her, and then kidnapping village children and setting them loose in the castle to unleash her hunger."

I inhale, sick to my stomach at the depths of Vlad's malice.

"Irina began to lose more and more of herself. She lay in bed for weeks, stewing in self-hatred." Thabisa sighs. "It was she who taught me to survive on animal blood. We spent decades building our resistance to humans, and in time, the villagers grew to tolerate, if not trust us. But always he would return and force us to drink human blood. We unlearned that diet over and over, the cycle unending. That, Lucy, has been our immortality: utter exhaustion and misery."

The mist clears on another memory, of the mountains in spring, with flowers blooming and birds singing in the thicket. A cozy hamlet is tucked into the shoulder of the peaks, farmland sloping downward as goats and sheep graze. High on a hilltop stand Irina and a broad, stocky village man, his eyes shining down at the baby boy in her arms.

This idyllic tableau is everything society has ever asked of me. That could have been me, presenting our firstborn to Arthur, and now I know that it could *still* be me, if I somehow escaped and went to be with Arthur again. I imagine the face of Irina's lover, suffused with joy, to belong to Arthur instead. To see my dear one so content, would a child be such an impossible price to pay? I remember how he had cradled his old dog, loving and protective, and picture him doing the same to a son or daughter with all the love he has to give.

"Did you ever want this for yourself?" I ask Thabisa, not taking my eyes off the family.

"No. I have never desired romantic love, nor do I long to be a mother. And you?"

"It repulsed me once," I admit. "I think it was the expectation that disgusted me, as though I had no right to choose my own life."

"But if you could choose? Would you still want this?"

In my mind's eye, I see Arthur hugging a roly-poly child, both of them laughing up at the sky with eyes that are the exact same shape and color. "Not for myself, no," I say softly as Irina hands the baby to her lover and he beams down at the boy, his ruddy face aglow. "But perhaps for another."

"There was a long period of time in which Vlad grew tired of us and went abroad," Thabisa says. "We were left in peace, and Irina fell in love. It was everything she had longed for as a human, for even Russian princesses are not free to choose their own lives, and her family wished her to marry for political power. They disdained Vlad, and so in death, he sought out Irina merely to possess her. But then she found this one true, fleeting joy."

I can hardly bear to ask the question. "How long did she have it?"

Thabisa's smile twists. "Five years. Less than the flicker of a dragonfly's wing to us. We knew he would return at some point, possibly during Petyr's lifetime. I urged her to pass the boy off as a village orphan she had adopted in her kindness. It was a plausible story, we thought."

"But he did not believe it?" I ask, and she looks at me in silence as the shocking revelation overcomes me. "The child's tomb in the chapel. That belonged to Petyr?"

"It was over the minute he laid eyes upon the child. Whether he knew the truth or not, Irina's love for the boy was too strong and the center of her world . . . and that would not do."

The mist unveils a final memory. We stand on the castle balcony, jutting over a river that slices the mountain like a deep blue knife. It is autumn, and the peaks are scarlet, tangerine, and gold. Irina stands with her hands on the railing, staring down at the roaring water. The wind whips her long, unbound hair across her angelic face as the younger Thabisa paces back and forth, her features twisted with grief as she speaks in rapid Russian.

The Thabisa beside me translates it into English, her voice almost a whisper. "'I will kill him, Irina. I will destroy him, once and for all, for what he has done. To take both your lover and your son from you . . . He has gone too far this time. He will pay. I swear it to you.'"

Irina turns to look at the girl. I am startled by the change in her beauty, by the sudden translucence of it, as though the light of her spirit has faded. She speaks, low and vehement.

"'Wash not your hands in his blood,'" Thabisa translates beside me. "'Baptize yourself not in evil. Not for me. You have been as a daughter to me, my dear one . . .'" She turns her back on the memory, and I lay a hand on her shoulder, watching the scene with growing dread.

Irina embraces the girl and returns to the edge of the balcony. The girl lifts her chin and does not utter a sound as Irina swings her legs over the railing. She looks back one last time, murmuring something before picking up a wooden stake, fearsomely sharp, and plunging it into her own heart. And then in a flash of sunlight, she is gone, her gown a streak of white against the mountains. She is a dove, a fallen flower, a star drifting in perfect silence toward the river below.

Thabisa keeps her back turned on the memory. "Strange, is it not? That I could have once hated and mistrusted this woman, as I did all white people, particularly one who seemed arrogant enough to try to save me. But she made me love her. With her, I had a mother again. Someone to care for me, protect me, and make me forget the hell in which I was trapped."

With a sweep of her arm, the mist dissolves, and we are in the chapel once more. Hong, who is still standing beside Petyr's tiny tomb, comes over and enfolds Thabisa in her arms.

"Why, oh why, was I chosen for this suffering?" Thabisa asks, her face stained with tears. "Why Irina? Why you, Hong? What did we do to deserve such a destiny?"

I watch them embrace as something hot and slow and burning fills my chest.

Thabisa is sobbing. "Why, of all families, did Irina belong to the one he hated above all? Why, of all ships, did I stow away on *that* one? Fate is nothing but cruel. I thought to escape torment and disease, but instead, I only embraced it."

"No," I say, my voice ringing through the chapel, and they turn to look at me. "You did not know what you were doing. You were only a child, and your home was being torn apart by European invaders. There was nothing else to be done. You would have died if you stayed."

"And did I not die anyway?" Thabisa asks bitterly. "Has it not ended worse for me?"

"No, it has not," I say. My voice is calm despite all that smolders underneath. My fury is taking shape inside of me, gaining form and purpose. Resolve snakes through it like blood dropped into water, dark and sinuous and staining. "You have friendship and hope. Your story, Hong's story, and Irina's story might as well be mine. We are the same, and we will find a way out of this. An answer, an escape. By the grace of God, we will end it all, here and now."

Hong's smile is both approving and ferocious. "I am glad, for his sake, that he intends to reside in England for a very long time."

"My friends say he is on his way here at this very moment," I say quietly, and they exchange glances of dismay. "I thought I was too sick and weary from my journey to sense it, but surely the two of you must have felt him?"

"We did not," Thabisa says, clenching her fists. "We have shut him out for so long, finding peace in the silence, but perhaps that was not wise."

"Then let this be an opportunity for us," I urge them. "What shall we do, we three? How can we right his endless wrongs?"

They are both silent for a moment, and then Hong speaks. "So often have I wanted to burn this castle to the ground," she says, her voice low and intent. "I have dreamed of pushing him into that abyss of darkness and decay where he gave up his soul five centuries ago. That hole in the mountains where the fallen return not as themselves but as something else entirely, and I would close it up with tar and holy water and hear him choke on his screams."

"No. He would find a way back out," I say, pacing back and forth. "We must rid the world of him entirely. Destroy him utterly, body and soul."

Hong laughs. "You speak a language I love, Lucy. By all means, continue your poetry."

"This curse he gave us," Thabisa interjects. "We don't know enough about it. Say your far-flung plots of destruction work. Say we manage to kill him. What happens to us? What if the venom inside us cannot survive without him? Have either of you thought of that?"

There is a long silence.

"It behaves differently in us," I say, thinking aloud. "I can walk in the light. I can enjoy the food I once loved. I can see my reflection in a mirror. I need not sleep in a box of earth."

Hong nods. "Crosses, holy water, and wild roses do not hurt us. Nor do garlic or powerful smells, which are unpleasant only to those unaccustomed to the foods of our homelands. Notice," she adds with a cynical smile, "what kind of women he prefers for his brides. Thabisa and I have long believed there is something in the taking of our souls that incurs a price upon him alone."

I shake my head in silent wonder, almost amused. I spent so many years obsessed with death, longing for a romantic version of it in which I would be with everyone I had loved and lost. I relinquished my mortal life to escape it only to discover it haunts me still. But too long have I cowered in its shadow, and I am tired of running away. I am tired of being afraid of the inevitable. "Then I, for one, am willing to take the chance," I say firmly. "If by my death, I can protect the people I love more than life itself, then I will do it."

"As will I," Hong vows.

After a moment, Thabisa nods. "And I will as well. The cloak I weave at the loom," she adds, "is something I began without even knowing my own intention. But over time, it became clear to me that I am crafting it with a purpose. All the spells and incantations on the trinkets the village children give me are no more than superstition, and yet—"

"You are making a weapon, Thabisa," Hong tells her. "It is perfectly fine to admit it."

We laugh, and something blossoms in the space where my heart once beat. I take my new sisters' hands in mine. "We will start by exploring how the venom differs within us. I have felt for some time that the key to ending him lies there."

Hong exchanges glances with Thabisa. "We may have a solution for you, Lucy," she says.

CHAPTER EIGHTEEN

Hong leads us through the maze of corridors and up a flight of stone steps. This wing of the castle is grander than the one the women inhabit, with a muted, ancient splendor. The deeper we immerse ourselves, the more agitated I feel—a discomfort I can see is shared by both Hong and Thabisa, who wince and grimace as the smell of Vlad surrounds us. His essence permeates these quarters like a pall of dark ocean water, but nowhere is it stronger than the door to which Hong is taking us. His scent is almost tangible, glowing like a bloodred halo of hellfire around it.

The door is made of yew wood, its surface covered in masterful carvings of shapes and figures and symbols. I look at it, and I can hear screams and sobs. Victims pleading for their lives, and young fragile brides whimpering before falling into dazed silence, for it is always, always easier with him to choose resignation over rebellion.

Even courageous, vindictive Hong, a woman with a spirit of flames, trembles before it. When she speaks, it is with an effort to keep her voice steady. "I told you he sleeps in the chapel when he is at home, but this wing is his residence. We are never to intrude without invitation."

Thabisa stands sideways as though unable to face the door head-on. "Before he left, he had me promise I would not come here in his absence. For my own safety."

That piques my interest. "Safety?" I repeat.

"He never warned *me*," Hong informs us, glowering at the massive door.

"You have made no secret of your animosity toward him," Thabisa tells her with a faint smile. "He knew you would not come here of your own free will. But there is something inside that may pose a danger to us. And if that is true, then perhaps it might harm him as well."

I ignore my own shudder as I approach it, my excitement growing. It is unpleasantly cold, as though it were crafted from solid ice. I see neither knob nor handle, so I push inward, hard, feeling the complex carvings bite into my palm. But the door does not budge, and the edges fit so snugly into the surrounding stone that I cannot dig my nails in to pull it out toward me.

"It is the door of hell itself," Hong says. "We have tried to open it by any means possible. Pushing, pulling, pressing for a secret panel, searching for a keyhole that may not be immediately apparent. Speaking all sorts of phrases that may serve as a password, including his favorite." In a vicious and guttural voice, she intones, "Die Toten reisen schnell."

It's something I seem to remember from the deepest corners of my mind. A phrase, once spoken into the frigid air, that spurred four coal-black horses onward, dragging me behind them.

"Translated roughly from German, the phrase means 'the dead travel fast.'" Hong speaks it once more, making Thabisa and me recoil, and gives the door a vicious kick. "Not that it helps at all. The only thing that does is feed the carvings our blood."

I flinch. "The door drinks blood?"

“Examine it if you will, Lucy,” Thabisa says, looking sick to her stomach as she moves to the wall opposite the door. “You will excuse me if I stand over here.”

I take a few steps back to study the carvings. A skillful hand has etched scenes of torture, violence, and pain into the yew wood: here, a man boiling alive in a pot of oil; there, a woman’s body impaled on a wooden stake, the point entering between her legs and exiting her mouth as her sightless eyes stare upward; decapitated heads and severed limbs adorn the spikes of a fence; wolves and bats and snakes devour humans, entrails dangling like ribbons from their jaws; and peasants writhe in pain as they endure sexual atrocities with spiked wooden clubs and swords.

“Surely the wood-carvers went mad after making this,” I say softly.

Hong gives a sharp gunshot laugh. “I doubt not they were all killed before they even had the chance to go mad. Surely he did not allow anyone who laid a single stone of this place to survive, but forced them to endure those very deaths you see before you. Where else might he get such artistic inspiration?”

In the very center of the door, I see a human heart etched into a particularly frigid spot, the four chambers scooped out and concave. The wood there is stained and dark, and the smell is unmistakable. “Vlad’s blood,” I say. “And both of yours as well.”

“That is how he opens the door,” Hong says, glancing at Thabisa. “We do not know how much he feeds it, but we have tried varying amounts to no avail. The door *does* creak slightly as though considering opening for us. But no matter how much we give, it is never enough.”

“It is not the amount, I think,” Thabisa says, her voice like a taut thread. “But the strength of the venom. His blood carries much more of the infection than ours does.”

I straighten. "Then try again, and let me add my own blood this time. Perhaps with all three of us feeding the door, there will be enough venom to open it. But open, it *must*. I think you are both right," I add, my muscles tense with anticipation. "The answer to his defeat lies within."

From a pocket of her dress, Thabisa produces a pair of sewing scissors, the points small but sharp. "This is all I have," she says reluctantly. "Otherwise, we will have to procure a knife."

"This should do." Hong takes the scissors and digs them into her palm without hesitation. Blood spurts out of her skin, a red so dark it looks almost black, and the scent of tropical flowers—thick and cloying in the breath of humid air—surrounds us. I marvel at how my hunger, almost uncontrollable in the presence of humans, does not even rear its head for the blood of another vampire, as Hong tips her bleeding palm into the concave heart.

The door groans.

Thabisa takes the scissors from her friend and cuts a small X into her own palm, her full lips pressing tightly together as she feeds the door in her turn. The wood makes another keening sound, like the hull of an ancient ship, as the essence of brine and saltwater fills the air.

"Now you, Lucy," Hong says as Thabisa hands me the scissors.

I dig into my palm and feel the bright sting of pain as my blood spills out. I press it to the carving of the human heart, and there is an odd sensation as my skin meets the door that I am pouring my blood into a ravenous mouth. I now feel a hot, eager, moist warmth where there was unpleasant cold before, and something is *sucking* my blood from within the yew. The deep red-brown stain is pulled straight into the wood, and Hong and Thabisa and I watch as our blood slowly travels through the deep grooves of the door, staining the dreadful scenes of violence.

The door creaks open, moving so quickly I almost fall backward. I exchange glances of triumph and apprehension with the other women, and then we stare into the blackness beyond. I smell wet sand, rotting roses, candle wax, and smoke, all underlined by the musk of freshly turned earth. Vlad's residence has the scent of a tomb by the sea, and the air that wafts out is so reminiscent of him that we all instinctively step backward, as though to flee.

But I stand my ground. "Come, sisters. Let us see what lies beyond," I say, feeling braver with the other women behind me as I cross the threshold. My skin prickles. I expect teeth to sink into my neck, fire to sear my face, a blow to strike me down where I stand. But nothing happens.

We are standing in a suite of rich, luxurious rooms. My eyes take in ancient furniture of heavy wood, including an enormous bed hung with tattered blue-green velvet and an expansive well-worn desk; spindly black candles in crooked sconces; and another library full of books with cracked spines that hail from every nation in which Vlad has ever set his pale and arrogant foot, swaggering about as though it could be possible to discover a place where people already lived.

The others are silent, as surprised as I am by the commonplace nature of his residence.

"So this is Bluebeard's chamber?" I ask, disbelieving. "This warranted the protection of such an evil door?" I step forward and knock something over with a clatter.

It is then that we realize that every inch of floor space is littered with objects. There are books in different languages, some lying open to reveal maliciously shredded pages; chalices, urns, goblets, and vases of every metal, many marked with symbols; scrolls made of cloth and yellowing paper, a few unrolled to show images of saints, cathedrals, or lines of faded script; strings of wooden beads and ropes affixed with totems and pendants; reams of fabric resembling the flags, banners, and altar cloths of holy institutions; drums constructed of animal skins pulled taut over wood frames;

and dozens upon dozens of crosses in every material imaginable, from wild rose branches and twigs lashed together to gold and silver encrusted with precious gems.

Hong finds her voice first. "What is all this?"

"Those look like gifts the village children would give me." Thabisa indicates the amulets of oak, brass, and stone. "Why would he keep such things in here?"

I bend down, reaching for a goblet of dark brass embedded with emeralds.

"Lucy, don't!" Thabisa cries. "It may be cursed! Or poisonous, or—"

But my fingers have already made contact with the goblet. I wait, not breathing, for it to singe my skin or turn my eyes to dust. But nothing happens. I feel only the hefty weight of metal in my hand. "These are holy relics. Objects from many different religions across the world." I stare at a beautiful crystal mirror on the wall that has been smashed beyond repair. Its face is jagged with lines that dance outward from the point of impact as though it had been punched.

Thabisa wraps her long, elegant fingers around an ivory cross studded with diamonds, her dark skin contrasting with its pale surface, while Hong lays a tentative hand upon a branch of wild rose that has been twisted into a cross. "Why would he warn you to stay away from this room?" she asks Thabisa. "It sounded as though death awaited us. And yet we are all unharmed."

I run my fingers over prayer beads, a scroll etched with what might be Arabic script, and the bronze sculpture of a goddess, the entire back of which is charred as though fire were applied at one point. "Religious relics do not hurt us," I say. "But how can he not know that? After all this time? And all of the women he has stolen and infected?"

"Our prince is self-absorbed," Hong says tightly. "You know that. He has all the time in the world, but only uses it to poison new countries, not reflect over what he has done."

"I think he *does* reflect," I say slowly. All around us, I see evidence of burning, breaking, scratching, or smashing of the relics. "But only on matters that affect him directly. He must have gathered these items here, objects that *hurt* him, to try to destroy them."

"He can neither touch nor look long upon objects of faith," Thabisa says thoughtfully. "Any faith or religion. It is a punishment for his deeds, while we, the innocent, are unaffected though we carry his venom."

"What interests me," Hong muses, "is that he is unable to destroy the objects. If only *we* could repel him thus. I would keep him from entering the castle at all, and when dawn broke—" She goes absolutely still. A moment later, she lays down the cross of wild rose branches across the threshold, near the yew door, and steps over it. "Anyone else would be able to do this."

A smile spreads across my face. "But to *him* . . ."

"It would be as good as a gate of fire," Thabisa finishes, her eyes alight.

"He believes he is all-powerful," I say. "He has the strength of a dozen mortal men. He can fly, disappear, and transform at will . . . but always, he must hide. In shadows, in corners, in boxes of earth. My friends have been burning his coffins in England, like smoking a fox from its den, and we shall do the same here. We will block every door, every window, every possible entryway into this godforsaken castle and keep him in the path of the sun."

"And if he survives and escapes to one of his other castles?" Thabisa asks. "What then?"

"Then we follow him," I say grimly. "The three of us, in full daylight. Until it is over."

Hong's lips tremble with emotion. "He took our lives from us. Our homes, our hearts, our freedom. And now we will take his safe places from him until there is not a corner of this earth he can use to hide." Her laugh is the most joyful sound I have heard her utter.

"The end is near, and his last day will be a memorable one. My sisters, let us turn this sanctuary . . . into a trap."

Within days, we render the castle impermeable to Vlad. Not a door, window, or secret passageway is left unmarked by a sacred relic, and we scour the villages for dead rose branches and garlic bundles to use as additional barriers. Thabisa, who has lived here the longest, is an invaluable resource for hidden tunnels and underground passages. She shows us a labyrinth of caves deep beneath the catacombs, some of which hold rickety boats on shadowed waters.

"Why are there so many doors in this place?" I complain on the fifth evening of our task.

"Because he is riddled with paranoia and must be able to flee in any direction," Hong says matter-of-factly. "By the way, have you made contact with your friends?"

"No, not for more than a week now," I say as the familiar worry settles like a stone in my belly. Each night, I have attempted to find Mina, Arthur, or even Jonathan through the mist, and each night, not a single one of them has answered me.

"I was in the village buying flour and one of the women mentioned seeing two foreigners," Hong tells me. "I wondered if it was anyone you know. She gave no description, only that they were men."

My hope surges at the possibility of Arthur here at last. I ache to see him, and my longing drives me to seek solitude soon after supper. I leave Hong reading and Thabisa weaving in the great room and settle onto my bed, letting the mist surround me and trying to clear my head of all else but Arthur and Mina. My worries, however, seem to forestall any attempt to reach them.

After an hour or so, I roll over and stare up at one of Irina's tapestries. Across the top corner is an elaborate cobweb, gossamer strands shining in the candlelight. I watch the spider busily working away at the silken strands and think of Thabisa—so gentle, yet so full of emotion and rage—weaving deadly tokens for Vlad into her cloak of faith. I think of Irina, her lover, and their baby on the mountains in spring, so blissfully happy and unaware of impending disaster. I had pictured Arthur and me in their place, and watching him experience that joy.

Somehow, it is this that sends me into the dream state.

The ancient splendor of my bedroom dissolves into a tiny room so small I can scarcely move for fear of knocking over the furniture. No sooner have I turned, wondering where I am with such homely curtains and a bitterly cold draft from the windows, than Arthur is gathering me to him so tightly it feels that we have fused together. Only when we separate a long moment later do I realize that I am weeping with relief at the sight of him.

He looks exhausted but just as ecstatic to see me. "Lucy," he breathes, and then we are holding each other, our bodies melded tightly with the urgency of long separation. "I tried to find you. But the journey has been so difficult, not even Jack's hypnosis could lighten my sleep."

I press my face to his chest, fighting electric tingles of desire. "Where are we?"

Arthur pulls away, stroking my eyelids, nose, and mouth as though to ensure that all are in order. "The home of a nice grandmother who took pity on two foreigners. Jack and I went through village after village, but no one would give us a bed until we found her. They are wise not to trust strangers here, I think. Considering what lives on this mountain." His face darkens.

"Have you heard from Jonathan and Mina?"

He shakes his head. "I'm sure they're all right. Mr. Harker would never put his wife in harm's way. Which brings me to my point." He sits on the bed, creasing the threadbare blanket, and wraps his arms around me, looking up at my face. "I want you to leave the castle.

Run away as far and as fast as you can. It won't be safe for you with that monster coming back."

I hold his face in my hands. His cheeks are rough with stubble, but the walnut hair at the back of his head is unbearably soft. "Why would I leave just as you and Mina come to me?"

"Listen to me, my love," he pleads.

"My love?" I echo. It is difficult, even with the gravity of our situation, not to be playful with him. I want to laugh, to smile, to dance. "I thought you wanted to be friends."

"I am serious, Lucy." Arthur tightens his hold on me. "You are in danger, and I could not bear it if this creature hurt you again. I would rather you be lost to me, somewhere out there in the world, than taken from me forever. Go and be happy. Experience every joy you can."

"Without you?" I whisper, aching at the look in his eyes.

He leans his forehead against me. "I was angry with you before. I felt betrayed by your refusing a life with me. But I understand now. Strong and brave and adventurous as you are, you would never have been content tied to a stolid goat like me. You are meant to be free, so *be* free. Go and live some far-flung dream of a life." He looks back up at me with wet eyes. "I was never going to make you happy, my love. So I give you up, willingly and with my whole heart."

"You love me so much?" I ask, moved to tears.

"To listen to what you need? To get over my own stubbornness and wounded pride so that I can see you live as you wish? That is only a fraction of what I feel for you." Arthur leans his chin against me, head tilted up to meet my gaze. "Why love someone if you cannot accept all that they are? And I do love you, Lucy Westenra, and I shall miss you forever."

I sink down into his lap and bury my face in his neck, both of us weeping now, clinging desperately to each other. "I left you for something that does not exist," I murmur when I am able to speak again. "A mere fantasy I concocted in my yearning mind. But if I am able to rectify this . . ." I pull away to look at his beloved face, nose to nose. "If I am able to fix what I have done and to protect you all, I . . . I want to go home."

Arthur stares at me, uncertain.

"I want to go home with you," I say, smiling through my tears. "Because I love *you*, Arthur Holmwood. I want to spend the rest of your life with you. I want to be your wife, and to share your home and make you happy. You, my gentle, tenderhearted soul, who would so readily give up his own happiness for mine, are the one I should be with."

He snatches me to him again, sobbing, this time from joy. He does not need to ask me if I mean it. He can hear it in every syllable of my voice, and every hitch of my breath, and every kiss I imprint into his lips as he cradles me in his arms. If I am able to accomplish what I hope to, then immortality and everything I have ever hoped to experience still await me—and a fragment of it, heartbreakingly fleeting, will be spent by Arthur's side.

Suddenly, Arthur pulls away. "What do you mean, if you are able to rectify this?" he asks. "If you are able to fix what you have done? What do you have planned, Lucy? I thought we made it clear . . . we agreed that you would leave the castle—"

"*We* agreed? No, my love, you instructed me to leave, and I have given you no promise to do so." I place a finger over his protesting lips. "This is my mess to put to rights. I will not run away with my tail between my legs when I have a chance to see you and keep you safe."

Suddenly, the room begins to waver. It is as though the heat of the miniature fireplace has risen, pushing waves of air through the mist and blurring Arthur's face.

"Lucy?" he asks, concern stretching out the vowels of my name. "Lucy, you—"

In a heartbeat, though my eyes are closed, I know I am back on my bed in Vlad's castle, but I am not disappointed by the sudden parting. I know Arthur loves me, and I love him, and we will be together—soon, and then for many, many years afterward. I lie still, thinking of him as the smells in my room lull me into peace: the pleasant charring of firewood; the herbs Hong cooked for supper; the sage and mint soap Thabisa uses on her clothes; and the mildew emanating from the ancient bones of the castle. But underneath these scents, which have become so comforting to me, is an odor I cannot quite place. And yet I feel certain I know it as well.

My drowsy mind struggles to remember where I have encountered it before. A childhood memory resurfaces: I am in the kitchen as Papa and our servants open a stack of newly delivered crates. "What on earth are these?" Mamma asks, and Papa proudly holds up a clump of papery white bulbs, pleased that our cook will be able to make his grandmother's dishes, the recipes she carried from her homeland after her English husband swept her across the sea.

Garlic. I smell garlic, perhaps lingering on my hands after placing it around the castle. But the fragrance seems to be growing stronger, accompanied by other scents: plain soap, clean linen, and medicine, bitter and cloying. It is how a hospital might smell.

Or a doctor.

Someone inhales quietly, their muscles tensing.

My eyes fly open, and before I even have time to register the man leaning over my bed with garlic in one hand and a wooden stake—long and brutally sharp—in the other, my body has flown across the room. "Hong! Thabisa!" I scream.

Dr. Van Helsing, undeterred by the speed with which I narrowly escaped his attack, lunges for me again, aiming the stake at my heart with unerring precision.

CHAPTER NINETEEN

Not for nothing do I have the reflexes of a supernatural predator. Once again, I sense air moving, Dr. Van Helsing's brief intake of breath, and the bunching of his muscles well before he even has time to move in my direction again. I fly out the door and into the great room as the doctor crashes into the dressing table, sending glass bottles shattering to the floor. He wears a thick wool coat pulled up to his ears against the cold and is almost unrecognizable under a hat of dark brown fur. His narrow dark eyes, however, are clearly visible and afire with determination.

In the great room, Quincey is struggling to free himself from Hong's powerful grasp as Thabisa ties him to a stone pillar, her knots in the rope mercilessly tight. It is a testament to the strength of the vampire as I watch Quincey—bigger and broader than the two women together—strain against his bonds, the veins in his face and neck bulging with fury. He attempts to land a kick on Thabisa's shins, which she dodges neatly before proceeding to secure his legs as well.

Hong grabs Dr. Van Helsing, taking care to avoid the stake. He rails and shouts, but he is no match for her or Thabisa as they tie him to the same pillar as Quincey. He spits at them, hissing like a cornered wildcat, and Hong calmly slaps him across the face.

"Don't hurt them," I plead. "I know them, and they do not mean us any harm—"

"Do not mean us any harm?" Hong sputters. "Lucy, he almost stabbed you in the heart!"

"At least loosen their bonds a bit. Dr. Van Helsing, we do not want to hurt you." I stand before him but keep my distance—not out of fear that he might get loose, for Thabisa's knots are perfect and brutal, but so as not to frighten him further. I have never seen his steady, appraising eyes so wild with terror as he regards me. He is almost foaming at the mouth.

"To hell with you, demon," he says, his voice thin and strained. "I have holy water—"

"Ah, is that what this is?" Thabisa asks thoughtfully. From Dr. Van Helsing's pocket, she has taken a glass bottle filled with clear liquid. She uncorks it, and just as she holds it up to smell, Quincey manages to free one of his elbows with impressive speed. Thabisa, of course, senses the movement, but in avoiding the blow, splashes a bit of the holy water onto her face. The men stare at her in anticipation as drops slide down her cheek.

"Well?" Hong asks with a touch of dark humor. "How do you feel?"

Thabisa tilts her head, considering the bottle. "Refreshed."

Quincey's elbow is still free. He manages to put two fingers into the breast pocket of his coat, flicking white granules in Hong and Thabisa's direction. Some of the crystals stick to the drops of holy water on Thabisa's face, and his mouth falls open in disbelief when Hong dabs a fingertip along her friend's cheek and tastes the granules.

"Salt?" she asks disdainfully. "What do you hope it will do to us, precisely?"

Thabisa hurries forward to tighten the ropes that bind Quincey's arms. "Lucy, I am sorry to do this to your . . . friend," she says as the man thrashes violently. "But if we let him be, I'm afraid he or his companion really will stake one of us through the heart."

I nod at her to continue. "Dr. Van Helsing, please," I say, facing him. "This is for your own safety. I genuinely do not wish to hurt or restrain you—"

"Safety?" His hat has fallen off, revealing jet-black hair that stands on end, and his face is bright red from exertion. "Each and every one of you is a monster! You care nothing for my safety! You want only to drink my blood and contaminate me the way you yourselves have been. It is the virus inside you. It wishes to propagate, it—"

"My good man, have no fear," Hong says, bored. "Your blood is not to my taste. I can smell the self-righteousness in it, and believe me, I want no part of that." The doctor scowls at her, and then his expression changes into astonishment at the sight of her jet-black hair and olive skin. Clearly, he has not studied her or Thabisa with any attention. We *are* simply monsters to him, creatures to be destroyed, and not people with our own histories, our own features.

"Holy water and salt do not affect us, Doctor, and neither will your crosses," I tell him as frustration creeps into my voice. "Please conserve your energy. You will need it, but not to fight any of us." I look him in the eyes. "Nothing I say will convince you that I am still the Lucy you knew. I cannot persuade you to believe that I have her heart and her mind and her soul, even after everything that has happened. All three of the women you see before you have been seduced and tricked and infected by the *true* monster. But you will persist in blaming us, both of you," I add, looking at Quincey, "and I must tell you that my considerable respect for you both has eroded."

The doctor glares at me through sweat-dampened locks of hair. "Of course we blame you. You would have harmed that little girl in the churchyard had we not happened upon you. That, I know for a fact. The old Lucy would never have done that. You cannot fool me or Quincey, however much you have managed to hoodwink the Harkers and Arthur and even Jack Seward."

"Did you see me bite that little girl?" I ask angrily. "Did you see me hurt a single hair—"

"It was the intention!" he roars.

"And you can read my mind, can you?" I shout back. "That is why you have pursued me on land and sea? Shot at me? Tried to stab me through the heart? Because of *intention*?"

Thabisa touches my shoulder. "Lucy, someone else is here," she says quietly.

At that very moment, the smell of lavender and lily soap reaches my nose, followed by a whiff of shaving cream and male sweat. Boots run down the corridor toward our wing, and I hear Jonathan Harker call, "This way! The footprints in the dust lead here—" And then I am staring at Mina and her husband, who skid to a stop in the doorway of the great room.

Mina rushes into my arms, and our embrace is like feeling sunlight on my face after only ever knowing the heat of a candle. She is wearing so many layers to protect against the cold that I can barely feel her warmth, but it is enough for me: the sweet floral smell of her hair beneath her hat, the feel of her cheek against mine, and her arms around me.

"Thank God," she gasps. "Lucy, Lucy. Oh, thank God."

Jonathan is right behind her, and when I reach out a hand, he takes it and squeezes it. "We were camping a short distance away," he says, panting slightly. "I set up a tent and a fire and told Mina to sleep, thinking I would enter the castle alone and meet whatever I found there."

"He does not know my sheer stubbornness like you do," Mina says, pulling away to look at the others: Quincey, still struggling against the ropes; Dr. Van Helsing, red-faced and breathing hard; and the other women, standing off to one side as though to give us privacy.

"These are my new sisters, Hong and Thabisa, and they want to destroy Vlad every bit as much as I do," I say. "But there will be time for all of this later. How did you get into the castle? And find this wing? We took care to barricade every door."

Mina and Jonathan exchange glances. "We saw footprints in the snow," her husband says. "Two men wearing boots, leading directly up the peaks. The entrance must have been locked, for the prints went around the side of the castle, back down a slope where there was a cave."

"There was a raft, almost completely rotted through. We managed to paddle it down a narrow waterway and made it by the skin of our teeth." Mina's teeth chatter slightly, and only then do I notice that her skirts and the bottom of her coat are soaked through. "We saw a rickety boat pulled to shore before an unlocked entryway covered in garlic and wooden crosses."

"Unlocked," I hear Thabisa whisper to Hong. "We did not think of preventing humans."

Mina looks appealingly at Quincey and the doctor. "Please, as I have written to you, you *must* know Lucy is not trying to harm you—"

The doctor frowns. "And as I have written to *you*, Madam Mina, she has tricked you—"

"She bit dozens of people in Paris!" Quincey cries. "Van Helsing and I both witnessed it. Men were fainting, carried out with wounds on their throats. We cannot trust her, Mrs. Harker."

"Here is something the two of you did *not* witness, Mr. Morris, for neither of you were in England, helping us as we asked," Mina says coldly. "The count controlled me. He reached into my mind and made me leave my room to wait for him in Jack's garden. Another night, I was in my bed, helpless with longing for him, as my husband and Lucy watched. I—" She closes her eyes, her cheeks burning with shame. "Do you think I am careless or stupid? Do you consider me a woman who would violate the sacred laws of my marriage to the husband I adore?"

Dr. Van Helsing sighs. "No, Madam Mina, but—"

"You believe me when I tell you the monster possessed me, body and soul?" Mina asks, her voice strident, and the men nod reluctantly. "Then why can you not believe that he did it to Lucy? Or to these two women, whom I do not know yet am willing to believe are as blameless as I am? No. Oh, no, gentlemen." She gives a derisive laugh. "You are not to be the self-appointed jury on which lady to blame. We have a common enemy, and it is *not* any of these women. If you cannot force that through your stubborn skulls, then we are all in more danger than you think."

"Your friend," Hong tells me in an undertone that everyone can hear, "is magnificent."

"I know it well." I turn urgently to the Harkers. "Listen to me. You must remain here in this room, where it is safer. Hong and Thabisa and I have blocked every window and passageway against him, except for the exterior door leading into the chapel. Stay and—"

The Harkers both speak at once.

"And enjoy the fireplace while you risk your lives? I'd like to see myself," Mina snaps.

"Absolutely not," Jonathan says vehemently. "We came to help you."

"Well, then," I say, wanting to weep with gratitude, "Arthur and Jack are in the village and will be here presently. As for *him*, we have had no sign. We do not know where he is."

"Perhaps he has drowned," Hong says brightly. "The ocean may have swallowed him whole and saved us all from the trouble of waiting for him."

"I doubt even the sea can rid us of him," Thabisa says. "He would find a way to claw up from the depths. No, I should like to see the life leave his eyes for my own comfort."

It is as though the mention of Vlad reconnects us to him. My chest begins to burn like I have swallowed a coal straight out of the fire. I press my hand over my breast, dizzy and weak, as the scalding heat spreads outward from my heart. It feels like uncontrollable rage. Thabisa cries out, and Hong bends over, panting, as Mina gasps, "What is this? What's happening to us?"

"He is here," Thabisa says, her voice a fragile thread. "He has come home."

A steady pounding begins to shake the foundations of the castle. It thrums in my head like a relentless drumbeat, and Hong and Thabisa and I instinctively cluster together with Mina, staring at the trembling ancient bones of the fortress. It is as though a pair of gigantic fists are beating the windows, doors, and every entrance that has now been rendered useless to Vlad.

The men cry out in fear and confusion until the pounding eases, and now we hear a gust of wind propelled by fluttering dark wings. I close my eyes, sick with dread, knowing that Vlad is now a bat flying to the highest towers of the castle. The heat in my chest intensifies as he sails and dips, searching in vain for a way to enter before plummeting to the ground. A moment later, we hear the howl of a great grey wolf. Its cry scratches the inside of my mind like fingernails on wood as the animal scurries through the snow, moving from one secret passage to another.

And then there is silence.

"He has given up," Thabisa says quietly. "He is waiting in the chapel."

The end is here. The confrontation has arrived, and it will take every bit of strength we have. Hong and Thabisa each take one of my hands. I look at these women who have become my friends, who know better than anyone what it is to live this curse. I am afraid, but I am not alone.

"Mr. Harker," the doctor addresses Jonathan. "Cut Mr. Morris and me loose. You need every man available, and we cannot be tied here like lambs for the slaughter. Let us go."

Mina holds up a hand to stop her husband. "Only if you promise not to hurt Lucy or her friends. That stake and any other weapons you carry are meant for the count alone."

Dr. Van Helsing's eyes meet mine. He still thinks that I am Vlad's creature, and that I led them all here to die. But there is doubt in his gaze, too. "Very well, you have my word," he says at last, and Jonathan and Mina hurry forward to free him and Quincey of their restraints.

"Come, sisters," Hong says, her dark eyes flashing. "Let us meet our destiny."

CHAPTER TWENTY

The chapel is pitch-dark when Hong, Thabisa, and I enter, passing under branches of wild rose and garlands of garlic. Outside the windows, restless clouds smother the moon, and I can see only the vague outlines of the tombs. Vlad, however, stands out as clearly as though lit by unholy light, tall and broad and built for war. His long white hands are folded, and his dark cloak flutters in the breeze. He does not speak but looks at each of us without expression. When his eyes land on me, I stare calmly back at him with my chin lifted high.

"This is a most unusual welcome," he says at last. His voice soothes my agitation at once. Suddenly, I want nothing more than to press against his broad chest and feel his arms around me, protecting me as only he ever can. It is only the bottle of holy water clutched in my hand—given to me by Thabisa before we entered—that keeps my mind clear, and I tighten my grip on it.

Thabisa is shaking from head to toe with the effort of resisting his power, and Hong actually takes an involuntary step toward him. "No," she says through clenched teeth.

"My sweet Hong. Let me hold you as I did the night you ran away. Do you remember? We stood in the shadow of the trees and listened to your aunts wail and mourn your loss, but you refused to return to them. You chose the shelter of my embrace over them." Vlad's blue-green eyes on her are kind and soft. "Come, my love, and stand with me as you did then."

Hong's body moves jerkily toward him. And then her slipper catches on a loose stone, sending her sprawling against a tomb. She braces herself, and her eyes find the tiny unmarked coffin of Irina's son. Though she quivers like a leaf, she manages to walk away from Vlad and return to where Thabisa and I are standing, and I squeeze her cold, clammy hand.

"Very well. I see you have forgotten your gratitude. I saved you from a cruel, miserable marriage, and this is how you treat me? I know Thabisa will not be so unfeeling." Vlad directs his attention to the tall girl. "After all, I saved her, too. I could have let her die with her people, but instead, I took her for my own. I gave her a life of comfort and security, far from danger and disease. *She* will certainly come to me." His smile is irresistible, both warm and affectionate.

Thabisa does not move. Sweat streaks her temples as she stares him down with the face of a queen. "I would not come to you," she says, her voice taut with restraint, "if you held my salvation in your hands and I was drowning in the sea. I would rather meet my end at the bottom of the ocean before ever calling you my *savior*." She speaks the word with such anger that Vlad reacts at last. The color of his eyes abruptly shifts, darkening like a ravenous undertow.

"After everything I have done for you, you still blame me. I am disappointed." Vlad looks at me, and it feels like sitting in moonlight, dreamy and sensuous and captivating. I feel my body move toward him like a wanderer in a dream, stretching out her yearning hand.

"Lucy," he breathes, and my name on his lips is a symphony. "You are my youngest bride and have surely not allowed *your* memories to fade. The cliffs in the wind, the stars above the sea, the tree whispering above us as I held you. We spoke of so many subjects . . . of seeing the world before our feet, of ships and foreign lands and cities drenched in light. Come to me, Lucy, and I will take you to places beyond your darkest dreams."

I go to him readily, ignoring Hong's muffled gasp. "You told me you would show me the world and spend eternity teaching me all that you know." I stand before him, gazing up at his brutally beautiful face. "Will you? Can you be that man I cared for again?"

Vlad's gaze roams over my face like a feather-light kiss. "The people you call *friends* have burned every last box of earth I brought to England, ensuring I would have no safe place to rest. They are pursuing me as we speak." His hand hovers over my cheek, and I ache to lean into his touch, sinking into it along with the warm velvet of his voice. "Prove you are mine. Forsake those people and stand beside me in my fight, and I will keep every vow I have made to you."

"Why did you come back, knowing they pursued you?" I ask, staring up at his chiseled white features. "Why not escape to one of your other sanctuaries and leave us to our fate?"

He strokes my face as though I am very precious to him, beyond value, and though half of me leans gladly into his touch, the other half wants to recoil. "The other two, I leave to their fate," he says dismissively. "I came back for you and you alone. After all, you are my kindred soul, Lucy. We share a bond I have only experienced once in all my long years."

With Irina? I think. *The woman whose one glimmer of happiness you destroyed?*

Vlad lays his other hand on my face as well. "Be my bride, my *only* bride, once the hunters are through with *them*. Be the wife I envisioned since first you found me in dreams."

I place one hand over his. "Yes," I say as my other hand clenches on the uncorked bottle of holy water. "I will be everything you want me to be."

He and I stare at each other, the distorted image of a couple locked in a loving caress.

And then we both move.

I lift my hand to fling the water at him at the same moment that he wrenches my head to the side so cruelly, I believe at first that he has torn it from my shoulders. I fall, and he kicks me in the side. I wheeze in pain, and the bottle rolls away as Vlad kicks me again and again.

"Lucy!" Hong screams.

And then Thabisa—gentle Thabisa—is by my side, clawing at his eyes with her face like a mask of fury. Hong runs after her, tearing his brutal hands away from her friend. He snarls as they fall against his tomb, sending the heavy stone lid to the ground with a tremendous crash.

Painfully, I crawl toward the exterior door through which Vlad had entered. My hands shake uncontrollably, but I manage to grab the bottle and spill what is left of the holy water across the threshold. It spreads over the dusty stones, leaving an impenetrable gleam in the doorway. I hear Thabisa shriek and turn in time to see Vlad throw her against one of the tombs. Her bones crack against the marble, and she lies motionless as Hong hurries over to her, pale with terror. Vlad looks at me and the stream of water that now prevents him from leaving the chapel.

"What did you do?" he asks, low and dangerous.

I struggle to sit up. "I trapped you," I say, my jaw clenched. "The door leading outside is blocked by holy water. The door leading back inside the castle is covered with garlic and wild roses. And as for the windows, they are limned with holy relics from your secret room. What shall you do now, our bold savior and defender? What will you do when the sun rises?"

Vlad is going to kill me. I know it as surely as I know my own name as he strides toward me, particles of air shifting as he prepares to deal the killing blow . . .

A man is bellowing outside the chapel. "Mina! Mina, where are you?"

I hear shouts and the screams of horses as fire blazes up beyond the windows. Torchlight flickers, sending the shadows of people fighting over the silent tombs.

"Harker! To your left!" another man cries, and I recognize the voice at once. The pull of it is enough to send me flying out of the chapel, even in my pain.

"Arthur!" I call. Hong follows me into the frigid night air, supporting a limping Thabisa, as Vlad roars for us to come back, pacing inside the chapel that is now his prison.

The dark castle grounds are a maelstrom of confusion and violence. The snow is stained with ruby splatters of blood and the imprints of boots and horse hooves, and the torchlight moves in dizzy patterns as men punch and kick and wield weapons, everything from axes to clubs.

Jagged light cuts across Arthur's face as he fends off a dozen attackers with an enormous wooden cross. One enemy, a bald, heavyset man with pale skin and an unsettling grimace, jabs at Arthur's ribs with a dagger, missing by spare inches. But then he goes flying as a broad body charges straight into him, sending the blade into a snowdrift. Arthur's rescuer rolls back onto his feet gracefully, and in the light, I recognize the handsome, dark-skinned face of Quincey Morris.

"Watch yourself, Arthur!" he yells.

Arthur gives him a nod of thanks before swinging the cross into another attacker. Jack Seward, who has been keeping his own foes at bay, rushes over to help.

Near the castle wall, I see Jonathan running toward Mina and Dr. Van Helsing, who have just emerged from a side entrance. The Harkers embrace, and though Mina's face is pressed into her husband's chest, I see one of her eyes wide with terror at the horrific scene. "No! Don't leave me," she pleads, but Jonathan kisses her and heads in Jack and Arthur's direction. As he sprints, I see him pull out a massive, lethal-looking silver blade from its sheath and aim it at the attackers.

"Come, we must help them," Thabisa says.

"You are hurt!" Hong protests.

But the girl breaks away from her and flies into the air, floating in the mist like an avenging angel. She sweeps her hands, and the mist cracks like a rope, whipping a torch out of one man's hand and sending it cracking against the skulls of two adjacent attackers.

Dr. Van Helsing joins the fray as more enemies swarm across the snow like a cloud of red-mouthed locusts. One of them passes me with a torch held high, and I see unfocused eyes, loose features, and a mouth twisted in a scarlet snarl, with two long, protruding fangs of pale bone. These men are vampires, I realize, or close to becoming so. Vlad must have turned them on his journey across the sea and up the peaks, for they all wear the garb of sailors or peasants.

Bullets ring out to my right. Quincey Morris opens fire on the monsters circling him. His aim lands true, but he is outnumbered and empties his pistols within seconds. His cheeks gleam with sweat as he scrabbles desperately in his pockets, fending off the attackers whose teeth glint white as snow. Even in their half-vampiric state, they are much stronger and faster than he is. He will have no chance at all to reload his guns before one of them bites him.

I do not stop to think.

With a ferocious movement of my hands, I gather up a boiling cloud of mist and launch myself into the air above them. I send a gust with full force to push them back, catapulting them beneath the hooves of frantic horses or over the steep cliff that spills into the river. I do not know if it is enough to kill them, but at least I will buy Quincey a bit of time.

I land, placing myself between him and three enormous sailors charging at him with axes held aloft. They may have more strength and speed than a human man, but they are no match for me. I hear their hearts beating and the rhythm of their breath changing, and it is all I need to predict their movements. I seize one of their sharp axes and swing, decapitating all three in one merciless blow. I watch their mutilated bodies tumble to a stop, blood steaming in the snow.

Both Dr. Van Helsing and Quincey stare, slack-jawed, at me. In the time I bought him, Quincey has reloaded his pistols . . . and they are now pointed at my heart. I have grown used to seeing him look at me with fear and hatred, but it still hurts after a friendship so true.

And then he says gruffly, “This doesn’t change anything.”

I shake my head. “Of course not. Other than the fact that you are still alive.”

He utters a frustrated growl before turning away to shoot at the foes closing in on Jack.

I search for Mina and am relieved to see her safe in the shadow of the castle wall.

“Lucy!”

I whirl toward the voice. Jonathan Harker perches on a burning wagon, lit like a bonfire from fallen torches. He cannot jump to safety, for there is a wall of vampires waiting for him. They bite and snap, their unsettling red mouths stretched wide. They do not seem afraid of the cruel silver blade he wields and dodge the blows from his tiring arms without difficulty.

With the axe still in my hands, I get to work. Soon, the vampires are nothing more than a pile of wet, writhing entrails smoking in the snow. Jonathan leaps off the wagon, and we stand back-to-back as a fresh wave of monsters descends upon us from all directions. With his grit and determination and my supernatural agility, we make quick work of them.

"Why are there so many?" Jonathan asks, panting.

"He was building himself an army," I say, glancing at the chapel. I catch sight of Arthur lying in the snow, weighed down by a pair of vampires whose mouths dribble red saliva on him. He barely manages to wrench his hand away when one of them tries to bite his fingers.

Dropping the axe, I grab the men by their napes. They thrash wildly as I soar higher and higher and fly them toward the tower, hurling them at the stones with deadly speed. I watch the contents of their skulls stain the ancient parapets before floating down to rejoin Arthur.

He is on his feet now, coat gone and shirt torn. The smile I crave is nowhere to be seen, but in his eyes is the light I remember the night he asked me to marry him. We are like puzzle pieces snapping into place as our arms enfold each other, natural as breathing. I press my ear to his heartbeat as he murmurs into my hair, "Lucy, Lucy, Lucy."

A scream of rage shakes the glass and stones of the chapel. Vlad is still trapped inside behind the barriers of garlic, holy water, and sacred relics. His anger burns like poison inside my mind as I stumble away from Arthur. I let my eyes tell him everything I do not have time to say before I run toward the chapel, joined by Thabisa and Hong. Both women are covered in the blood of a pack of sailors who were trying to bite Jack Seward, and they carry heavy clubs and axes confiscated from the vampires.

"Well?" Hong asks. "Shall we execute the next stage of our plan?"

Thabisa looks up at the sky. "If only we could hurry the sunrise," she says anxiously. "The horizon is brightening, bit by bit, yet there is no light over the mountains."

"God help us if he somehow escapes," I say. "Let us prepare."

We run as a pack through the fighting men, cutting down enemies as we go. The herd of vampires is finally thinning as my friends, led by Jonathan and Quincey, tackle them with methodical brutality. I see Jack and Dr. Van Helsing apply torches to the dismembered bodies, ensuring they do not return. Hong, Thabisa, and I hurry to the grove of dead trees where we stored our secret weapon earlier that day. It is very near the burning wagon on which Jonathan had stood not long ago. I notice a large pile of nails in the ashes, which must have come from Vlad's final box of earth, now disintegrated in the flames. Hope stirs in me at the sight of them.

"There will be justice," I say as we race back to the chapel and not a second too soon.

A tremendous shattering pierces our ears as every window explodes into shimmering shards of stained glass. A monstrous bat with hairy, muscular wings sails into the night. Had it been a true bat, it would have escaped unscathed. But Vlad in this form is so large and heavy that he cannot help brushing against the sacred cloths and amulets lining the window. He shrieks in unbearable agony as smoke rises from the parts of his body that touched the relics, and then he turns back into a man. Burning red weals steam on his moon-white skin, and his eyes—hellish pools of blood-rimmed onyx—are full of boundless hatred, strong enough to send him out of the chapel and into the path of the rising sun to . . . what? Escape somewhere until night falls once more? Destroy Hong, Thabisa, and me? Enact vengeance upon the hunters?

His eyes find mine through the commotion. Slowly, his hand lifts. Something floats in the air behind him: an enormous piece of stained glass, oblong and pointed, the tip razor-sharp. The other brides and I tense, ready to protect ourselves and whichever of the men Vlad might impale.

But he does not aim the shard of glass at any of us. Instead, he sends it with inexorable speed toward the shadows of the castle wall.

It barrels directly at Mina's heart.

CHAPTER TWENTY-ONE

"No!" several voices scream as one.

Hong and Thabisa's hands lift with my own, pushing the mist between shard and victim, but it is too late. There is a sound like a pillow being punched as the glass sinks deep into flesh.

Quincey falls to his knees in the snow. The shard juts out from the right side of his chest, spurting blood down his coat. Breathing hard, he moves his big hands to the glass buried inside him, while an unhurt Mina cries out and hurries to help him. The brides and I had slowed the shard enough for him to leap in front of Mina, taking the attack that had been meant for her.

Vlad watches them, eyes blazing. The sight of such pain and suffering enraptures him enough that in the spare few seconds of his distraction, the other women and I move as one. We raise the weapon Thabisa has spent endless days and nights weaving for Vlad's return: a heavy cloak of altar cloths, stitched cleverly with bells, totems, amulets, crosses, and bulbs of garlic into every square inch. We bring it down upon him, pulling the ends taut around his body.

The mountains quake with his roar of excruciating torment, and through the gaps in the cloak, I see smoke swirl upward wherever the material touches his skin. He falls forward, almost weeping with agony, as we gather the relics and wild rose branches that flew into the snow when the windows shattered. We lay them in a tight ring, trapping him where he lies writhing in pain.

"Come, let us help them!" Arthur shouts.

While Mina and Dr. Van Helsing care for Quincey, the others help us surround Vlad with objects of faith. The cloak has rendered him immobile, and I see his strength depleting with each passing minute. Thabisa hands Jonathan a large crucifix to add to the barrier, while Jack, Arthur, and Hong rescue wild rose branches from the fires that rage around us.

All the while, the sky is growing lighter, softening from navy to rose as a glow touches the mountains. Even Vlad looks upward, his mouth stretched in a grimace of terror and fury.

Jonathan's eyes meet mine. Even panting and covered in blood, Mina's husband is the image of a hero as he walks toward me with his head held high. He holds up his wicked silver blade, curved and flashing in the light, and offers me the handle.

"My father was an explorer, Lucy," he says. "He traveled the world in his youth and brought this kukri knife back from Southeast Asia. I never questioned his right to possess it, nor my own. That is a failing with which I must come to terms." He looks at each of the other brides and then back at me. "This knife was stolen, just as you yourselves were. Please take it."

I hold the handle for a moment, feeling its sturdy heft, before giving it to Thabisa. "You are the oldest among us, my sister," I say, bowing my head. "Yours is the right to begin."

Thabisa's beautiful face looks even more otherworldly as she accepts the blade with both hands. She looks at Vlad, who appears gaunt and wasted as though the cloak has leeched the very essence out of him. "I was young, lost, and in search of refuge when you found me," she says. "The shores of my home were burning thanks to foreigners who had claimed the land as their own, spread their disease, and raped and murdered my people. I stowed away on your ship, hoping to find what family had been taken to the white man's lands. And instead, I found *you*."

"My love." Somehow, Vlad's voice is still as magnetic and musical as ever, and even now I feel my heart stir with desire. "I only wished to save you. To give you a life you deserved."

"You did neither," Thabisa says. "You did to me what those foreigners did to my land, and now you must answer for it." From the pocket of her gown, she takes a vial of clear liquid. More holy water, and from the nod she gives Dr. Van Helsing, I know how she acquired it. She pours half onto the blade. And then, with a sound that is half snarl and half sob, she plunges the kukri knife into Vlad's back, aiming for his cold dead heart. I hear metal hit bone as he jerks forward. She pulls the knife back out, cleans it in the snow, and offers the handle to Hong.

Hong takes it with hands that do not tremble.

Vlad, lying on his side in a pool of blood, gazes at her with pleading tenderness. He looks as though he loves her, and it is frighteningly convincing. "You are the bride of my dreams," he says. "The queen I chose. Remember how it was between us."

She stares at the man she once loved, tears staining her exquisite face. And for a moment—even knowing the depth of her hatred for him—I fear that she will give in to the love she had once felt for him, drop the knife, and allow him to live for countless centuries more, all for the tenuous thread of hope that one day he will care for her as much as she does for him.

But then she speaks. "I do remember how it was between us," she says, calm and steady. "Followed by decades, *centuries* of derision and neglect. Tell me, what will ever change? Aside from the fact that *you* are the one cowering before me and I can, at last, reclaim my own fate?"

She does not give him a chance to reply. She pours the remaining holy water over the blade, and then, with a great cry of sorrow and relief, she stabs him in the center of his chest. She kneels before a writhing Vlad, weeping, as Thabisa holds her and murmurs words into her hair.

Gently, I bend to pick up the kukri knife.

I do not look Vlad in the eyes, for he does not deserve it. Instead, I turn my face to the sky, to the east, to a new beginning. The dawn is shining, turning the snow-covered mountains into a bright mirror of spun gold, and all around us, the mist sparkles like the endless sea.

"Look around, Vlad," I say. "It is the first day you will never see."

"You would never be so cruel, Lucy," he says, his voice strained at last. "I made you your true self. I showed you a way out. I opened a door for you and prized you above all my brides—"

I laugh. "I agreed with everything you said up until that lie." He is dissolving, fading like a pile of bones disintegrating to ash. I crouch down beside him. "It is true. I am now my most genuine self. I have found fulfillment and friendship in people who understand the very depths of my soul. But you are not to be credited for that. It is *I* who have triumphed."

The sun begins to rise, casting the first of its rays upon his face.

"You say that you saved us. But, Vlad, the truth is that we never needed you. You only see women as a means to an end. Well, now we look at you in the same way. You are but a tool to be used and discarded. For pleasure, for entertainment, for immortality . . . which I assure you we will not waste as you have. You squandered your gift, and now your time has run out."

"You hate me that much?" he whispers. "To sacrifice your own selves in the light of the sun and burn to ash whilst witnessing my demise?"

I rise, standing between him and the sun, and he almost sobs with relief in my shadow. "Oh, you need not worry," I say lightly. "As self-obsessed as you are, you never noticed that your curse treats us with more leniency than it does you. We can still see our reflections, enjoy food, and learn to survive without harm. Perhaps best of all, we can also walk in the sun." I bend to run a finger down his face, his skin smoking and scalding in the light. "It is a gift to inhabit two worlds as we are able to. And it is something at which you have never been adept."

"Take me inside," Vlad gasps. "Bring me into the chapel, Lucy, and I will cherish you above all. I will repay you a thousandfold for eternity."

I cock my head. "No. I think not." And then I step away, removing my shadow from him.

Dawn blooms in a brilliant wash of peach and rose gold, cleansing the land with its light. All around us, the dead vampires wither into dust, crumbling like sand. The wind blows away their remains and the snow shifts, covering the carnage and bloodshed in sparkling white.

And when the sun bursts out in its full strength, I use the kukri knife to cut the cloak off Vlad, exposing every inch of him to its merciless light. He has no voice left to scream. His skin sears off his bones like curls of paper in a bonfire, melting all along his wasted body.

I wait, allowing him to suffer as much as possible. Soon, he, too, will dissolve like dust in the wind. But before that happens, I bring the wicked blade down with all my strength upon his neck, severing his head from his body. Hong and Thabisa watch without blinking as his head—obsidian eyes still gleaming and fanged mouth still gaping—rolls to their feet before crumbling.

And then there is nothing left of either the man for whom I had once cared or the monster who had tormented me.

I lift my face to the sun. "We are free," I say. "It is over."

* * *

In the great room, the fire roars in the hearth as Hong spoons soup into bowls, which Jack and Arthur help distribute. Mina and Jonathan sit together on a sofa, wrapped in one blanket, while Thabisa uncorks a bottle of wine and divides it among the group.

Earlier, the men carried Quincey to the softest chaise before the fire, where he rests in a nest of blankets as Dr. Van Helsing puts a roll of bandages and liniment back into his medicine bag. They look up as I approach, still tense in my presence despite the relief I know is on my face upon seeing Quincey's large chest moving up and down with his steady breaths.

"Is he all right, Doctor?" I ask. "Did he lose much blood?"

Dr. Van Helsing's gaze on me is shrewd. "Quite a bit, but I am not concerned. The shard was not deep, thanks to Mr. Morris's fortunate habit of carrying objects inside the breast pockets of his coat. They prevented the shard from doing maximum damage. His injury is fairly superficial, and he will heal well now that it has been cleaned and bandaged."

"You saved Mina's life," Jonathan tells Quincey fervently. "It is a debt I can never repay."

"Thank you," Mina adds, her eyes wet. "I only sit here because of you, my friend."

The old Quincey, modest and cheerful, might have joked to deflect their gratitude. But *this* Quincey keeps his gaze on me. "I would not have had time had Lucy and her friends not helped," he says gruffly. "Never let it be said of me that I don't give credit where credit is due. I saw them push the fog in front of Mrs. Harker to protect her."

"What was in your pocket?" I ask him. "What kept the shard from impaling you?"

Quincey holds his hand out to me. I recognize the two items at once: a round grey stone, veined with red and gold, and a triangular piece of dark flint, both cracked from impact. Not long ago, when he still believed my soul was worth saving, he had shown me three talismans of protection that he carried with him always. The stone comes from his ranch, symbolizing the family he loves and the hardship they endured when brought by force to America, and the Indian arrowhead reminds him to respect the stolen land upon which he has built his life.

He gasps when I take his third talisman, a charred lump of silver metal, out of my pocket. "I believe this bullet is yours," I say, placing it in his palm.

"You kept it all this time?" he asks in disbelief.

"Of course I did. This is the bullet you dug from your leg after a run-in with bandits. You gave it to me as a reminder that life can end in the blink of an eye. The stone means faith and the arrowhead means respect, but *this* is a symbol of strength. You told me that. And it helped me find mine in the end." I smile into his wet eyes. "I have never forgotten your kindness, Quincey. And I will always think of you as my friend, no matter how your opinion of me has changed."

To my surprise, Quincey returns my smile. I had not thought to see it again, not for me.

"Besides, I promised to return it to you at my wedding." I glance at Arthur, who sits a bit apart from the others. It feels so natural to go to him, pulled into his arms like water running down a slope. I notice the others engrossing themselves in conversation to give us privacy.

"Your face has not changed at all," Arthur says, studying me in his customary almost shy way. "As beautiful as ever, though your skin is cold. Your smile is exactly how I remember it, and that look in your eyes . . . like you are holding a torch and lighting your own way while everyone else is content to wait for the sunrise. That, too, is the same."

"You have changed."

"Have I?"

"Yes," I say, unable to resist teasing him. "You came readily to my bedchamber to wash up just now, even though we were alone and unchaperoned."

Arthur laughs. "I am glad, too, that you still have a light heart."

I lean forward to kiss his dimple, but he turns so that our lips meet instead. This gentle kiss speaks volumes above any of the passionate ones we have shared. It is an exchange between a man and a woman who have been separated by death itself, only to come together again. When we pull apart, I tuck my head into his shoulder, feeling the deepest, most profound peace.

"If anything about you has altered," Arthur says, "it is your spirit. I see it in the way you move and hear it in your voice. There is an ease to you now. A contentment that was not there before." He presses his lips to the top of my head. "When my pride healed and I stopped being angry with you, I was disappointed in myself. I wished I had tried harder to understand you and what you needed before it was too late and I had lost you. I was full of grief . . . and then joy, seeing how peaceful and free you have become." I look at him, at the ever-changing hues of green and brown in his eyes. His smile is a thing of heartbreaking beauty as he tucks a strand of hair behind my ear. "What will you do first, my lionhearted Lucy, with the limitless years before you? Will you wander the world and sail ships to uncharted lands?"

"Someday. But first, I will go home with you." I look down at his big, comforting hand in mine. "I will pay my respects properly to Mamma, and speak to her lawyers and handle her affairs. I will be near Mina and Jonathan and see their family grow. And most of all, Arthur Holmwood, I will marry you and be with you as long as you live. I have limitless years ahead, as you said, to do everything I have ever dreamed of and to be selfish—"

"You are not selfish," Arthur interrupts. "Loving yourself enough to choose a life on your own terms is something we all ought to do."

"Listen to you, Lord Godalming!" I exclaim, my heart filling for this good, kind, loving man beside me. "A proper, well-respected viscount and a pillar of society such as yourself, touting revolutionary ideas of female choice and independence!"

"A new century is coming," he says seriously. "The times are changing, and I must change with them. After all, when I refused to do so, I lost you."

I take his face between my hands. "You have never lost me, and you never will. I have an eternity ahead of me now. I have the opportunity to live many different lives. I want to share this one with *you*, my Arthur, whom I love so very dearly. Will you accept my proposal of marriage?"

He laughs, pulling me close. "I shall. Everyone will approve, even Dr. Van Helsing," he adds in a whisper. "Have you noticed he has not looked over at us *once* to ensure you are not biting me?" We both laugh at poor, well-meaning Dr. Van Helsing's expense. The physician seems to sense our attention, for he clears his throat, beckons us both over, and moves to stand solemnly before the group, as though preparing to lecture a classroom full of medical students.

"My friends, I have something I would like to say." To my surprise, the doctor's narrow dark eyes find me. "Lucy Westenra, I owe you an apology. I believed you to be a monster like the creature who had turned you. I assumed the worst of you and discouraged Lord Godalming and the Harkers from communicating with you, though of course, they ignored me." Jonathan winks at me, and Mina laughs, both of them looking happier than ever. "Along with Mr. Morris, I did everything I could to destroy you. I am a physician, tasked with protecting the lives of the living, but I should have done more to understand your condition. I pride myself on my open mind, and yet I clung so stubbornly to my prejudice that I could not see the danger you were in. I should have helped you, Lucy, and I am sorry that I did not."

I hold up my hand. “No, Doctor, you could not have helped me. Only I could do that. I hardly knew the rules of what I had become, so how could you? What I *did* know was I did not wish to be like *him*. Hong and Thabisa showed me that there is a better way to live forever,” I add, looking at the women. “To do good, to hope, and to love, as we did when we were human.”

Dr. Van Helsing shakes his head in wonder. “I was astonished to see all you fighting alongside us and protecting us. I knew then that I was wrong, and that the curse has not affected your heart or your character. Your love for your friends shone through.”

“I forgive you completely,” I say, looking at him and Quincey. “And I do not think it will be difficult to lead a life of which my parents would be proud. As I told Arthur just now, I intend to return to England, marry him, and spend the rest of your lives with all of you.”

Mina chokes out a sob. “Oh, Lucy!”

“And I would like Hong and Thabisa to join us, if they wish. I know a good lawyer who could help them.” I raise my eyebrows at Jonathan, who grins. “But I would not blame them for choosing to see the world first instead, trapped as they were in this castle for so many years.”

The women look at each other. “We will each return to our homelands first,” Thabisa says, her dark eyes shining. “But we would love to visit our sister in England afterward.”

“There are things I must attend to, but I will find you again,” Hong promises me.

“What I wonder,” Jack says, musing, “is how this condition of yours will manifest from now going forward, seeing as the one who caused it is dead.”

“A question I myself ponder,” Dr. Van Helsing says, looking at me.

“We were surrounded by blood last night,” I say, frowning. “Yet I did not hunger for it.”

Thabisa gestures to Quincey. "What's more, an injured man sits before us with the smell of his blood filling the room, and I have no craving for it. In fact, the idea repulses me."

"I cannot think of anything I want less," Hong agrees, startled. "Do you suppose the virus has left our bodies following his demise? My skin is still cold as marble . . ."

"And my heart does not beat," I add.

Thabisa lifts her fingers, summoning a thin ribbon of fog. "I can call to the mist, and I am certain I still have my strength and speed. Our powerful senses remain."

"But my reflection has returned!" Hong cries, staring into a mirror on the wall. Thabisa and I hurry over to her, and I must fight the absurd urge to cry when I see my unstained skin. All evidence of Vlad's venom and of my unspeakable deeds has disappeared from my face.

"The virus may not have left," Jack says thoughtfully, "but perhaps it has changed. The death of the original host may have caused it to mutate so that you no longer consume blood."

"Jack may be onto something," Dr. Van Helsing agrees. "It seems you have all retained the benefits of being a vampire without the unnatural hunger. The disease may differ in you because it was forced upon you. Your lives were, after all, stolen. It is almost as though the virus is . . . making amends by leaving the good and taking the bad."

Hong smiles at Thabisa and me. "To live forever with our beauty and abilities, but no need to drink blood or hide from the sun," she muses. "That, I think, is a rather fair apology on behalf of the virus, is it not? I think I shall accept."

I laugh with them, even though in the mirror, I see a sadness that will never leave my eyes again. It is grief for everything I gave up, for the regard I had once held for Vlad, and for every loss I have suffered on this journey. Papa, Mamma, Nell, the baroness.

But it is a balance, I know.

This gain for these losses.

In the afternoon, the castle bustles with activity as we prepare for departure. We borrow wagons from the villages below and load them with our belongings, as well as jewels and other valuable items to sell from around the empty castle.

The women and I stand in the great room, which already looks abandoned. "Can you believe this is the very last time we will ever see this place?" Hong asks.

Thabisa takes in the pots and paintings and vases of holly. "I once found some measure of happiness here. But it is time for us to go." She puts an arm around each of us. "Come, my sisters, and we will close the door on this old chapter of our lives."

In front of the castle, Mina finds me as the men prepare the horses. "It crossed my mind, Lucy, when he was biting me that night," she says solemnly. "I imagined becoming like you and giving up everything to be with you forever. But I knew I could not, however much I love you."

I take her hands in mine. "And I would never let you do it, however much *I* love *you*. That is the life I would want for you. You dreamed of a future with Jonathan, and mark my words, I would have given my very last breath to ensure you got it."

"But you did not give your last breath," she says fiercely. "There will be no last breath. You will be my friend, my sister, my love, the aunt to my children."

"So long as you live, we will remain in each other's lives. This I swear to you, Mina Murray-Harker." We press our foreheads together, and peace and contentment fill my weary body.

She climbs onto Quincey's wagon, fussing with his blankets like an overzealous nurse.

"I'm fine, Mrs. Harker," the cowboy says, laughing. "You and your husband don't need to coddle me forever." He raises his voice so that Jonathan, who is tightening the horses' harness, can hear him as well. "If you want to show your gratitude for me saving Mrs. Harker's life, you could name your first child after me. Quincey! Now that there is a fine name, if I say so myself."

"Oh, honestly!" Mina exclaims, blushing, and we all laugh.

"Quincey Harker," Jonathan says speculatively. "That *does* have a certain ring to it."

Jack raises his eyebrows. "But what if the child is a girl? Shall it be Quincia instead?"

"Quincine? Quincette?" Arthur adds.

"Honestly!" Mina repeats as everyone laughs even harder.

The cheer is infectious as Dr. Van Helsing helps Hong and Thabisa into a wagon.

But I do not join them just yet. I turn to look at the castle, at its sprawling stones and ancient towers and the slopes where Vlad had met his fate at sunrise. I do not regret him and I never will. My remorse is all for the yearning, trusting, and naïve girl I once was. But I will not look back on her unkindly, for she led me to myself. My *true* self.

I smile at seeing my friends' joyful faces, especially Mina's. She sits beside Jonathan in the front wagon and links her arm with his, looking so content that my heart lifts at the future I can see for them. Warm windows alight on a winter evening, a fire in the hearth, steaming cups of tea, cakes stacked on a plate, and children playing with a dog. There will be so many days of laughter and so many years of joy for my Mina, and I will be there to share in all of them.

Dr. Van Helsing and Jack Seward sit chatting with Quincey on the second wagon. My friendships with these men will be renewed, and they will become my family. I imagine them gathering in my home as I go out to welcome them, with Arthur following close behind.

Arthur offers me his hand. "Well, my love. Shall we go home?"

"We shall," I say, and he helps me into the back of Mina and Jonathan's wagon.

Hong and Thabisa are there, waiting, and though none of us feel the cold any longer, they still gather me under their blanket as we descend the mountain. Soon enough, Vlad's castle and the memories trapped within are far behind us, hidden by trees and blinding sunshine.

I meet the eyes of these women with whom I will share my immortal life. Only they know exactly what I have been through. Only they understand what I have lived, what I have lost, and what I will always be. I can see our future, too, theirs and mine. I can see decades and centuries of fulfillment and of joy. Of living life for ourselves, of doing good, of celebrating our courage and our freedom. I see us roaming the world if we choose; settling down with someone we love, if we choose; and being anything and everything a little girl has ever dreamed, if we choose. And best of all, we will be *together*. Never alone again.

I close my eyes, and behind my lids, I see a crowd beneath an enormous silken tent lit by candlelight. I hear music from an organ, joined by the poignant, sweet voice of a violin. Mamma, who had been a girl as reckless and wayward as me, had once dreamed of running away with the circus, and I smile as I picture, in my mind's eye, a tangle of ropes from which I dangle, my long dark hair spilling beneath me as I swing from the trapeze and the audience gasps in awe. My body moves with the utmost grace and confidence of a woman who belongs in this world.

In my future, I am boundless.

In my future, I fly.

ACKNOWLEDGMENTS

It's hard to believe that *Now Comes the Mist* and *So Blooms the Dawn* are both out in the world when they were once stories written just for me, blooming in the darkness that was the pandemic. I am infinitely grateful to the people who helped turn them into a reality.

The first thanks goes to Tamar Rydzinski. Look at all of the beautiful books that have come out of our partnership of ten years! I'm proud of each and every novel and I can't wait to see what comes next for us. A big thanks to the fabulous Context Literary team, especially Celsie Moseley and Monica Rodriguez, for their guidance and support.

Thank you to Melissa Frain for helping me polish this duology to a high shine, alternately fangirling over my characters and yelling at Vlad, and making me laugh with your comments in the margins of my Word documents. I'm so grateful to have worked with you!

Much gratitude to the folks at Podium Entertainment for their hard work on these books, including: Cass Dolan, Stephanie Beard, Taylor Byron, Tierney Ulrich, Laura Vorhees, Mindy Fichter, Cole Antos, Griffin Spurr, Hannah Grenfell, Gina White, Keara Wood, Nicole Passage, and the rest of the team. You are all fantastic! Thank you to the artists at Damonza and to Leah Zink for this jaw-droppingly gorgeous pair of book covers, and thank you to Ainsleigh Barber for lending your spectacular voice to the audiobook.

I don't know what I would do without my friends. It means the world to see them in the audience at book events, to spy my books proudly displayed on their shelves, and to have them by my side whether I need to cry, vent, or shout with joy. Thank you for being in my life.

Thank you to our co-agents overseas and to my foreign publishers, Azbooka Atticus and Niezwykłe, for getting *Mist* and *Dawn* out to even more readers around the world!

Huge thanks, as always, to the readers, librarians, booksellers, influencers, and bloggers whose passion and dedication for books inspire me so much. Words can't express how grateful I am to you for boosting my work.

Thank you to my film team, especially Jon Cassir and Andrew Wang at JuVee Productions, for everything you do on my books' behalf.

Dawn will be my ninth published book since 2017 and my family has been there for the whole ride! Their journey to America is on my mind a lot these days. Their experiences—from the pain of having to leave home, the uncertainty of growing roots in a new country, and the trauma of never quite belonging—directly influenced the way I wrote Lucy and the brides. Their sacrifices made every possible every novel I have dreamed up and written. I love you all!

Last, but not least, thank you to my bear for your love, understanding, and unwavering faith in me. Every romance I have written up until now has been foreshadowing for the real one I am now living with you. I love you.

ABOUT THE AUTHOR

Julie C. Dao is the critically acclaimed author of many books for teens and children. Her novels have earned starred reviews from *Booklist*, *School Library Journal*, and *Publishers Weekly*, and won recognition as Junior Library Guild Selections and Kids' Indie Next List picks. *Now Comes the Mist* is her adult debut. A proud Vietnamese American who was born in upstate New York, Dao now lives in New England.

Podium

DISCOVER MORE

STORIES UNBOUND

PodiumEntertainment.com